KNOCKED OFF

THE LUCIE RIZZO MYSTERY SERIES

ADRIENNE GIORDANO

THE LUCIE RIZZO MYSTERY SERIES

Dog Collar Crime

Knocked Off

Limbo (novella)

Boosted

Whacked

Cooked

Romantic suspense books available by Adrienne Giordano

PRIVATE PROTECTOR SERIES

Risking Trust

Man Law

A Just Deception

Negotiating Point

Relentless Pursuit

Opposing Forces

HARLEQUIN INTRIGUES

The Prosecutor

The Defender

The Marshal

The Detective

The Rebel

JUSTIFIABLE CAUSE SERIES

The Chase

The Evasion

The Capture

CASINO FORTUNA SERIES

Deadly Odds

JUSTICE SERIES w/MISTY EVANS

Stealing Justice

Cheating Justice

Holiday Justice

Exposing Justice

Undercover Justice

Protecting Justice

Missing Justice

STEELE RIDGE SERIES w/KELSEY BROWNING

& TRACEY DEVLYN

Steele Ridge: The Beginning

Going Hard (Kelsey Browning)

Living Fast (Adrienne Giordano)

Loving Deep (Tracey Devlyn)

Breaking Free (Adrienne Giordano)

Roaming Wild (Tracey Devlyn)

Stripping Bare (Kelsey Browning)

KNOCKED OFF

A Lucie Rizzo Mystery
by
Adrienne Giordano

For Kelsey and Tracey.
Your constant and unwavering support means more to me than I can express.

1
———

Lucie paused in front of the Lutz's garage while the door made its ascent. The heat from the tiny cobblestone driveway scorched right through the bottom of her sneakers, and she rocked back on her heels. For what this brownstone cost, the driveway should have come with air-conditioning. After all, Chicago in August? The humidity alone could suffocate her.

Once the door silently halted, Lucie pointed toward the interior door. "Stay alert, Lauren. This is where it gets tricky."

The newest part-time member of Lucie's dog walking team studied the door and waited for instructions. Lauren seemed like a nice kid. Well, at twenty, she wasn't really a kid. Lucie was only six years older. Still, Lauren was new to Coco Barknell and needed to understand the intricacies of working with the dogs.

Particularly this dog.

"The door," Lucie said, "is your friend. Otis is the deadly combination of a jumper and a runner."

Lauren scrunched her face. "What?"

"When you open the door, you have to do a body block so he doesn't squeeze through. He's an eighty-five pound Olde English Bulldogge. If you're not careful, you will either A) wind up flat on your butt with Otis on top of you or B) be chasing him around the neighborhood. I've done both and it's not fun. Plus, it'll destroy your schedule."

And with the number of clients Coco Barknell serviced in a day, the schedule was the Bible. As happy as Lucie was about the growth of her dog walking and upscale-dog accessory business, she hated turning the dogs over to others. Of course, she'd done a thorough background check on Lauren, but these animals were almost her babies and she couldn't trust just anyone with them.

Lucie stepped to the door and planted her feet, weight on her heels. "Are you ready?"

"Ready."

Lauren smiled and maybe that smile had a bit of lady-you're-a-fruitcake in it, but the first time Otis did one of his Underdog leaps, she would learn.

Lucie opened the door and the howling began. "Hi, boy," she said, her voice firm and level, no excitement that would cause a doggie mindmelt. "I'm coming in."

Slowly, she inched the door open and slid through with Lauren bringing up the rear. Otis did his normal jumping and Lucie steadied herself for the onslaught. "Off!"

Finally, he sat, but he tracked Lauren with his eyes. Then —*here we go*—unable to withstand the pressure of a new person in his space, he leaped, his long tongue flying in search of a cheek to lick.

"Off!"

But Lucie would never be Cesar Millan when it came to making Otis understand who the alpha was. That was Joey's specialty. It helped that he was six-foot-four and weighed somewhere in the vicinity of two-thirty.

"Sit, Otis," Lauren said, her voice calm, yet assertive in a truly enviable way.

Otis sat.

Cripes. Nothing like the newbie showing the boss up. "Perfect," Lucie said. "He likes you. Come in and I'll show you where his leash is."

Dressed in micro shorts, a tank top, and sneakers, Lauren epitomized the wholesome, yet sexy college co-ed. Her heart-shaped face and long blond hair only added to the morphing of girl-next-door and sexy vixen. If Lucie wasn't careful, the girl might drive Coco Barknell's male clients insane.

But the risk was worth it. So far she'd been a responsible employee who showed up on time, ready to work.

Lucie led her through the kitchen to the utility closet, strategically placed in a nook between the kitchen and the adjoining dining room. Otis's leash and various other dog supplies—poop bags, treats, shampoo—were all stored there and it made Lucie's life a whole lot simpler. Too bad all her clients weren't this organized.

"Whoa. Is this an Arturo Gomez?"

Lucie turned and spotted Lauren a few feet away studying the new painting near the dining room entrance. Lucie had seen the painting for the first time last week and marveled at the rich tones. She'd been drawn to the woman's long, auburn hair cascading over her shoulders as she concentrated on the lute in her hands. The deep red of her dress brought out the smoky archway behind her, and Lucie imagined music echoing off the stone on the surrounding walls.

They shouldn't be snooping, but the painting was right

there. Plus, Lauren was an art history major and probably couldn't control herself. Lucie decided to let it go. Except the schedule was quickly falling apart.

"I don't know who the artist is, but the leash is in this closet."

Ignoring her boss, Lauren inched closer to the painting. "I did a paper on Gomez once. Pure genius at Renaissance."

"Uh-huh," Lucie said.

"It might not even be a Gomez, but it looks like one. I don't think this would be an original though."

Lucie rolled her eyes. The only fake thing in Mr. Lutz's world were his wife's boobs. And those had probably cost a fortune. The man never did anything on the cheap.

"If this is a copy," Lauren said, "it's amazing."

"Lauren, we need to go."

The girl straightened up. "Right. Sorry. I've just never seen one in a private collection. I remember something weird about Gomez's paintings and how they were sold. I could be wrong though. I'd love to know where he got this one."

Lucie knew exactly where Mr. L. had gotten it. She'd introduced him to Bart Owens, an art gallery owner who was also a Coco Barknell client. Mr. Lutz had mentioned he wanted to invest in art. Lucie connected him with Bart, and next thing she knew, Bart offered her a finder's fee for the sale of the painting. And all she'd done was make an introduction. If the amount of the finder's fee were any indication, that painting was most definitely an original.

After that hefty commission, Lucie—a business owner with escalating expansion expenses to deal with—found herself dropping Bart's card off with every client she serviced.

Lucie reached into the closet for Otis's leash. "I think it's an original. Here's the leash. Always grab a few of his treats. If he gets loose, it's the only way to lure him back. He's a sucker for peanut butter. Trust me, you don't want him to get loose. He's an animal."

At the sight of his leash, Otis leaped, knocking Lucie back a step, but she held her hand out. "Yes, baby. I know. It's Lucie time."

When Lucie shoved the leash at her new dog walker, Lauren tore her gaze from the painting. "Sorry. I promise I'm not this flighty. It's like meeting my favorite celebrity. Total fan-girl here. Would you be able to find out the name of this painting for me? Would that be okay?"

She looked back at the painting with a wistful longing and something in her expression reminded Lucie of herself at twenty. She'd been at Notre Dame back then and dreaming of a future in banking. She'd worked hard, graduated with honors, and landed a job as Mr. Lutz's assistant at one of the city's top investment banks. During that time, she'd lived her dream of being more than mob boss Joe Rizzo's kid. In the world of investment banking, she'd moved beyond the title of mob princess.

For a little while.

Being downsized had certainly humbled her. Reminded her, as if she needed reminding, how easily life could change. It had also busted her back to living in her parents' home.

That aside, she was now living a different dream. Building her own company. Who would have imagined her little side business of making high-end dog accessories would take off? But take off it did.

In a big way.

Now Lucie, along with her mother and her best friend, Roseanne, had a major department store pressuring them for more dog coats and collars. The faster they made them, the faster they sold and Lucie's panic meter had shot to the red.

All in all, a nice problem to have considering she could still be unemployed, but as with any growing business, time had become scarce. Speaking of...

Lucie checked the time on her phone. Eight minutes behind.

If they didn't make up some of that eight minutes, by the end of the day, it would be an hour. "Let's hit it, Lauren. Plenty more dogs to see today. I'll ask Mr. Lutz for the title of the painting."

AT FOUR O'CLOCK, AFTER SPENDING THE AFTERNOON SHOWING Lauren her route, Lucie headed southwest back to her hometown. Depending on the day, she either loved or hated Franklin. In Lucie's mind, the town carried the stigma of her father's lifestyle. When she moved back home, she'd moved back to life—at least she thought—as a mob princess. And that, she hated. But Franklin also had a familiarity she loved and a sense of closeness she couldn't get living in the city.

She strolled Franklin Avenue with the hot August sun at her back and spotted her BFF, Roseanne, standing in front of the vacant store at the corner. Ro wore a red pencil skirt so tight it must have taken her ten minutes to wiggle into. But Ro had the curvy, lush body to pull that off. To complete the look of the circulation-modifying skirt, she'd added a white peasant-style blouse and stiletto-heeled sandals. She was, in short, stunning.

As usual.

Lucie, also as usual, smelled like dog. And she was

sweating like some other sort of animal. A farm animal most definitely.

As she approached, Ro waved her expertly manicured hand toward the storefront. "Sister, this is a hot-ass mess."

For this, Lucie had prepared. "It's been empty for a while. All it needs is for you to do your magic. Fresh paint and a good cleaning."

Ro made a gagging noise. "A good cleaning? You're delusional. It needs to be firebombed."

Lucie took in the sight of the filthy plate glass windows and the broken realty sign hanging inside. Doing some quick math, she computed that it had been at least ten years since Carlucci's had closed. Pops Carlucci died in 2004, and his family had no interest in running a shoe store that had been a mainstay in Franklin since the fifties.

Lucie stood next to Ro, staring at the filth and cracked glass and years of disrepair that awaited them inside.

It's cheap.

And close to home. So close, in fact, that Petey's, the luncheonette where her father's mob cronies hung out all day, was right down the street. If ever there was a reason to run screaming, that might be it.

Still, the other locations Lucie had scouted were out of Coco Barknell's measly budget. For now. If they kept up the current pace, by this time next year, they'd be able to afford space in downtown Chicago.

Soon.

She focused on the front door. "Let's just look at it. See if it'll work."

"Luce," Ro said. "Please. We have to be able to afford something a little better. We've been working our asses off."

Indeed they had. When the accessory line had started to take off, the production schedule had become too much for

Lucie and she'd brought her mother in to help with the sewing. Ro, with her blazing style and queen-of-all-things-fabulous attitude, had also been added to the payroll. Basically, Ro was in charge of making sure nothing looked gaudy or cheap. Something she excelled at. Rounding out the employees was Lucie's brother, Joey. He drove her insane with his constant teasing and general harassing, but he always came through for her if days ran long and she needed help walking the dogs.

"We *have* worked hard," Lucie said. "Which is why I'm not overextending us. Besides, I wouldn't even be looking for a place if my father weren't being released early. He'll have a coronary if he walks in and sees the dining room has turned into Coco Barknell's headquarters."

Her father's early release from prison should have come as good news. *Should have.* And for her mother's sake, Lucie wanted her dad home. But with Dad came his opinions on how she should be living her life and, most times, those opinions didn't mesh with Lucie's. In her father's mind, the dog walking and accessory business was a waste of her MBA. Being old-school, he didn't see the big picture. The picture that included building a brand from the ground up. In *his* mind, she should still be looking for a banking job.

"He'll understand," Ro said.

Ha. Right. "Think about what you just said. You've known me and my father for twenty years."

Ro see-sawed her head. "Okay. Maybe the term *understand* is a stretch."

"Yeah, forget it." Lucie dug the keys she'd picked up from Mrs. Carlucci out of her messenger bag. "We're just looking."

She unlocked the door, wrapped her hand around the gritty handle, and imagined she'd need a bucket of antibacterial soap to rid her skin of the germs.

"I'm not touching that," Ro said.

Whatever. Lucie held the door open for her. Ro took two steps, peeled back her lips, and halted. "Dear God, the smell."

True. The aroma of mold and possibly a dead animal or two wasn't exactly pleasant. "The place has been closed for years. What'd you expect? Lavender?"

She gave Ro a light shove. "Move it."

Ro didn't budge. "I will not. That floor is disgusting and I'm wearing Prada sandals. They'll melt off my feet in this pit."

"For crying out loud!"

Lucie shoved her aside and propped open the door with the rubber doorstop sitting just inside the entry. If the dog poop hadn't destroyed her work sneakers by now, this floor had nothing.

Ignoring Ro, Lucie scanned the interior and immediately saw the possibilities. The large open space—fifteen hundred square feet according to the realtor—could do double duty. They'd put a couple of desks or cubicles along the one side and then work tables and sewing machines on the other.

She turned back to Ro, standing painfully erect so she didn't brush either side of the doorway. "You look like you're in vertical rigor mortis."

"I might be. The smell probably killed me."

"Forget the smell a minute."

"And the dirt."

"And the hole in the wall."

Ro laughed. "I'll just close my eyes and hold my nose."

"Perfect. Think about how we could put the administrative area on this right side here. We'll splurge on a couple of comfy chairs and make a little waiting area." She glanced back at Ro, who indeed had her eyes closed. Such a maniac.

Lucie wandered to the other side of the room and motioned with her hands. "Over here we can set up work tables. Sewing machines along this back wall." *And the money shot.* "If you had your eyes open, you'd see where I want to set up an office for you so you can work on designs and dealing with the clients. This could be your area."

Lucie dared a glance back at Ro, still with her eyes closed, but nodding. So damned stubborn.

"If you do that," Ro said, "we'd need screens to separate the two places. People don't need to see a messy work area when they come in."

That's my pal. Ro might moan a little, but she had a sense of style that would rival the Versace's. Precisely why Lucie gave her a job designing doggie accessories. Making this place look good would be just the challenge she craved.

By now, Ro had one eye open. As if opening both might tax her. Lucie held out her arms. "Well?"

"We'd have to replace the floors. Under all this dirt, the linoleum is broken. We'll do laminate. It's easy to care for, and if you get a decent one, it looks like wood."

"Sure. And we can repaint."

"Of course. You realize Petey's is two doors down."

Lucie had long despised Petey's. The food was terrific, but throughout her life, Petey's had been the place her father and his crew ran their "business." She'd spent years trying to rise above being Joe Rizzo's daughter. Her father's current prison stint hadn't helped her anti-mob-princess campaign or their sometimes-strained relationship. Lucie had dealt with it. For her mother's sake. Her mother had been the consistent parent. No matter what, she'd always been present, attentive, and loving. She'd nursed all wounds —physical and emotional.

"There's nothing I can do about Petey's. If this place were on the other side of town, I'd be thrilled. But it's not. This is what we can afford."

"Despite the possibility of seeing Frankie every damned day since he can't go twenty-four hours without a meatball sandwich?"

Yeah. That too.

Frankie, her currently off-again boyfriend of four years was also a family friend. His father and Lucie's father were the closest of friends. At least her father thought so. Lucie? She wasn't sure she understood anything about her father's relationships.

Regardless, Ro was right. Petey's was the epicenter of bad Karma.

Including the day three months ago when she'd gone to Frankie's, Petey's meatball sandwich in hand, and he'd hit her with *the news.* And now, Lucie stood in the mess that was Carlucci's, trying not to think of that day. Even if her mind battled the memory, her heart ripped itself open and wailed.

Damned broken heart bringing it all back to her.

She'd been standing in Frankie's living room, holding that stupid bag with the stupid meatball sandwich while he stared at her, his eyes a little sad.

"Luce," he said, "we need to talk."

No. They didn't. Because every time she'd said those words to him, it meant she needed a break. Not necessarily from him, but from *the life.* Taking a break from the life included Frankie because, despite his determination to stay legitimate, his sense of loyalty bonded him to his family and friends. And those people had no interest in going legit.

That loyalty extended to his father, even after he'd put Lucie in danger to protect a twenty-year-old secret.

She set the meatball sandwich on the end table, and with her head pounding and a bead of sweat rolling down her shoulder blades, she slid to the sofa. "Oh, Frankie."

Ignoring the sandwich, he sat beside her, grabbed both her hands. "Luce, I need a break."

And, oh, those words imploded her chest, just *boom*, total annihilation. Worse? She'd done this to him countless times. Always using that exact I-need-a-break phrasing. As the pain ripped her apart, she finally understood how those four little words could decimate a life. She squeezed her eyes closed, fought the tears. Each time she'd done this to him, he'd been downright supportive. Not making a fuss or hurling insults or laying on guilt. Knowing her demons, he'd simply let her go.

Which she would now have to do. She couldn't be mad. Not at him.

"It's okay, Frankie."

"I've been loyal to everyone for so long, I've become a doormat."

"That's not true."

"Yeah, it is. I'm done with that. I don't want to leave you, but I've waited years for you to get comfortable. Now, I'm not comfortable. I need to walk away and get my head together. We just had this major blowup with my dad and I need to figure out how this thing with him and your family will play out."

She nodded. "I don't want to let our relationship go. I love you too much for that. So this time, I'll do the waiting." And then, that sadness in her chest surged and she breathed in, closed her eyes. No tears. Please. He deserved to be happy. Even if it hurt her.

"Luce—"

"You don't have to explain. Not to me. I'm just... sad. But I'll wait, and hopefully, you'll come back to me."

He leaned forward and brushed his lips over hers. "I love you, Luce. Always will."

"Excellent. Then I have nothing to worry about."

He grinned. "Wanna have sex? Leave me a reminder of what I'll miss."

She rolled her eyes. Some things would never change. "I'll do better than that."

A spark lit in Frankie's eyes and she was sure it involved something leather and kinky.

"I'm listening," he said.

She propped her elbow on the table, extended her fingers and waited for him to entwine his hand with hers. "Are you ready for this?"

"Ready."

She squeezed his hand. "This will be a sacrifice, but I will let you keep that meatball sandwich I brought you."

And she had. She'd handed over the bag and walked out of his house, hoping the break would be a short one.

That had been three months ago, and she'd been doing her best to avoid seeing him. Not that either of them was bitter. On the contrary, they often spoke on the phone. But right now, Frankie needed his space. For the first time in their history, he was the one who'd called off their relationship.

So, Lucie killed time until they eventually worked it out and got back together.

That's how it was with them. The love between them was a potent thing and they both just plain stunk at resisting it.

"What about the back room?"

Ro's voice broke through Lucie's mind travel, and she turned to see her friend still standing in the doorway.

"The back room? It's a mess. A bunch of boxes in there. We'll have to go through them. I'll do that."

"What about a bathroom? God help us, I can only imagine what that looks like."

Lucie wandered to the doorway leading to another smaller room. Probably the old stock room. Yep. Five short rows of shelving units filled the much smaller space. They'd store their accessory supplies back here. Or even make it the sewing room. She'd have to think about it. To her left was another door. She opened it and found a small bathroom with a white sink—circa 1965—and a toilet that should have had a pull cord. The sink and toilet were both rust-stained and the grout on the black and white checked floor looked like it had seen the wrong end of a chain saw.

"How is it?" Ro asked from the doorway.

"The bathroom is... um... It needs work."

"Hey," came Joey's voice from where Ro stood. "What are you nutty broads doing?"

"Your sister is thinking about renting this dinosaur. I refuse to enter."

"Seriously?"

"Yes!" Lucie said. "Come back here. I need you to see this."

Her brother had become fairly handy since their father's incarceration two years ago. If she could negotiate the owner replacing the floor and paying for a new toilet and sink, Joey might be able to install them.

"Roseanne," Joey said, "your ass looks *great* today."

Ro made a *pffting* noise. "You'd better believe it does."

"Hey! She's married."

Ro laughed. "But my ass still looks good. That's the important thing."

"And last time I checked, Luce, my vision was still twenty/twenty."

Terrific. Barbarian flirting. What more could a girl want?

"This place," Joey said, "is a hole."

"I know. But it's cheap. With a little elbow grease, it'll be a palace."

He stuck his head in the bathroom and his tight-lipped expression, so classically their father, temporarily stunned her. Joey had always had her father's dark features, but as he got older, he'd become more and more the angles of Dad and less the softness of Mom.

After sniffing once, he winced. She couldn't blame him. The smell could gas a town.

"If I get the owner to pay for the supplies, can you install a sink and toilet?"

Joey shrugged. "I'll do you one better. I got a plumber who owes me money. I'll have him do it. "

"Is this one of your bookie-ing"—*was bookie-ing a word?*—"clients? I don't want to be associated with your degenerate gamblers."

Although her brother sometimes filled in as a dog walker at Coco Barknell, his main source of income was a bookmaking business. And Lucie hated that.

"Listen, goody-two-shoes, how do you think Ma's plumbing gets fixed? The next time you take a dump, thank my degenerate gamblers."

Still in the entryway, Ro laughed. "I do adore you, Joey."

He leaned back and wiggled his eyebrows at her.

Good God.

"Does Mom know that? Not that Ro adores you. About the degenerates?"

"I guess. She tells me she needs a plumber and I tell her I'll take care of it. We're lucky this guy can't pick a winner. She hasn't paid a plumbing bill since Dad went away."

"Luce," Ro said, "you'd better take him up on this. Fixing this trap up will cost you. Save money where you can. Besides, since you pee at your mother's, your integrity has already been compromised."

Joey jerked his thumb in Ro's direction and gave her one of his smart-ass perfect teeth smiles. "Good point."

"Okay. Fine."

"Joey," Ro called, "what other contractors owe you money? She'll need a flooring guy and a painter."

Slippery slope, this one.

With Lucie on his heels, he left the bathroom and headed for the door. "Let me see what I can do."

On the way out, he lightly smacked Ro's ass. The one that looked great today.

She waved him away. "Hands off, big boy. Looking is one thing. Besides, you had your chance."

Ew.

"Don't remind me," Joey said.

Recently, Ro had admitted to Lucie that she and Joey were an item for a few months while Lucie was in graduate school. But her brother couldn't commit and Ro had moved on. Lucie wasn't sure she was exactly comfortable with her brother and Ro having done the nasty. So she stood in the middle of the filthy floor, avoiding eye contact with her best friend because the visions swimming in her mind were too much.

Lucie stifled an ick face. "Sometimes I wish I still didn't know about you two."

Ro shrugged. "He really has a sweet side. You don't see it

because you're his sister. But that's old news. And with the state of my life right now, not worth rehashing."

Ro loved her husband. Prior to a month ago, he'd been a good, solid guy and that's what she needed. Someone to cool her fire once in a while. Except, last month that good, solid guy, who was also president of the Franklin town council, got caught in a strip club doing things he shouldn't have been doing.

"How are things at home?"

Ro let out a heavy breath, then studied the molding around the ceiling for a few seconds before finally meeting Lucie's gaze. "You mean my stripper-banging husband? He's lucky I don't stab him in his sleep. It takes incredible restraint, you know. I keep telling him not to close his eyes."

"I'm sorry, Ro."

She rubbed her nose a couple of times, sniffled, and shrugged. Ro wasn't a crier. Hated it. She'd sooner cut off her own leg than cry in front of anyone, but Lucie knew the signs. Inside, Ro was coming apart.

"Eh," Ro said. "It's only a broken heart. It'll get better. What do you think about this dump? Is it our new headquarters?"

"Depends."

"On what?"

"If you can get it cleaned up in roughly two weeks because that's when my father comes home."

"Two weeks!"

Lucie raised her hands before Ro started yelling. "It could be three. I'm sorry! I just found out. They're having an overcrowding issue and they're paroling him early."

Lucie's father had been locked up over an income tax issue. Not exactly the violent offense the government would have liked to have nailed Joe Rizzo on, but they took what they could get. Lucie suspected the feds were still trying to build a case on her father—they'd been at it for years—but they obviously didn't have enough evidence to bring him to trial again, and since he'd been a model prisoner, they were letting him out early. Go figure.

And now she had to move her company headquarters from the dining room. Her dad would take one look at the boxes of fabric and sample racks and start yelling about getting that crap out of his house. *Thanks for the support, Dad.*

"It's a good thing I love you," Ro said. "Two weeks!"

"It doesn't have to be finished. It just has to be usable." Lucie moved to the side of the store where the design area would be. "Let's get this half going. Then I can move all the stuff from the dining room here and set up a desk in the corner. We can work out of this half while the other half is being renovated. That's doable, right?"

Ro put one finger up. "Cleanup." Another finger. "Paint." Another finger. "New floors." Her pinkie. "Bathroom."

"I'll take care of cleaning out the back room. Joey will line up the contractors. All you'll have to do is pick out the floor, fixtures, and paint. Is it a deal?"

"It'll be a *miracle.*"

With that, she spun on her Prada sandals and marched away.

"Thank you," Lucie called after her.

Finally alone in the store, she turned back and took it all in. In a few weeks, this broken-down mess would be the new corporate headquarters of Coco Barknell.

And her father would be home from prison.

2

THE FOLLOWING AFTERNOON, LUCIE STORMED DOWN ASHLAND Avenue with Bear, an overweight Great Dane who totally lacked an aggression gene, pulling her along. Bear may have looked like a force, but the dog was a complete lover. On the rare occasion someone approached to pet the behemoth, he'd go up on his hindquarters, drop his front paws on the person's shoulders, and nearly knock them backward, aiming for a lick or twelve.

Their first week together, Lucie had learned not to give him much slack. As in any at all. Considering the heat today, and the melting asphalt, a dog his size shouldn't be moving fast anyway.

In the subtle mayhem of Chicago traffic, a taxi driver sat on his horn. Bear halted, turned toward the offending sound, and let out three rapid-fire barks. *That'll teach him, Bear.* Having added his opinion, Bear went back to searching the pavement for a good spot to relieve himself.

Oh, these dogs. If there ever came a time where she'd have to be in the office full-time, hopefully running her Fortune 500 company, she'd miss the quirky rascals. She wouldn't miss schlepping around in snow in the winter, but being outside during the other three seasons, getting the air and exercise, wailing through the streets on her scooter from client to client, all of that she'd miss.

Somehow, even on busy days, it relaxed her. Made her feel not so trapped by life.

A chirp sounded from her pocket and she moved the leash into her other hand to check her phone. Mr. Lutz. Ahead of her, a group of pedestrians parted like the Red Sea to give Bear room, so it was as good a time as any to take a call.

"Hi, Mr. L."

"Lucie? Hi. I got your note about the painting."

After the conversation with Lauren, Lucie had taken pity on the eager student and left Mr. L. a note regarding the title of the painting. "Thanks for calling. You could have left me a note though."

"It's fine. What's up?"

"My new part-timer is an art history major. She's enthralled and wanted to know the title."

A man in a suit, also talking on his phone, headed straight for them, obviously not paying attention to the giant dog in front of him.

Without a free hand, Lucie pulled the phone away from her ear and waved it at the guy to grab his attention. "Hey, there. Lady with a giant dog coming through."

Just before going ass over elbow, his eyes shot wide and he veered left.

On the other end of the phone, Mr. L. laughed. "The painting is called *My Darkest Night*. My wife says it's a Gomez, whoever the hell he is. She knows more about art than I do, but Bart convinced me it would be a good investment. He says modern art is hot right now and no one is buying the old classics. I'll make a fortune."

"I guess art is like real estate. When the market is dead, you invest and wait for it to come back."

"Let's hope so."

At the corner, Bear stopped to inspect a garbage can and finally let fly a stream of urine so strong it could wash away a small village. The dog, quite literally, peed like a racehorse. While waiting, Lucie went back to Mr. Lutz. "Either way, it's a beautiful painting. I'll let Lauren know the title. I'll be by this afternoon to walk Otis again. He's my last stop today."

Lucie ended her call with Mr. L. and swung a right at the corner to head back. Except, the parked car must have appealed to Bear. He tugged, dragging her so he could inspect a tire.

"Don't you pee on that car."

But he kept sniffing and she knew what was coming.

He lifted his leg.

"No, Bear!"

Too late. He squeaked out another shot of urine. Terrific. Lucie glanced around, praying the owner wasn't nearby.

"Glad that's not my car," a passing woman said.

"No kidding, lady," Lucie muttered.

A beat-up Crown Victoria came to a stop on the other side of the defiled car. Other drivers zoomed around, honking at the Crown Vic, but Lucie knew that didn't matter. Not in this city.

Out of the double-parked car stepped Detective Tim O'Brien. As with the last time she'd seen him, O'Brien wore a suit, gray this time, and a white shirt sans the jacket and tie. Maybe those were in the car. She hadn't seen him in over three months, but he appeared bigger, more beefcake than the lanky guy she'd first met. And the lonely side of Lucie liked the beefcake look on O'Brien—a lot.

Helloooo, Detective.

Because of a little issue a few months back with some stolen diamonds, she hadn't quite figured out if Detective O'Brien was friend or foe. But he liked to flirt with her, and given the serious lack of Frankie in her life, flirting wasn't such a bad thing.

He stepped onto the curb. "Hello, Lucie."

Bear made a move to maul O'Brien, straining against his leash. Lucie planted her feet, leaned all her weight back, and held on. She was only 105 pounds, so Bear could take her for a ride if he insisted, but she'd at least make it a challenge. Really though, she couldn't blame the dog. Where Frankie was dark-haired and a lean, 5'10" movie-star handsome, O'Brien was fair-haired but rugged and...alpha.

Extremely alpha.

He also had that half-cute, half-deadly handsome face inherent to fair-skinned Irish boys. Add the green eyes, the strawberry-blond hair that was more strawberry than blond, and the broad-shouldered build, and a girl could be done for.

"Nice to see you, Detective."

He grinned down at Bear. "Who do we have here?"

Bear lunged and Lucie gave him a little slack. Maybe too much because he raised up on his hind legs, dropped his paws on O'Brien's shoulders, and launched into an all-out lickfest.

Holy crap, the dog was a menace. Lucie couldn't help laughing at the rude behavior, but still found it embarrassing. "Bear! Off!"

O'Brien set his hands on the dog's back and patted. Slow dancing. With a Great Dane. How funny was that?

Must have been darned amusing to the hottie detective. The deep rumble of his laughter—first time she'd heard that—shot a zing right to her core.

Seriously? She *had* to be lonely. When had she ever had that feeling about anyone other than Frankie?

She didn't like it. Well, she liked the *feeling*, but not having it about anyone other than Frankie. Talk about your tangled web. But spending her evenings alone hadn't been a picnic. It seemed these last few years, they'd spent more time apart than together, and if she were being truly honest with herself, it was getting old. Working day and night to kill time didn't exactly make an exciting life for a twenty-six-year-old. Even Mom had a more packed social schedule.

How the hell did that happen?

All she could hope was that she and Frankie, as they had countless times before, worked through this break-up fairly soon because her lusting after cute Irish cops was a disaster in waiting.

Her father would have a stroke. She didn't know which would be worse, the he's-not-Italian part or the cop part. Her father wanted his grandchildren—all of them—to have an Italian last name. In short, he wanted Frankie, a nice Italian boy from the neighborhood, who had a successful—i.e. legitimate—career. On paper, in Joe Rizzo's eyes, Frankie was the gold star of husband material.

"Um, Lucie?" O'Brien said. "How about calling off the atomic tongue here?"

"Ooh, shoot. Sorry!"

She reached around Bear's ribcage and hauled him off, her feet moving backward in perfect sequence with his hind legs.

O'Brien stepped back and slid his big hand over his cheeks. "Helluva greeting."

Obviously exhausted—*shall I get you a cigarette?*—Bear dropped to the pavement for a nap. Unbelievable.

Lucie squatted and gave him a good rub. "Sweet boy." She smiled up at O'Brien. "He's such a mush it's hard to get mad at him. At least you're tall." Somewhere about six-foot-one, she figured, but who paid attention? "A couple of months ago, he knocked a teeny-tiny grandma on her butt. It was a nightmare."

O'Brien grinned and that little squeeze in her belly happened again.

"How are you?" he asked.

"I'm great. Business is good."

"I saw your stuff in Frampton's a few weeks ago."

Ah, yes. The big Frampton's order. Roseanne had taken it upon herself to send Chicago's largest department store samples of their doggie collars and before they knew it, they were producing thousands of diamond-studded collars and coats.

She stood again, but with his height, she barely reached his chest. "It's been insane. We're so busy. It's good though. And fun."

"That's great." He tilted his head and studied her for a second. "I, uh, heard you and Frank Falcone split up."

Heard that, did he? She wouldn't bother asking where or how he came upon this information. What did it matter? "Yes. A few months ago."

Right after you thought I stole a million dollars-worth of diamonds.

"Sorry to hear that," he said in that voice that telegraphed he wasn't sorry at all.

Lucie shrugged. What else could she do? She'd cried enough tears over Frankie to fill Wrigley Field. Now she just had to wait and hope they once again found their way back to each other. With both of their fathers in *the life,* she and Frankie understood each other. There was an acceptance between mob kids. Except, sometimes that didn't quite measure up and they found themselves in a place where they couldn't agree on how much interference from their families was too much.

For Lucie, it was always too much.

Bear rose from his power nap, sniffed the parking meter, and squirted a few measly drops on it. This dog was a never-ending pee factory.

The radio clipped to O'Brien's waistband squawked. He stared at the ground for a second while he listened to a dispatcher throw around a stream of codes. The radio once again fell silent and he looked up, all the amusement from a second ago now gone.

"I gotta go."

"Oh, no. I hope it's okay." She stopped, then smacked herself on the head. "Of course it's not okay. It's a crime. Forget it. Dumb thing to say."

A corner of his mouth quirked. "How about I call you? Maybe we can grab a bite and catch up?"

"Sure."

Sure? What did she just do? Pretty positive she just agreed to go out with the Irish cop. And considering the only man she'd gone out with in the last four years was Frankie, this was a problem.

But she didn't hear herself backing out. Nope. She just stood there—*mute*—while the hunky cop drove off.

Bear stared at her with disappointed eyes.

"It just slipped out," she said. "And I'm lonely. You think that's easy to admit? Besides, it's not your business."

It wasn't anybody's business. Particularly Frankie's.

Or her father's.

"AN IRISH COP," ROSEANNE SAID. "HAVE YOU SUFFERED A HEAD trauma?"

Lucie propped her elbows on her mother's dining room table, shoved her dinner plate aside, and dropped her head into her hands. "I don't know what happened. One minute the dog was mauling him, the next my stomach was flip-flopping, and O'Brien was asking me for a date. I think it's a date anyway. It's been so long since someone asked me out I'm not sure."

Across from her, Ro pushed food around her still-full plate. "Go out with him. I only saw him the one time, but he's a hot one. Besides, you're not getting any from Frankie."

Lucie gasped. "I'm not having sex with him. It'll be a date. That's all."

"All I'm saying is you shouldn't turn into a nun because you and Frankie broke up. Again. This is what? The twelfth time? Go out with the cute Irish cop and let Frankie find out. He'll come back. Men are stupid that way. They always want what they can't—or shouldn't—have."

Ro knew men, for sure, but her current attitude had more to do with her cheating husband than Lucie dating someone new. No. If Lucie decided to see O'Brien, it wouldn't be to lure Frankie back. It would be because she was lonely and O'Brien, bless his handsome self, made her feel something she hadn't felt since Frankie dumped her.

She lifted her head. Behind Ro an antique mirror spanned the length of the short wall and Lucie stared at her best friend's reflection. That mirror, like Ro, had been around since Lucie could remember. Its unchanged presence somehow anchored Lucie. Gave her a place to belong even when she didn't necessarily want to.

She brought her gaze back to Ro, who continued playing with her food. Her friend's marriage was in crisis and Lucie was moaning about a date that might not even happen. What kind of friend did that?

"I don't know why I'm worrying about this. He hasn't even called yet." She picked up her notepad and pen. "Let's get back to the timeline on the new office space."

"Is it official?"

"Yes. I called Mrs. Carlucci. She'll pay for all the fixtures if we handle installing them. She's also covering the paint but not the floors."

"Good work. I'll pick up some samples and run them by the store tomorrow. Maybe I can get the flooring cheap."

Cheap to Ro meant something that fell off a truck in a dubious location. "It has to be legitimate."

She rolled her eyes. "I was talking about remnant flooring. Have you forgotten my louse of a husband is president of the town council? Maybe he can do something through one of the city contractors. Those guys always have leftover stuff from jobs. Right now, he'd probably do anything I asked. Even if I asked him to cut off his own penis. Rat bastard that he is."

"That would be fine." Ooof. She needed to focus here. "Yikes! Sorry. Not the penis part."

At least her mother wasn't around for this conversation. Because yes, once again, Mom was out to dinner with friends, proving Lucie's theory that she had a more active social life than her unmarried daughter.

Ro made snoring noises. "Whatever. I knew what you meant."

Grand day so far, an Irish cop, and now she'd insulted her dearest friend's husband's penis. "Anyway, I'm still training the new part-timer, but I could meet you tomorrow afternoon to look at the samples. Or you can just do it. You have a better feel for that stuff anyway."

"I'll narrow it down and then you can pick. How's the new girl working out?"

"So far, so good. I have to work on her about keeping on schedule. She got sidetracked yesterday staring at that painting Mr. L. bought from the crazy gallery owner."

"The one who called my Gucci purse gauche?"

"Yes."

Ro tossed her long, sable hair over her shoulder. "That guy is an ass."

"Yes, but he's a good client. I've picked up several dogs because of his recommendation. Plus, he gave me a finder's fee on the painting Mr. L. bought. And that little hunk of cash is helping to finance our new headquarters."

"Really?"

"Yep. He said he'll make it a standing deal. If anyone I introduce him to buys a painting, he'll give me a commission. And we need a whole lot more paintings like that to fuel our expansion."

Ro stood, gathered her plate, then walked around to Lucie's side and took hers as well. "Doesn't sound like a bad deal."

"It's an excellent deal. And the extra cash will come in handy as we're expanding Coco Barknell."

"Then why do I think you have a problem with it?"

Huh. Her friend knew her too well. "Eh. Not really a problem. I guess it feels a little smarmy. Like I'm using my clients."

On her way to the kitchen to dump the plates, Ro made snoring noises again and Lucie threw her napkin at her. A napkin. As if that would do any damage. "I can't help analyzing this Gomez thing. It's what I do. But heck, when I was in banking, a lot of stuff felt smarmy. What's the difference?"

Ro came back into the room and stood beside Lucie. "Think of yourself as a recruiter. They get paid for matching employees with companies all the time. You're doing the same thing, only with a product."

In a twisted way, it made sense. "Exactly!"

"Glad we once again agree. Now let's ditch this subject and run down to the hardware store and see about paint samples. You can show me what colors you like. That college kid who wants to do me usually works evenings. If I give him a little cleavage, he ponies up a discount." She ran a hand down the side of her halter-top. "I'm dressed appropriately for this mission."

Lucie shoved out of her chair. "By all means, if your boobs will save us money, let's use them."

She glanced down at her Notre Dame T-shirt and cut-off shorts, and contemplated a wardrobe change. Eh. Why bother? Lucie didn't have the wow factor Ro had. Not that this was a pity party. She knew she was attractive. If she tried hard enough, like she'd done for Frankie a few months back, she was downright pretty. Alluring. But she didn't have that sexy, I-will-destroy-you-in-bed look that Ro possessed.

Ro bent over, gave her boobs a shimmy to get them boosted in her top and flipped back up, adjusting where necessary. "All in a day's work, girlfriend. You can thank me later. Let's move."

"BRACE YOURSELF, LAUREN."

Lauren stood frozen, a feat considering the blazing late-afternoon sun in front of the Owens Gallery. "I'm so excited.

I've never been to this gallery. And to actually *meet* the owner? You have no idea."

"Well, we don't actually go into the gallery. The dog stays in the office at the back of the building."

She swiped her hands over her jeans and bobbed her head, sending her ponytail flying. "Still, it's exciting."

Lucie laughed. This girl was a nut, but her enthusiasm was nothing short of enviable. "Bart might be in the office though. If so, I'll introduce you."

Couldn't hurt to give her employee a potential networking contact in her field of choice. Lucie had learned that from Mr. Lutz. Despite being forced to downsize her, he remained one of her biggest supporters. For that, she'd always be grateful. And would also pay it forward.

Lauren followed her through the alley between the gallery and the boutique next door while Lucie dug in her messenger bag for the key. "The office door stays locked, so you have to remember the key. I'll keep it in the office. Whoever has Oscar on their schedule that day can pick it up. Bart isn't always here, and if you don't have the key, you can't get in to walk the dog. Got it?"

"Got it. Does he leave the dog where the art is stored?"

"Absolutely not. Bart is obsessive about that. All the art is kept in a climate-controlled area. Oscar isn't allowed anywhere near it. He can walk through the gallery only because he can't reach the paintings. That's it. He's a good boy, but he's still an animal."

"He's the Maltese-poodle mix, right?"

"Yes. Two years old and cute as can be. Just pray he likes you because he can be a real hater."

Lucie had an arsenal of small, but mighty dogs on her route. Josie and Fannie, a couple of shih tzus a neighbor had nicknamed the Ninja Bitches, could chew off a man's leg in one bite. Well, maybe that was an exaggeration, but only a fool would mess with those girls. Being petite herself, Lucie liked their spunk.

Sometimes she even encouraged it. *Bad, Lucie. Bad.*

Inside the office, Oscar, in all his fluffy, white glory, scampered to them and immediately sat. Lucie bent to nuzzle him. "Good boy, Oscar."

"Well trained."

"Yes, but I'm telling you, there's a switch in his brain. If he doesn't like someone—*bam*—he turns into the Incredible Hulk."

"Let's see if he likes me." Lauren stuck her hand out and let Oscar sniff. "Good boy, Oscar."

Lucie closed one eye. *Please let him like her.* As if reading her mind, Oscar leveled his big brown eyes on Lucie—*did he just smile?*—before licking Lauren's hand.

But then he blew it by turning to Lucie, mounting her lower calf and hanging on for the ride while he humped her.

"Wow," Lauren said.

Lucie gently pushed him off. "He's a total horndog."

A loud voice came from behind the office door that led to the gallery. Sounded like Bart's voice. Something about someone getting screwed.

Ouch.

"Whoa," Lauren said. "That didn't sound good."

No fooling there. But they were dog walkers, not eavesdroppers. "We should go. We only have thirty minutes to walk Oscar and he's fussy about the route."

The voices drew closer to the door. Lucie hustled to the spot on the wall where Oscar's leash hung. *Time to go, kids.*

"You keep ducking me!" a deep-toned voice—definitely

not Bart's—came from what sounded like just the other side of the door.

"Stop, Robert." Bart's voice. Definitely. "How incredibly offensive. I'm not ducking you."

They're close. Yikes. If Bart walked in now, he'd think Lucie and Lauren were doing exactly what they were doing. Eavesdropping.

Lucie bent low to clip Oscar's leash. "Good baby, Oscar. Here we go," she whispered, but Lauren's attention was plastered to the door. "Psst, Lauren."

She spun to Lucie, who jerked her head to the door.

"You get on the phone with that gallery and get my paintings back!" Robert—whoever he was—hollered. "They've been on loan for six months. They either need to buy them or send them back. I want my money."

Lauren made an *eeekkk* face and the veins in her neck popped. Time to go. Lucie paddled her hand to the door and Lauren did a half-run, half-walk to get there. Who knew life as a dog walker packed this much drama?

"Robert, it's almost eleven at night there. I'll call them in the morning for God's sake. Calm down."

"Don't tell me to calm down. I'm losing money on those paintings. Get. Them. Back."

Lucie nudged Lauren through the door. Once outside, Oscar trotted along beside Lucie until she led him to the tree in front of the gallery. Right about now would be the appropriate time to warn Lauren about maintaining discretion when it came to overhearing things related to their clients' businesses.

"So, obviously," Lucie began, "you'll sometimes hear things that maybe you shouldn't."

"Um, I guess."

"And I'm sure I don't need to tell you this, but part of

Coco Barknell's excellent reputation comes from our discretion."

What a load of bull that was. First off, Coco Barknell wasn't quite established enough to have a reputation for discretion. Second, half the time, the dog owners weren't even home, so there wasn't a whole lot happening to feed the gossip mill. And third, they'd just narrowly avoided being locked up for hiding stolen jewelry from a twenty-year-old heist.

Great track record so far.

"Sure." Lauren took the leash from Lucie. "I understand. My lips are sealed. I can talk to you though, right?"

"Of course."

Oscar finished peeing and began his trot down the block.

"Sounds like Bart Owens lent someone's paintings to another gallery. And now he can't get them back. That's juicy. I should write a paper on the pitfalls of lending. I wonder who Robert is? I bet we could find out."

Oh, boy.

Moving fast, Oscar sniffed the ground, his snout swinging back and forth, back and forth. Lucie clutched Lauren's forearm, squeezing enough to let her know not to wreck this moment. "Sshhh. This is it. Don't rush him. He's getting ready to poop."

Wide-eyed, but apparently understanding the importance, Lauren nodded. Oscar pooping in a timely manner meant keeping the already-blown schedule from completely slipping out of control.

Finally, Oscar picked the winning spot and did his business while Lucie readied the atomic plastic baggie that hung from a holder on her belt loop. Having learned the hard way that she could wind up with a hole in a bag and poop smeared over her fingers—not fun when in the middle of a walk with nowhere to wash up—Lucie provided her own industrial bags. Just one of the many perks of Coco Barknell's services. She also now carried an extra water bottle, wipes and sanitizer in her backpack. For emergencies.

"About the paintings," Lucie said, "this is what I'm talking about. We need to pretend we didn't hear that. So, no, you shouldn't write a paper on it. Please."

A car honked—*I know that horn*—and Lucie turned, spotting Frankie jogging across the street from where he'd parked in a no-parking zone. He wore dress slacks and a dress shirt, no tie. His office look. Meaning he was probably on his way to the newspaper. His hair was a little shorter than usual, and even from the ten-yard distance, the sharp cut of his cheekbones, the perfect jaw and dark eyes sent her body buzzing. Nothing unusual there. She'd missed him horribly. Mind-torturing missing him, and then he showed up and her body nearly purred over his closeness.

The two of them were stuck. Broken-up but still talking and feeling the feelings that people in love felt.

He squeezed between two parked cars. "Hey, Luce."

"Hey there. You're in a no-parking zone."

"Yeah. I'll only be a sec."

What if this was it? Him telling her he was ready to try again. A spark of adrenaline flooded her brain and she whipped around to Lauren. "I'll just be a minute. Why don't you walk ahead and I'll catch up."

"Got it."

Lucie waited for Lauren and Oscar to get out of earshot and turned back to Frankie. "Are you heading to work?"

"Yeah. I knew you walked Oscar around four and figured

I'd catch you before I headed in. You know," he said tapping his watch, "you're a little behind schedule."

Oh, ha-ha. Funny man. More than anyone, he knew her obsession with managing her time. "Hardy-har. I'm training my new part-timer, so it's taking longer. What's up?"

"Joey told me about your dad. I was thinking about you. And him. Living under the same roof. Are you gonna be okay?"

And apparently, this little impromptu visit wasn't for him to pledge his undying love and tell her he couldn't live without her. So much for the adrenaline rush. But he'd cared enough to stop and see her. That was something at least.

Lucie shrugged. "I have to be. It's his house. If things get rough, I'll rent an apartment. I just have to see what kind of budget I can manage."

"If Ro and Tommy split, you could move in with her. It's eight to five Tommy is gonna get slaughtered in that settlement."

Oh. My. God. That damned Joey. "Please, Frankie. You have to tell me Joey is not taking action on Ro getting divorced."

"Really, Luce? He takes action on everything."

"I'll kill him."

"Technically, it's not his fault. The guys at Petey's started it, but it got too big and they needed Joey's help. He's not one to refuse money, so he caved."

And here she'd hoped her degenerate gambler brother was getting out of the bookie business by helping her walk the dogs a few days a week. If things kept up with the accessory orders, she'd need Joey to help her run the dog walking end of the business.

One thing she knew about her brother, he was good with numbers.

"Still," Lucie said. "I think it's a little twisted that he's accepting bets on Ro's divorce considering they were once... whatever they were."

"Eh. It's Joey. What are you gonna do?"

"Nothing. He's like my dad. I love him, but he makes me crazy."

"When your dad comes home, don't argue with him. It never gets you anywhere."

"I'll try." She smiled for the first time in this whole misbegotten conversation. "You know that's never been my strong point."

Frankie blew air through his lips. "You're telling me."

"All I know is that house will be crowded with Joey and my dad under the same roof again. But hey, I rented Carlucci's for Coco Barknell's new headquarters."

"No way."

"Yep. You know my dad is a control freak. If he comes home and sees the dining room is Coco's headquarters, it'll start a war. If we move the stuff, maybe he won't wig out."

Since Frankie was an early investor in the business, she owed it to him to clue him in. Let him know his investment was in good hands. Although, after all the years they'd known each other, she'd hoped he knew that. Plus, she'd spent four years moaning to him about her career ups and downs. Why should now be any different?

Breakup aside.

"Anyway," she said, "Ro is flashing cleavage all over Franklin, trying to get us deals on supplies."

That made Frankie roar. That great laugh she loved caused a little flutter in her belly. *I miss him.* Her breath caught and she smacked her hand against her chest. This semi-meltdown hit her every once in a while. A fierce longing for him that she hadn't quite figured out how to navigate in his absence. All she knew was it hurt. Like a flash mob inside her, ripping at her heart, tearing the pieces away.

"That girl is a total pisser," Frankie said. "She gets it done though. Should we, uh, celebrate?"

Having no idea what to do with that suggestion, she forced out a long, slow breath, tilted her head back and stared at the open sky. *Relax.* Would it be nice to spend time with him? Yes. But she missed him and there were moments, like now, when the physical ache split her in two. If they were going to remain broken-up, being out with him would be pure torture.

Plus, whenever she got near him, her hormones whacked out and the insanity usually propelled them right to Frankie's bed.

"Luce?"

"I don't know. I mean, yes, we should celebrate. I just don't know if we should do it alone. Or together even. God, Frankie. I don't know."

For a few seconds he stayed silent, those dark eyes of his on her in that way that let her know he was contemplating his next statement. Deciphering just how much to say and if it would get him in trouble.

It was your doing this time, bucko. But she wouldn't say that. Not after all the times she'd been the one to say the four little words. *I need a break.* Each time he'd been understanding. Ridiculously so, she now realized.

Lucie glanced behind her to where Lauren and Oscar wandered by a tree.

"I know, Luce. This sucks. I miss you."

"Me too. That's the problem."

"I wake up every day and want to call you, but I think it's

been good for me. Suddenly, there's no pressure to make anyone but me happy. Is that selfish?"

She didn't need to know he was happy without her. "Frankie, you're always everyone's rock. Always keeping the peace. You deserve some time to yourself."

"But it hurts. Not being with you. I want to go back to the beginning."

Nice thought, but they never had a beginning. They went from being lifelong family friends to having a couple of casual dinners alone. Those casual dinners churned the Franklin gossip mill and soon the entire town had planned a wedding.

Then his father betrayed them by mixing Lucie up in a jewelry heist, and now everything was off. How she and Frankie would ever recover from the rift with his father, she couldn't fathom.

She sighed. "I think we need to concentrate on moving forward, not backward. That's what I'm focused on. And now, with my father coming home? My life is a little nuts."

Lauren stopped at the corner and motioned to Lucie about which way to turn. "Go left," she called. "I'm finishing up. Be right there." She shifted back to Frankie. "Sorry. I need to go."

He glanced back at his car in the no-parking zone. "Yeah. I know you're working. Should we talk later?"

Yes. *No.* She shrugged. Indifference. Great. "I'm not sure what there is to talk about. Nothing has changed. At least that I know of. Why torture ourselves?"

More of that filthy, awkward silence drifted between them, and Lucie's heart slammed. It would be so easy to give in. To have a night out with Frankie, but if they weren't getting back together, she'd just be ripping her heart open for another stab. Wounds never healed if they were picked open.

"You're right," Frankie said. "I guess."

He guessed? He was the one who wanted this. She shook her head. Tried not to feel angry. As understanding as he'd been all those times she'd broken up with him, she never expected him to spend time with her. Not when they weren't a couple.

"Frankie, I need to go."

She went up on tip-toes and kissed his cheek like she used to do before they were lovers. She breathed in, taking the woodsy scent of his soap with her. This is where they'd wound up. Cheek kisses. Dammit, it felt like that stab to her mangled heart had already happened. She glanced over at Lauren, patiently waiting for the dog to finish inspecting one of the giant trees entrenched in the sidewalk.

No need to glance at the time to know they were further behind schedule. "I have to go," she said.

"Right. Bye, Luce. Keep me updated on Carlucci's."

She nodded, gave him a little wave, and jogged to meet Lauren and Oscar. When she reached them, she heard Frankie's car door slam and then another honk. Frankie saying goodbye like he always did.

Lucie didn't look. Instead, she focused on Lauren and work. Because that's what she did when things went awry with Frankie. She focused on work.

"Sorry about that, Lauren. How are we doing?"

Oscar swung his head in her direction, stared a second, then went back to the tree. "Move it along, Oscar. You've got five minutes before we turn back and you're nowhere near your favorite bush."

Lauren laughed.

"I know," Lucie said. "But these dogs can be so

predictable. This one? If you try to turn back before he squirts on the bush that's just around the next corner, he'll dig in and refuse to move. I try to get him to that bush in a hurry so he can take his time going back."

Of course, had she not been distracted by Frankie, she'd have explained that.

And then her phone rang. "Yeesh!"

She pulled the phone from the pocket of her shorts. A 3-1-2 number. Downtown.

"Go ahead," Lauren said. "I've got Oscar."

"Thanks. Hello?"

"Lucie?"

She knew that voice. Her stomach did that crazy flip-flop thing. After the last few minutes with Frankie, her emotions couldn't be trusted.

"Yes."

"It's Tim O'Brien."

Yep. The hunky cop. "Uh, hi." Lordy, she'd need a solid shot of scotch. And she didn't even drink scotch. "How are you?"

"I'll take Oscar to his bush," Lauren announced.

Apparently hearing what Lauren said, O'Brien laughed, all deep and sexy—*rrrowr*—and the weight of her conversation with Frankie lifted. So did her hormone level.

"He's being processed," O'Brien said to someone on his end. He came back to her. "Sorry. Finishing up here. So, Lucie, can I buy you dinner one night? I can quiz you on all things dogs since my sister is trying to unload a stray on me. The damned thing is cute as hell, but it needs to be about fifty pounds heavier."

"Because you're a manly man?"

"Because I carry a big freakin' weapon and I can't be seen

with a midget dog. Then again, carrying a big freakin' weapon means I can have any dog I want."

"Whatever you say, Detective."

"Oh, ouch. Did I not just ask you to dinner?"

"Yes."

"Then how about calling me Tim, because there's something off about you calling me detective when I'm trying to take you on a date."

Just wait until you get me into handcuffs.

Mother of God! Lucie threw her hand over her head. She had to be insane. Or lonely. Or just plain horny. Or maybe she simply needed someone to touch her. In a good way, a loving way that made her feel safe and secure and not... heartbroken. Sitting at home, waiting for Frankie to come back to her was hard. Brutally so. And Tim seemed like a nice guy. What could it hurt to go out for dinner?

"Sure. That sounds fun." *Handcuffs notwithstanding.* "Tim."

"I'm off this weekend. How about Friday night?"

Friday night. Hmmm. She'd been out of this dating thing a while. Maybe she should pretend to be busy?

Nah. Who had the energy for that?

"Friday night is good."

"Great. I'll pick you up at seven. Does that work?"

"Yep. Sure does."

Just that fast, she had a date. With someone other than Frankie. Did anyone else hear that? The sound of her heart crumbling like an abandoned building? *Think about the handcuffs.*

Lauren turned the corner. "Oscar did his thing in the bush."

"Okay!" She went back to Tim. "Sorry. The dog just made a deposit in his favorite bush."

She smacked her hand against her head. "Did that sound as bad as I think it did?"

"I didn't hear anything."

"You're a good man, Tim O'Brien."

"You haven't seen anything yet, sweetheart."

3

—————

LUCIE SAT AT HER MOTHER'S DINING ROOM TABLE, HER LAPTOP open in front of her, researching Gomez paintings. After overhearing Bart Owens' argument, a niggling feeling of him being involved in something crooked wouldn't leave her. For the Lutz's sake, she decided a little research on that painting was necessary.

Across the table, Mom was dressed in a plain white T-shirt and lightweight modern cargo pants. Her poker night outfit. She liked the extra side pockets for holding her chips. She sat quietly, hand-stitching a sample faux fur vest for one of the Ninja Bitches to test. If Mom and Ro could get the design on the first one right, they'd pitch a line of fur accessories to Frampton's Department Store, their largest client.

The front door—one of those vintage oak ones that weighed slightly less than a ton—flew open and smacked against the inside wall. Lucie flinched and Mom's entire body jerked.

"Ow!" Mom dropped the vest and shook her hand out. "Stuck myself."

Ro's dramatic entrances were nothing new, but one day, she'd give someone in the Rizzo family a heart attack.

"Ro!" Lucie said. "You just bludgeoned my mother."

Stomping toward them in a micro mini, a tank top, and her typical mile-high strappy sandals, Ro went straight to Mom, threw her arms around her and started bawling. "I'm sorry."

Lucie wasn't one to swear, but crap. Ro. Crying? "Ro, it's not that big of a deal. Just take it easy next time."

"There, there," Mom cooed, rubbing Ro's back. "It was just a little stick."

Still sobbing, Ro straightened up, grabbed a piece of loose silk Lucie had bought from the overpriced-but-worth-it fabric store in Lincoln Park and blew her nose on it.

Had she lost her mind? "Hello? That was silk. Do you know what that stuff costs?"

"I'll pay you back. After I get my settlement check from my stripper-banging husband."

"No!" Mom said.

Ro wailed again. "Yes! I'm done. He expects me to pretend like nothing happened. Like he didn't humiliate me in front of an entire town. All for his re-election. If he'd act the least bit sorry, maybe I could stand by him. He's only sorry he got caught."

The back door slammed. Again nothing new because Joey slammed every door he walked through. Between him and Ro, they'd take the whole house down.

He rushed into the room arms up and ready for battle, his head swinging left and right. "What the hell? Sounds like a goddamn slaughter."

"Joseph," Mom said. "Language."

"It *is* a slaughter!"

Ro. Heavy on the drama.

Joey looked at Lucie, nudged his head in Ro's direction. "What's that about?"

"She and Tommy." Not wanting to say the word divorce and risk more wailing, Lucie slashed her hand across her throat.

"She's dumping him? My odds just hit nine to five the other way."

"Whaaaaaaa," Ro wailed.

"Joseph!" This from Mom. "Leave. Now. Go to your room."

This place is an asylum. Twenty-nine years old and his mother was sending him to his room.

Rushing around the table, Lucie wrapped her friend in a hug and flipped Joey the bird behind Mom's back. What an idiot.

He held up his hands. "I'm sorry. I'm sorry. You're right. Priorities. Ro, you want me to kick his ass? I'd do that for you."

Finally. Some concern about their friend. This was the Joey she adored. Idiot or not, sometimes, in his own fatalistic way, he could be sweet and protective. Apparently, Ro responded to that because she pulled away from Lucie, turned to face Joey, and threw herself into his arms.

"I know you would," she said. "But no. If I'm taking him to the cleaners, I have to be the loyal wife to pull it off. I've been so good to him and this is what he does to me? I can't believe it. The bastard."

At which point, totally behind Mom's back, Joey grinned at Lucie, slid his hand over Ro's butt cheek and squeezed.

As expected, because Joey knew Ro just as well as Lucie, if not better considering their sexual—*blech*—history, Ro snorted. Her brother had known just what to do to make Ro smile.

"God, you're a pig," she said.

Mom spun around. "What did he do?"

"Nothing," they all said.

"I made her laugh though."

Ro gave him a smacking kiss on the cheek then ran her fingers under her eyes. Her makeup was already destroyed, but she didn't need to know that. Why make things worse?

"Yes, you did," she said. "Thank you."

"Ooh," Mom said. "It's almost seven. It's poker night. I need to go."

Joey put his hand out to help Mom from her chair. "I'll walk you."

"It's half a block and still light out. Knock it off. Who's going to attack me on this block?"

"Hey, you never know."

"Leave her alone," Lucie said. "She'll be fine. No one is crazy enough to bother her. Of all people. Between you and Dad, they'd be numbskulls to try it."

Her brother pondered that. "All right. I'll watch you from the sidewalk. But it'll be late when you come home. I'll pick you up."

Mom let out a frustrated laugh. "I love you, but when your father comes home, you need to move out. I'll never survive the two of you."

"Uh, speaking of..."

Everyone in the room stopped moving. Just *bam*, frozen. Speaking of what? Moving out? Could that mean...?

Lucie gawked. "You're moving out?"

And then, shocker of all shockers, her brother nodded. "Yeah. I mean, with Dad coming home, Mom doesn't need me anymore. And Frankie's got that empty third floor flat at his house."

Two issues here. One, Lucie would be alone with her

father and her mother. After Dad being gone two years and her mother proclaiming her newfound independence, there was no telling the drama that would unfold inside this nineteen-hundred-square-foot house. Two, her brother was moving in with Frankie. It shouldn't have surprised her. They'd been friends—best friends—since grammar school. But—wow—if the lines weren't already blurred, they sure were now. As long as she and Frankie were broken up, she couldn't visit. Visiting meant walking past Frankie's apartment, a place she'd spent countless nights watching television, having dinner, making *love*. Each time she'd wonder what was going on inside. Whether he had a woman in there. Whether he was making love to someone else.

Oh. My. *God.*

"You're moving into *Frankie's?*"

"Oh, boy," Ro said.

Joey shrugged. "Why not?"

Mom stared up at him, her mouth partway open and her hazel eyes more than a little stricken. Lucie hadn't seen this look since Dad got convicted.

But she knew from conversations with Frankie that the only reason Joey still lived at home was because he didn't want Mom to not have a man around to help with the household stuff. That and, well, she always had a meal ready and his laundry done. That didn't matter though. Chances were, she'd still do the cooking and laundry for him wherever he lived.

But make no mistake, Joey had unintentionally just broken their mother's heart.

Lucie tore her gaze away from Mom and went back to Joey. "When did you decide this? I just talked to him today and he didn't say anything."

"I asked him not to. I wanted to tell you guys. Luce,

you've been a little—" Joey waggled his hand, "—whackadoo lately. I wanted to be sure Dad was coming home before I said anything."

Mom held out a shaky hand. "Joseph, I was kidding. You don't have to move out."

"I know, Ma. But it's time. I'm twenty-nine years old and I can afford it. I gotta go. I'm sorry."

Being the trooper she was, Mom waved that off. "Don't you dare apologize for living your life. If this is what you want, then you should do it."

"It is."

Finally, she stood, held her arms out, and her mountain of a son hugged her, holding on for a few seconds while Mom sniffled away unshed tears. "I'll miss you." She backed away and nodded. "You drive me crazy, but I'll miss you."

Joey hit her with the Joey smile that always got him out of trouble. "I'll still come by to eat."

And probably bring his laundry.

"Of course you will."

As she always did in times of crisis or heartbreak or just about anything that rocked her world, Mom lifted her chin, tugged on the hem of her shirt and faced Lucie and Ro. "I'm off to poker. You three behave."

"Will do, Mom."

Mom left and Lucie, desperate to be rid of the idea of Frankie having other women in his bed, turned to Ro. "Back to the issue that started this whole thing. Are you okay?"

"Yeah. I just needed to get it out of my system. You know me, I'll survive." Ro gestured to the laptop. "What are you working on?"

"I'm researching Gomez paintings."

"Who?" Joey asked.

"Gomez. The artist who did the painting the Lutzes bought from the gallery."

"That's an ugly-ass painting."

Her brother. The art critic. "It's a matter of taste."

"Bad taste."

Ro snorted. Great. Now she was encouraging him. "Don't start, you two. This is important."

"Why?"

"Well, you know our new dog walker?"

Ro nodded. "Lauren, right? How's she working out?"

Lucie held her crossed fingers up. "So far so good. She's a little nosey though. Yesterday she was all over Mr. L.'s painting. Today, we overheard Bart Owens arguing with an artist. Lauren couldn't stop speculating on what the argument was over."

"Something good?"

"I don't know. They were going at it though. It sounded like Bart lent someone named Robert's paintings to a gallery and now can't get them back."

"Luce," Joey said, "you gotta stay out of this crap. It's not your business."

In a way, it was. Her brother just didn't know it. "Just hang on with me for a second. Lauren said she kinda remembered something weird about how the Gomez paintings were sold."

"So?"

"*So*, after hearing him argue with this artist today, I figured I'd research Gomez paintings. Last thing I need is Mr. Lutz getting swindled after I hooked him up with Bart."

"Oh, no," Joey said.

Ignoring him, Lucie moved back to her laptop and pointed at the screen. "I found a Michigan gallery that sells Gomez's paintings. His will dictates that the gallery is the only one with permission to sell his work. Apparently, the owner allowed him to show his paintings there when he was a nobody."

"Wha... what?" Joey said. "Why are we talking about this?"

Ro shot him one of her hairy eyeball looks. "Shut up, Joey. Ignore him, Luce."

Gladly. "I took a finder's fee for the painting—a *Gomez*—that Bart Owens sold to Mr. Lutz."

"So?"

She'd like to smack that giant head of his.

"Well, smart-ass, Lauren wondered if the painting might be a copy. A *fake*. If it is, Mr. Lutz got scammed by Bart Owens. And I helped."

"Oh, boo-effing-hoo," Joey said. "Maybe the painting is real."

If she didn't murder her brother, it would be a miracle. "Okay, *fine*. Let's say the painting is legit. If Bart didn't get it from the Michigan gallery, I've accidentally brokered an illegal deal. Either way," Lucie flopped one hand out, then the other, shifted them up and down like scales, "I'm going to jail for fraud."

4

____

At oh-eight-hundred hours, Mission Lucie-Does-Art went into motion. Lucie-Does-Art? Ew. That sounded bad.

Whatever. Work to be done here.

Following protocol, Lucie entered the Owens Gallery via the back door. Keegan, one of Bart's part-time sales associates, sat at the desk in the cramped office scrolling through a spreadsheet.

"Good morning, Keegan."

He swiveled sideways, his stick-thin body swinging fast as he smoothed his tie. An Andy Warhol today. Keegan had a thing for ties imprinted with works from famous artists. So far, Lucie's favorite was *The Scream* by Edvard Munch. The original painting, a pastel, depicted an agonized person, hands pressed against their cheeks, belting out a scream. In short, it could have been Lucie.

Today, he'd paired the tie with a pair of black dress slacks and a funky light-green shirt. His short hair, as normal, had been gelled back and the overhead light reflected off its glossy glow.

"Hello, my little Lucie," Keegan said.

Barely thirty, just a few years older than Lucie, Keegan's delusions of sophistication and grandeur resulted in his calling her his "little Lucie."

Lucie glanced around. "Where's Oscar?"

"They haven't come down yet. Are you early?"

Bart and Oscar lived in an apartment over the gallery. And, yes, as a matter of fact, she was early. Mission Lucie-Does-Art required it because Keegan, bless his gossiping heart, had a tendency to babble. And if one showed the least bit of interest, the man would prove just how in-the-know he was.

She checked her watch. "Well, look at that, I guess I am. That's okay. I can wait."

"Coffee?"

"No. Thank you." She leaned one hip against the desk. "Have you met Lauren yet? My new dog walker? She's an art history major. She nearly drooled when we came in here the other morning."

Keegan gave her a wry smile. "I have *not* met her. Tell her to come by and I'll show her some work. What's on the floor isn't the half of it."

Un-huh. Lucie would just file that away in her tickler. That's what investigators did. They mentally filed things. "I will do that. She saw the painting the Lutzses bought and thought it was a Gomez. Said she'd done a paper on him once and thought his paintings were only sold in certain galleries. How cool is that?"

Investigators also didn't always admit what they knew.

"She's correct. The only gallery allowed to sell them is in Michigan."

"Huh, I'll have to tell her she was right. Any idea how much they cost? I'm sure I can't afford it, but I'm opening a new office and something about the artist's work intrigues me. Just think. It could be my first big girl art purchase."

"You are too cute, my little Lucie. The prices vary. Now, maybe Bart could work a deal with the Michigan gallery like he did for Lutz, but you'd have to ask him. I don't know how he finagled that." Keegan flapped both hands. "I about died —died!—when that painting was delivered."

Finagled. Interesting word choice. "Who delivered the painting?"

"A courier service. And the sender wasn't the Michigan gallery." Keegan pinched his fingers in front of his lips. "Tick-a-lock, my little Lucie."

"Of course, Keegan. But couldn't whoever sold Lutz and Bart the painting have bought it from the Michigan gallery and resold it?"

He shrugged. "Possibly. It would have been a private collector though. From what I've heard, the Michigan gallery will not sell to other galleries. Now, of course, there are probably ways around it."

He leaned closer and crooked two fingers. Assuming he was about to share something juicy, Lucie leaned in and cocked her head.

Before speaking, Keegan glanced over her shoulder. Obviously satisfied the coast was clear, he brought his attention back to Lucie.

"The art world, little Lucie, is ripe with side deals. If you really want a Gomez, you should talk to Bart."

Lucie opened her eyes wide, feigning excitement. Not hard, considering her shyster meter had once again tripped. Without a doubt, she needed to figure out how Bart had *finagled* that Lutz deal.

Above them, the tiny pitter-patter of doggie nails smacked against the floor and Lucie tracked the movement.

In thirty seconds, Oscar would zoom down the stairs into the office and hit her with some morning Oscar lovin'. Like most males, Oscar woke up with sex on his mind and liked to give Lucie's leg a hump before starting the day. If she had a nickel for every dog that humped her, she'd have ten Gomezes.

"Here comes your boy," Keegan said.

Lucie turned to the open doorway. Oscar rounded the corner, stopped, stared right at her, kicked his hind legs, and charged.

"Get ready," Bart hollered. "He just seduced the bed post."

And here we go. Oscar skidded to a stop, wrapped his front paws around Lucie's calf and went to work.

"It must be brutal," Keegan joked, "being objectified this way."

"You have no idea." Lucie looked down at Oscar, bucking away. "Off!"

Bart rushed in to haul his horny dog off her. "I'm so sorry, Lucie. I don't know what it is with him when it comes to you."

"Maybe it's my enormous sex appeal."

Keegan grinned. "You are too cute, little Lucie."

Oh, whatever, Keegan. She stepped over to the peg near the door for the leash. "Let's hit it, Oscar. I have a busy day ahead."

One that includes finding out where your owner got a Gomez.

LUCIE HAD AN HOUR TO KILL. ONE MEASLY HOUR BEFORE heading downtown to walk Buddy the Wheaten Terrorist and Mamie, the ever-regal labradoodle, who never got ruffled by anyone or anything. The dog had to have been the Queen of England in a past life. Totally unflappable.

After that, it would be on to Josie and Fannie, the Ninja Bitches. Thanks to Joey—when had she ever imagined saying those words?—who was handling Otis and Boots for her this morning, she'd get home early.

Even still, she'd fill her spare hour by meeting with Ro at the storefront to look at paint samples.

Lucie pushed through the glass door and found her BFF standing in the middle of the vacant space. She'd held strong to refusing to enter until the floor had been cleaned so Lucie hired a commercial cleaning company to come in and basically take a belt sander to the place. It still reeked of dampness, but it didn't look half bad.

Just in case she'd be called into action and sent to the hardware store, Ro wore another hormone-inducing outfit: a revealing V-neck top and a short, red skirt. She'd finished the ensemble with multiple strands of beaded necklaces and a pair of her designer stilettos.

"Ro, you're going to give that kid at the hardware store a stroke."

"You know it, sister." She waved her hand over the samples. "Look at these and tell me what you think."

"Where'd the desk come from?"

She jerked her thumb toward the back room. "I found it buried under a bunch of boxes in the back and dragged it out here."

Lucie would have liked to witness her dragging the desk around in that getup. "By yourself?"

"Sure. It's cheap so it's light. When we're done, I want it destroyed. No questions asked."

Ro. The Queen of All Things Fabulous.

"There's a bunch of junk back there we'll have to deal with."

"I know. I'll get to it." Lucie eyeballed the paint samples and held up two of the beige-ish ones. "I think I like these two."

"Well"—she tapped her nail against the one on the left—"this one might have a bit too much yellow. We won't know until we get it on the wall. I'll run by the shop and get a quart of each and we can look at them tomorrow."

"Good. Joey lined up a painter and a flooring guy."

Ro eased onto the desktop and swung one long leg. "I'll talk to them. See what we can do schedule wise."

Such a good friend. From the time they were kids, Ro had always been there for Lucie, taking care of her the way Italian girls did for their friends. A gift really. "Thank you. You're the best."

The front door opened and in tromped Joey. In his massive mitts, he carried Boots, a Yorkie-Bichon Frise mix. The dog had the face of a Bichon and the body and coloring of a Yorkie, but all that craziness added up to massive cuteness.

"We got a problem," Joey said.

A problem. Something new. *Not.* "What is it?"

"The flying nun."

The cuteness known as Boots had goofy long ears that went up when he got excited. Only, they didn't go straight up. They went sideways like airplane wings, leading Joey to nickname him the flying nun.

"What happened?"

Joey gave her a massive eye roll. "Are you kidding me?" He pointed to the dog's right ear. "How do you not see he's stuck in flight mode?"

Lucie lost it. Just bubbled up with laughter. What the hell was her brother talking about? *"What?"*

"Luce, I'm serious. One ear won't go down."

Ro wandered over, cocked her head one way, then the other. "He looks like someone shot that ear full of Botox." She nuzzled Boots's head. "I know your secret now, kid."

Growing concerned, Lucie scooped the dog out of Joey's arms, tried to guide the ear down. Nothing doing. It shot right back up and she got a nice little lick for her efforts. "How long has he been this way?"

"Forty-five minutes. I showed up to walk him, his ears went up, he whizzed all over himself—he's got to learn to control that—and when he calmed down, only one ear relaxed. I figured maybe he was still in some kind of quasi-adrenaline rush and it would wear off. No dice. What do you wanna do?"

How the heck should she know? "Maybe I should call his mom?"

Joey scoffed. "She's not his mom—she's his owner. And yeah, that's probably a good start. Maybe this has happened before. Either way, I can't be walking him in this condition. Bad enough I'm walking a pansy-assed dog, never mind one that looks like a freak."

Who the heck was he kidding? If he wasn't just as worried about that dog, he wouldn't be standing in front of her. "You are so full of it, Joey. You're always complaining about how scooping poop is bad for your image, and yet, here you are, schlepping all the way over here because you're worried about Boots."

"I'm not worried. I thought you should know. That's all."

"Un-huh. Got it." She handed the dog back to Joey and dug her cell phone from her messenger bag. "Let me call the *owner*."

Her brother. Such a dope. The big lug just didn't want to admit that he'd fallen a little bit in love with the dogs. Day in and day out, he'd moan about his bookmaking business suffering because he was busy helping her run Coco Barknell and yet, he always showed up. Always. Still, he had to be a PITA and make it seem like he was doing this for her. That she should be grateful to him.

Which, in fact, she was. And that was saying something with their history of sibling battles.

She scrolled her contact list, found Boots's mom's number and clicked. "I'm glad you're here. I need to talk to you both about this Gomez thing."

"That lame painting again?"

"Yes. And it's not lame." She held her finger up after the phone's second ring. "Let me leave this voice mail and I'll tell you while we're waiting for a call back."

She left a message and clicked off. Ro had moved back to sitting on the edge of the desk and Joey parked himself next to her, stretching his long legs in front of him. Today he wore baggy shorts and a loose T-shirt, his normal summer work attire and Ro rolled her eyes at him. Clearly, she expected better.

Lucie had seen Joey and Ro together hundreds, maybe thousands of times, but right now, sitting side by side like that, it hit her why they'd had a fling. They were stunning. All dark hair and olive skinned, they were a perfect match.

"Tick-tock, Luce," Ro said. "I have a meeting with my lawyer in thirty minutes."

"Right, sorry. I talked to the sales guy at the gallery about the painting. With the thing about only the Michigan gallery being able to sell Gomez paintings, he's not sure how Bart 'finagled'—his word, not mine—the sale."

"He said *finagled*?"

"Yep. Sounds a little fishy to me."

"It does."

Joey shook his head. "You two nutty broads think you're Charlie's Angels. Forget this crap."

Ro huffed. "And what? Risk your sister going to prison?"

"Come on with the drama," he said. "She's not going to prison."

"She could. Art fraud is a big deal. Especially if this Gomez guy is big time. She could get ten years for selling knockoffs."

Ten years? Holy cow. She'd never survive prison. Someone would make her their bitch and it would be all over. "Gee, thanks, Ro."

Joey waved that off. "How the hell do you know?"

"I looked it up last night. I was bored and had already polished off a quart of Chocolate Passion. If I keep that up, my rear won't fit through the door. I needed something to distract me."

At that, Joey smirked and Ro elbowed him. "What's that smirk?"

"Listen," he said, "even if your ass didn't fit through the door, I'd still love it."

In a Joey sort of way, that was awfully sweet. *Ew.*

"I love your attempt at charming," Ro said, "but focus here." She turned back to Lucie. "Go ahead, Luce."

Where was she? She'd lost track after that whole Ro's giant-ass conversation. If her brother started hitting on Ro, Lucie would lose her mind. Just go insane. In the last sixty seconds, she'd become someone's prison bitch and listened to them flirting gorilla style. *Welcome to my life.*

"The Gomez," Lucie said. "Ten years. I think I need to drive out to this gallery in Michigan and check it out."

Joey threw his hands up. "What's that gonna do?"

"I have no idea. But if I go there, I'll be able to see a real Gomez up close. Maybe I'll pretend to be a student, like Lauren, doing research."

"Nah," Ro said. "If you're going undercover, you need to be a buyer. That's when you get the good dirt. I'll go with you. It'll be fun. We can get all dressed up and pretend we're loaded."

Easy for her to say. She was the one with the designer shoe collection. But this idea might have merit. "The most expensive piece of clothing I own is the dress I bought three months ago for that date with Frankie. It cost what? A hundred bucks?"

"Then I'll be the loaded one. You can be my beleaguered assistant. I'll even go out and buy a new outfit. Maybe melt my rat-bastard husband's credit card."

"Remind me," Joey said, "to never marry and divorce you. You are wicked, girl."

"You know it, brother."

Boots wiggled around and Joey set him on the floor to wander, his one ear still poking straight out.

"That ear is screwed," he said before turning back to Lucie. "I don't like you two going alone."

"Why?"

"I don't know. Just feels off."

Oh, no. He wasn't about to talk her out of this. No way. She folded her arms, narrowed her eyes trying for intimidating. "Then you'll have to come with us because I'm going."

Ro smacked her hands together. "He could be our driver."

"Just shut it, Roseanne. I'm not playing chauffeur."

But Ro, in full-on excitement mode, hopped off the desk and stood next to Lucie, staring him down. "Think about it. We throw you in a suit and you drive my Escalade. Luce and

I will ride in the back. If I'm going to be rich and have an assistant, I'd definitely have a driver. And we wouldn't be alone. Problem solved."

He rolled his bottom lip out. Considering it.

At this rate, they'd be arguing over this all day and Lucie didn't have time. Or patience. "Joey, I don't care what you do. With or without you, I'm going to Michigan."

5

The stress alone of driving to Michigan with Roseanne and Joey might kill her.

"Driver," Ro snapped, trying for the thousandth time in the last fifteen minutes to annoy Joey.

He switched to the left lane and roared by slower cars on the expressway. "I'm ignoring you."

Needing a distraction, Lucie opened her window an inch and let the warm air blow in. They'd hit the road at eight-thirty for the two-hour drive to the gallery and managed to miss the worst of the morning traffic. Ro, of course, was dressed the part in a black, sleeveless sheath, her favorite pair of Gucci sandals and sunglasses that probably cost more than Lucie's laptop. Even if she hadn't gotten a chance to melt her husband's credit card, she'd managed just fine pulling something out of her expansive closet.

Joey glanced at Lucie by way of the rear-view mirror. "I don't see what the rush was on this trip. We just talked about it last night and now we're hauling ass out there."

"Blame it on Ro freaking me out over that ten-year prison sentence. I'm nobody's bitch. That's all I'm saying."

"Huh? And since when do you swear?"

"Forget it. Besides, Lauren was available all day to cover the dogs. Just pray she can handle it."

"Luce, it's dog walking, not biometric engineering."

That got Ro's attention and she whipped off her sunglasses. "Do you even know what biometric engineering is?"

"Sure. It's the combination of engineering and biological sciences."

Ro turned to Lucie. "I have no idea what that means."

"Basically, you nutty broads, it's measuring and analyzing human characteristics. Fingerprints, DNA, voice patterns."

"Oh my God," Lucie said. It was like an endless cycle of insanity in this car.

"Hey," Joey said, "she asked. And speaking of the dogs, Boots's ear finally went down. His owner took him to the vet. They're stumped. Go figure."

"Well," Lucie said, "at least the poor baby is okay. How much longer until we get to the gallery?"

He hit a button on the GPS screen. "It says thirty minutes."

Lucie checked the time on her phone. They'd arrive at the gallery at eleven o'clock. Figure an hour tops of being there, a quick bite to eat, and they'd be back on the road by one-thirty. Home by four. They *had* to stick to a schedule. Even if she wasn't working today, she didn't want to be late for her dinner with Detective O'Brien. Tim.

Wait. Panic shooting straight up into her eyeballs, she drew a sharp breath and turned to Ro.

"What?"

She couldn't say it. Not in front of Joey. He'd have a world-class meltdown about her going on a date with a cop.

Via the rear view mirror Joey glanced at her again and their eyes met.

"Nothing," she said, swiping the screen on her phone to text Ro. "I forgot an email I had to send."

A minute later Ro's phone whistled and she dug it out of the seat pocket. She saw the name on the screen and frowned. "You're—"

Lucie cleared her throat and smacked the side of Ro's leg to shut her up. Finally getting the hint, she read the text. The one telling her Lucie didn't have anything to wear for her date with O'Brien.

This got her an irritated sigh. "My work is never done."

Before Ro could fire back a text, Lucie turned the volume and vibrate on her phone off. If her phone even buzzed, Joey Big Ears would be on to them. A second later the text popped up. All caps.

UNBELIEVABLE!!!! IT'S FINE. YOU CAN WEAR SOMETHING OF MINE. I'LL FIND A SHORT DRESS. CROTCH LENGTH ON ME. KNEE LENGTH ON YOU. LOL.

Lucie snorted. This was friendship. THANK YOU.

Giving up on the rear-view mirror, Joey swung his head and glanced back at them. "What are you two doing?"

"Nothing, *driver*," Ro said. "Pay attention to the road. Precious cargo here."

Fifteen minutes later, Joey pulled into the gallery parking lot and parked just across from the entrance. The three-story brick building with scrollwork on the corners was probably reminiscent of some early style, but Lucie was hardly an architectural expert and couldn't fathom a guess as to the age of the building. It looked old, but that didn't always mean anything. The subdued, etched sign near the door read Montrose Gallery.

Right place.

Joey pushed open his door. "Okay, ladies. Let's get this done and get home."

Amen to that.

The three of them sauntered in the front door looking like some whacked-out version of a CIA team. Ro in her designer duds, Joey looking like the well-dressed muscle and Lucie the dour assistant.

A wiry-framed older man in an expertly tailored gray suit came through a doorway at the rear of the gallery and waved. "Welcome."

"Hello," Ro purred.

Joey nodded at the man then moved off to the side to let them do their thing while he leaned against the wall and scanned the framed pieces surrounding them. The large, open area contained three support columns leading Lucie to believe a few walls had been knocked out. The low-slung ceiling and subdued lighting gave the room a cozy, but unconfined feel. Whoever had designed the place had managed to display the artwork without any harsh light.

Then there was the art. At least thirty paintings—all in one long row—lined the walls. Beside each painting was a small plaque that Lucie assumed held information about the work.

"I'm Carlton," the man said. "The owner. How can I help you?"

Ro wandered to the far wall and stood in front of a pastel painting of a woman and young child. "I'd like to look around. I've been told you are the exclusive gallery for Arturo Gomez."

Prayerful hands and all, Carlton gave a little bow, then straightened up. "Ah, yes. Excellent taste. Are you interested in purchasing one?"

"Yes." Ro gestured to Lucie. "Delilah—"

Delilah?

"What's the name of that painting? The one we want?"

Uh. What was Ro doing? Lucie had seen the names of some of the paintings while doing research, but she hadn't memorized any of them. Time to punt and give the one title she did know. The one Mr. Lutz owned. *"My Darkest Night."*

"Oh. Lovely piece that one. Unfortunately, I don't have it."

Dang it. If he'd had it, they'd have proved in record time that Mr. Lutz's painting was a fake. Which couldn't be considered good news because Lucie would then have to tell her former boss, her current best client, a man who had mentored her and even tried to help her find other banking jobs, that she'd connected him with a dealer who'd sold him a fugazzi.

Her stomach rolled and she turned back to Joey, who met her gaze then drew his eyebrows together. He would never be Mr. Sensitivity but clearly knew when his sister was in distress. She perked up, plastered on a smile and faced Carlton again. "Oh, that's too bad."

"Maybe I can show you something similar?"

Ro wandered to the next painting on the wall, tilted her head this way and that, playing the role of a wannabe buyer. If she knew anything about art, it would be a surprise to Lucie, but she looked good. And in Ro's world, that's all that mattered.

Total method acting.

"Well," she said, "I had my heart set on that one."

Being the able-bodied assistant, Lucie cleared her throat. "Carlton, do you know who owns the painting? Perhaps we could contact them?"

Ro spun back, curved her lips into the I-am-beautiful-

and-you-will-do-what-I-say smile. "And then I can make the owner of *My Darkest Night* an offer. Delilah, you are a genius."

"Thank you, ma'am." She nodded at Carlton. "Of course, we would *very much* appreciate any help you can give on that front."

Hey, Keegan had said side deals happened all the time. Still, this method acting wasn't so easy, but hopefully Carlton got the message that the disgustingly wealthy Ro would compensate him for helping make this deal happen.

None of which would actually happen, but well, this was the life of undercover work.

"Let me check my list," he said.

"Your list?"

"Yes. The family has a private collection of Arturo's work. Whatever they don't have, I'm able to sell. They've been known to occasionally sell paintings. For charity auctions and whatnot, but they are diligent about notifying me when that happens. It helps us keep the master list of all works updated so all paintings are accounted for."

"How smart."

Carlton walked to the desk near the back wall and Ro turned her back to him. She winked at Lucie and blew a kiss. Lucie feigned a gag. *Hairball.* Her lunatic friend was having way too much fun on this adventure.

Thank goodness, at least, big-mouth Joey was staying quiet. If he got on a tear, no telling what might happen. Lucie gestured to the entrance. "You could run outside and get some air if you wanted."

He folded his arms and leaned against the wall. "I'm good right here."

Of course he was.

"Well," Carlton said, coming back toward Lucie and Ro. "I have good news and bad news."

Ro cocked one hip. "Carlton, you're not going to break my heart, are you?"

He smiled at her flirty tone and Lucie's hairball grew.

"I certainly hope not," he said. "I checked my inventory and I don't see that particular painting on the list."

"Is that bad?"

"Not necessarily. The family might still have the painting in one of their homes. In which case, you might be in luck and they'd sell it."

Lucie didn't like the dubious tone. "What are the chances of that? You said they usually only let the pieces from the private collection go when a charity is involved."

Carlton leaned closer. That was a little crazy pants considering they were the only ones in the room, but hey, maybe the place had recording devices or something. Ooh. Bad thought since they were undercover.

Now who was crazy pants?

Get a grip, Lucie.

"You didn't hear this from me," Carlton said, "but Arturo's youngest sister has, shall we say, financial issues."

"Really?"

"Indeed. Twice the family has bailed her out. Rumor has it she's a gambler."

Finding this fascinating, Lucie slid her gaze to Joey, who was hopefully listening to the tale of woe. He shook his head and topped it off with a massive eye roll. Whenever they got into a discussion about gambling and his illegal bookie business, he assured her his money was safe and grew steadily each year. Unlike the poor slobs who lost their butts in the stock market every day.

The sick part of it was that she had no argument. Zero. Considering she was an out-of-work investment banker.

Ro inched closer to Carlton, giving him a nice view of her cleavage. "A gambler, you say? Meaning if we contacted her and made a hefty offer, she might consider selling us the painting?"

"Uh." Carlton's gaze zoomed to Ro's chest as if an alien had popped out. "Perhaps."

This guy needed to be rescued. Oxygen anyone? Lucie cleared her throat. "How do we contact them?"

Dragging his gaze from the alien boobs, Carlton faced Lucie and handed her a sticky note. "This is the number of their estate attorney. He's usually the contact regarding private transactions."

"Wonderful," Ro said, finally stepping back. "You've been most helpful, Carlton. I look forward to doing business with you in the future."

The three of them high-tailed it out of the gallery. Joey held the rear passenger door open for Ro while Lucie hustled to the other side. She needed a break from all this undercover stress. She didn't like lying, even for the saving-her-own-butt cause. Lying was still lying.

With assistance from the side rail, she vaulted herself into Ro's Escalade. These monsters weren't built for diminutive people.

Next to her, Ro buckled in and fanned herself. "So, that was awesome. My God, what a rush. Seriously, Luce, I might be an undercover detective in my next career."

That would be a vision to behold. "Great. Let's see if we can focus on today though."

"You're right. We shouldn't get ahead of ourselves."

Joey hopped into the driver's seat and fired the engine.

"Hey, Ro. You almost gave that schmuck a heart attack. You gotta go easy working your assets. Some men can't take it."

"Please," she said. "A little flirting never hurt."

"It does if the guy drops dead."

Ro jerked her thumb in Joey's direction. "Again with the Mr. Charming act."

Joey pulled out of the lot. "Where to?"

"Home," Lucie said.

"Home? What home?" This from the future detective with alien boobs. "We have to call the estate attorney. You said the artist lived around here. Maybe the family is local. We could go there today." She held out her hand. "Give me that phone number."

Still holding the number, Lucie held it out of Ro's reach. "No. We're not going there. At least not today."

All of this was coming at her too fast and she needed to slow it down. Slow, slow, slow. Ro was the impulsive one, always rushing forward. Not Lucie. Lucie needed to plan and prioritize. Run scenarios. Ones that didn't include going to jail for fraud.

And being someone's bitch.

No. What she needed was to go home and think on this. Carlton had told them the family made private sales. Perhaps Mr. Lutz's painting was one such sale. Lauren would have no way of knowing about these private sales, so going on her limited knowledge, Lucie could see why she might wonder if the painting was a forgery.

Which meant, Lucie could be overreacting to the whole Mr. Lutz-got-scammed theory. She could be wrong. Even if her instincts, that little niggling on the back of her neck, told her she wasn't, she could be. Accusing an innocent man —a client no less—of criminal activity wasn't exactly the way to build a solid reputation.

"Luce!" Ro hollered.

"Ro!" Lucie hollered back, making Joey laugh. "I'm not calling that attorney today. As it is, my nerves are shot. Mr. Lutz could have bought his painting direct from the family with Bart Owens brokering the deal. I could totally see that. That's what we need to confirm before contacting this lawyer. Once we contact the lawyer, we're committed."

"To what?"

"I don't know. Something."

Joey gunned the gas as he hit the on ramp to the expressway. "Roseanne, leave her alone. This is her deal. And I know my sister. She's a pain in the ass when she gets dug in. You won't budge her."

"Thank you, Joey. I think."

Twisted compliment, for sure, but coming from Joey? It might be the best she'd get.

"Sure," Joey said. "Who's hungry? I could eat."

"We can stop for something quick. Maybe the drive-thru. I need to get back."

Joey shot Lucie a quizzical look in the rear-view then went back to the road. "What's your hurry?"

"I have things to do."

"So, do them tonight. It's not like you have plans. You've spent the last three months moping around the house. At least tonight you'll have something to keep you busy."

As usual, he thought he knew her so well. Predictable, Lucie. Never straying from her routine. Wouldn't he be stunned to know she had a date? With a cop. An Irish one to boot. Ha. Carlton wouldn't be the only one having a heart attack.

As much as she wanted to tell him, just hit him with it, she couldn't. Frankie was his closest friend and cluing Joey in on her date meant putting him in the middle. A scary thought if ever there was one because, knowing him, he'd feel compelled to tell Frankie. And that would be bad. No matter that they were broken up, neither of them would want to hear the other was suddenly dating. Their history didn't include dating others. In all the times they'd broken up, she'd never heard anything about Frankie seeing other women. Never once in all these past off-and-on four years.

"She's going out tonight," Ro said.

Lucie spun on her, gritted her teeth. Really, Ro? *Really?*

"Where's she going?" He looked back at Lucie. "Tell me you and Frankie are back together. Please."

"Are you wagering on how long we'll be broken up again? I swear I'll kill you. That is so rude."

Joey stayed silent, an absolute tell that he was, in fact, running another Frankie-Loves-Lucie pool on when the big reunite would happen. Now with Ro getting divorced, he was busier than ever.

When she'd first heard that he ran these pools, she'd been infuriated. As if her and Frankie's personal lives were plain fodder for the entire town. Even Ro had been known to get in on it. Then, after the initial anger, she'd realized the bets and the subsequent odds were indicative of the ups and downs of her relationship.

And the insanity that came with being part of *the life*.

"She's not back with Frankie," Ro said.

"Dammit. You got my hopes up there. If you were, that'd be five grand in my pocket."

Five thousand dollars? If the kitty was that much, maybe she needed to get in on this pool. After all, she shouldn't be exempt because she wasn't the one doing the breaking up this time. She had no control over when Frankie might want to get back together.

And she could use that five thousand dollars. Health insurance didn't come cheap.

She smacked herself on the head. A minute ago, she'd been outraged. Now? She was selling her soul for health insurance.

"Sorry, Joey."

"Eh. No big. What are you doing tonight then?"

"Just going out with friends."

"You're not gonna tie the bathroom up, are you?"

Ro took that one. "Keep talking and we might."

Lucie laughed. "You guys drive me to want to drink, but I do love you."

JOEY WOULDN'T LEAVE.

Ten minutes until O'Brien picked her up and her brother was still sprawled on the living room sofa. On a Friday night. Wasn't this indicative of her life? Usually, by now, he was at the bar around the corner watching the games on television and making his collections.

Tonight? Glued to the sofa.

And she couldn't have him here when Tim showed up. Who knew how he'd react to a cop taking his sister to dinner. Not that it was any of his business, but she wanted tonight to be a drama break.

Lucie stood at the top of the stairs, leaning against the wall that still had the mark from twelve years ago when she'd gone tumbling down with a marker in her hand. One floor below, Joey shouted at the television and didn't appear to be anywhere close to moving off the sofa.

Time for reinforcements.

She dug her phone from her purse and dialed Ro.

After one ring, Ro answered. "What happened? Don't tell me you ripped that dress already."

When Lucie had gone to Ro's to try dresses on, she'd picked out a red, sleeveless one with a V-neck that showed just a hint of cleavage. Although it was a little tight in the chest area and big in the hips, the belt helped control the extra material and accentuated Lucie's tiny waist. And, according to Ro, her big boobs. While there, Ro insisted on doing hair and makeup, and Lucie figured, why not? A little pampering would be nice.

It took almost an hour, but Ro did her magic and curled Lucie's drab brown hair so it fell in fat waves around her shoulders. For makeup, she added heavy brown liner to Lucie's eyes to "make the blue pop." Lucie imagined her eyeballs exploding from her head. But, Ro had been her best friend since grammar school, and one thing she knew how to do was slay a man.

All in all, the look was summer casual and classy.

"The dress is fine," Lucie told Ro. "And I didn't wreck my hair or makeup putting it on."

"Why are you calling me then?"

"Joey. He won't leave, and O'Brien will be here in ten minutes. My mom is out to dinner with one of her friends so I can't even have her distract him."

With Dad in prison these last couple of years, Mom had taken to enjoying her independence. These last few months, she had been happier than Lucie ever remembered. Her father, being old-school, would hate the newfound independence when he came home in a few weeks. At this rate, Mom might even make him cook his own dinner.

Wouldn't that be a sight?

"Ro, I need Joey gone. He knows O'Brien from when he was investigating the dognappings. If he sees him, he'll tell my dad. I know he will. And possibly Frankie. I don't need either one of them knowing about this. I mean, it's one date, what could happen? All I want is to be out of the house for a while and Tim is a nice guy."

"Relax, sister. I'll take care of it."

"How?"

Ro sighed. "I don't know. But I'll figure it out. I'll call his cell, tell him I need him for something."

Pig Joey would love that. The sexual innuendos would fly like migrating birds. But Ro would be able to get his giant butt off that couch. "Go to work, Ro. Have no mercy."

She laughed. "I love when you talk dirty. I'm on it."

Thirty seconds later, the song "Devil Woman" drowned out the television. What an idiot. He'd given her "Devil Woman" as a ringtone? *I'll kill him later.*

"Hello?" he said. "Hey. What's up? ... Come on. Seriously? ... Awright. Are you okay? ... Hey, relax...You're a pisser, Roseanne. I'll be there in a few minutes."

Lucie rested her head against the wall. *Thank you.* Whatever Ro had come up with, it got him moving. Which meant she'd either told him she was running around the house naked or she'd severed a limb.

"Luce!"

She jumped away from the stairway so he couldn't see her all dolled up. "What?"

"I gotta run. That lunatic Roseanne got her foot stuck in a hole in her yard. She didn't want to bug you. Since she threw that scumbag husband out, she called me to dig her out. She thinks her ankle is busted."

It wasn't a severed limb, but close enough. Lucie threw her hand over her mouth to silence the giggle. Ro had come through in spectacular fashion.

"Oh no," Lucie said, laying on a good bit of feigned horror. "Is she okay? Do I need to cancel my plans?"

"Nah. She's okay. She was sniffling though. I kinda feel bad. She's crazy emotional lately. I can't take that with her. She's always so tough. Seeing her sad like this? Total killer."

These were the moments when Lucie's heart exploded with love for her brother. The caring Joey. The one who wasn't constantly harassing her or making fun of her goodie-two-shoes ways.

"You're a good guy, Joey. Thanks. Have her text me. Okay?"

"Yeah. No sweat."

The back door slammed and Lucie leaned against the wall. Phew. Close one. Going on a date should not be this difficult. In this family, though, nothing came easy. A minute after Joey left, a knock sounded from the front door. *Eeeek*—that was close. Suddenly frantic, Lucie paddled her hands as she ran to her room for her shoes. In her bedroom, she stole one last look in the mirror, fluffed her hair, checked her lipstick.

"Wow," she said, still marveling at the change in her appearance. "That's me. Go, Lucie. Yay, you!"

She wasn't a man-killer, but she had something. Dating movie-star-handsome Frankie sometimes made her feel, well, less. He'd always told her she looked beautiful, but down deep, she knew her looks couldn't compete. Lucie didn't belong to the Stunning People of America club.

Lucie belonged to the Better-Than-Average People of America club.

She'd learned to live with it.

But every now and again, like tonight, Ro helped her. Transformed her into being a possible candidate for the Stunning club.

The knock sounded again. This time a little harder. "Ooh, gotta go."

She flew down the stairs, thankful for her flats. "Coming!"

Four and a half years had passed since she'd been on a date with someone other than Frankie.

Her stomach clenched. Just curled into a tight, gripping, pea-sized ball.

And, God! Why did she think of that now? She squeezed her eyes closed. *Get it together here, Lucie.*

It was only a date. A casual dinner between two friends. Easy.

At the front door, she stopped, gripped the handle. The cold metal hitting her palm focused her, gave her a second to compose herself. *Just a dinner between friends.*

She pulled the door open and looked up at Tim O'Brien. An extremely handsome Tim O'Brien in a pair of khakis, his big shoulders in a white pullover. Who knew she had a thing for cute Irish boys?

His gaze skimmed over her, and his lips, those beautiful full lips she'd never noticed before, curved into a slick smile. "Hello," he said. "I'm here for Lucie."

Oh, now he wanted to play? "Funny man. It's me."

Again, he ran his gaze over her and her woefully lonely body howled his name. *Tim, Tim, Tim!*

"It sure is," he said. "You look amazing. Am I underdressed?"

For once, she wasn't the one asking that question. It probably shouldn't have made her happy, made her more secure, because intentional or not, she never wanted to be the person who made someone else feel...well, less. Of anything. "No. I just felt like doing something...special. You look great. Perfect even. I've only ever seen you in a suit, so this is a nice surprise. I like this Tim O'Brien."

"Lucie Rizzo," he said, "keep talking like that and you might be in trouble."

This time, unlike the situations she'd seen these last five months, trouble felt awfully good.

6

———

Luscious Lucie Rizzo laughed at his comment about her being in trouble. Little did she know he wasn't kidding. Not one bit. From the second Tim put eyes on her five months ago, he'd been curious. She was out walking two dogs, a couple of shih tzus someone had boosted. He'd been working a case—still was—involving a show dog theft ring. The wily bastards were still out there, lifting dogs, probably to sell on the black market.

And he couldn't catch them.

But that first day with Lucie, she was dressed like a coed. Sneakers, jeans, and a jacket with a T-shirt under it. All cute and nice, but her big, blue eyes were the kicker. He'd always been a sucker for blue-eyed women. Had she been anyone other than Joe Rizzo's kid, once he'd closed her case, he'd have made a play for her.

The fact that her father was a criminal created definite problems. Problems that, each time he saw her, diminished because he was a guy and guys had needs, and certain women might be worth taking a chance on.

The ultimate surprise this evening was the new side of

Lucie. The sexy, vivacious look. Because, damn, Lucie had a body on her.

"So," she said as Tim jumped on I-55 heading North, "downtown?"

He merged into traffic, shot to the left lane, and hit the gas. "Yep. There's a place in the Loop I like." He looked over and grinned. "Irish Pub."

Lucie laughed. "As long as I can get some cottage pie, I'll be happy."

Second surprise of the evening. The lady knew Irish food. If he wanted reasons to knock her off the list of women to date, that wasn't one of them.

"Bam!" he said. "Nice, Lucie. Here I was trying to be a smart ass and you busted me. You like Irish food?"

"Just because my last name is Rizzo, doesn't mean I don't have a varied palette. My college roommate's mom was Irish. She used to bring us all kinds of dishes. I liked cottage pie the best. That sauce! So good."

He crept up on a slower car in the left lane and tapped his horn, urging the driver to get the hell out of the way. People. To survive in Chicago traffic, going forty in the left lane wouldn't cut it.

Lucie grabbed onto the door handle. "I guess you're not worried about getting a ticket."

"It's been known to happen, but yeah, I usually get out of it."

"Obviously your boyish charm."

"Or the badge."

"Right. The *badge*."

He didn't need to be an ace detective to know the way she said *badge*, the punch at the end held meaning.

A meaning he understood. Already they were on the same page.

It might be early in this date—the first date, no less—but he'd never been one to beat around the proverbial bush. "Is it a problem for you?"

"Nope."

Funny how she nailed that. Hadn't even mulled it over. Most likely because she'd, like him, already beat it to death in her mind. In the minimal time he'd spent with her, she didn't seem like the type to rush into things. No problem there. He liked a woman who could make up her own mind, take a risk if necessary and not look back.

He smiled the famous O'Brien smile that had been known to open more than a few locked doors. "You seem pretty sure about that."

"Trust me, I'm going into this with my eyes wide open. I wouldn't be here if I didn't want to be. So, as long as you're okay with my, shall we say *backstory*, then I'm okay with it. The way I see it, we're two friends out for an evening. That's assuming this date isn't some sort of undercover sting operation."

A what? He glanced over, remembered they were doing eighty-five, and swung back to the road before he caused a wreck. Did she think...? "Holy hell, no. It's not—"

"Because if it is, you're wasting your time. I've spent my life trying not to know about my father's business. And I've succeeded."

All righty then. He took a breath, ignored the throb in his jaw where that damned muscle jumped, and tried to put himself in her viewpoint. With her history and the years of cops, federal agents, and prosecutors trying to nail her father, what was she supposed to think when a detective suddenly asks her out?

Better to get this cleared up now.

"As long as you don't ask about my family," she continued, "I have no issues."

He shook his head. "Not interested in your family. You, I'm interested in. Have been for months." He looked over at her again, met her steady gaze for a long second to make sure she knew he wasn't lying, and went back to the road. "Okay?"

From the corner of his eye, he spied the smile and a solid head jerk. "Thank you. Sorry if I insulted you. I just wanted to be clear."

"Hey, I'd rather get it out of the way. Now, I just want to take you out for a nice dinner."

And maybe other things...

Nah. She didn't seem the type to let him get handsy on the first date. Something else he'd like. Call him old-fashioned, but certain women he didn't want to be easy. He wasn't against easy. Hardly. Casual sex was a way to have fun and blow off steam. But if dating a woman regularly, he wanted assurances she wasn't getting busy with other men.

Men like Frank Falcone.

Rumor mill had it that they'd broken up enough times to have their own soap opera.

This current breakup might be just one more in the line. A definite risk on Tim's part. Luscious Lucie Rizzo might eventually hand him his carved-up heart on a platter.

And he didn't care.

I'm so screwed.

AFTER A TWENTY-MINUTE DRIVE—NOT BAD FOR FRIDAY-NIGHT traffic—Tim held the restaurant door open and waved Lucie inside. Immediately, the aroma of cooking meat and spices hit her and her stomach growled. Straight ahead, a plump woman of about forty wearing a black long-sleeved blouse, probably to battle the air conditioner, stood at the hostess station, making notes on a board. Her long, silky, blond hair fell over one shoulder and she tucked it behind her ear as she wrote. To her left was the bar. The completely packed bar with oiled wood and polished brass everywhere. Each of the dozen or so high-top tables was full. Patrons were even wedged into the minimal open spaces between tables. To the right was the dining room. Equally polished, equally packed.

Hopefully, Tim had thought ahead and made a reservation.

"Hiya, Tim," the hostess said.

"Hi, Jaye."

She grabbed two menus and waved them. "Follow me. Saved you a table in that spot by the windows."

Yay, Tim. Her hero for apparently being a regular who carried enough oomph to warrant a reserved table on a Friday night when the wait list went twenty deep.

The hostess led them to a table at the far corner of the room along the front window. Outside, a couple holding hands and a mom pushing a stroller wandered by, heading toward the lake just a few blocks up.

One of the things Lucie missed about living downtown were the evening walks. *Soon.*

The hostess set the menus on the table and removed two of the four place settings. "Special tonight is Colin's Irish Stew. It's pretty good."

Tim smirked. "Glowing endorsement, Jaye. Thanks."

"Eh. What can I say? I don't want him to get cocky. Enjoy your meal, guys."

The woman strode away, swinging her ample hips as she

went, and stopping to chat with customers along the way. Sensing something, Lucie turned to Tim, who had those green eyes plastered to her face. Not in an annoying way that made her want to fold in on herself—or hide.

This look was all male and heat and appreciation. Immediately, her cheeks fired. It had been a long time, too long, since a man had looked at her with such open appreciation and...longing. Sure, Frankie loved her, but the newness had worn off. With the newness went the subtle anticipation of where the night might go. Which, in Lucie's mind, might have been one of their issues. No surprises. Everything just...was.

This?

All new.

And kinda fun.

"Sorry," he said. "I'm staring."

She picked up her menu. "You are indeed."

"I can't get over it. You look different. I like cute, wholesome Lucie, who walks her dogs in a ponytail and sneakers. This Lucie? Gotta say"—he held up his hands—"and please don't freak out. This Lucie? Seriously hot."

Another onslaught of heat rushed her cheeks. Darn it. She held the menu in front of her face, pretending to read, but knowing, without a doubt, the handsome detective understood exactly what he'd caused. After a second, the blood rush slowed and her cheeks cooled. *Phew.* She lowered the menu and grinned at the stupid smile on his face.

"You are too damned cute, Lucie."

"Thank you. And I'm not freaking out. It's nice to have someone notice when I put in a little extra effort."

He shoved his menu to the side, blew out a breath. "Oh, I noticed."

She had to look away. If she didn't, she'd have another surge of blushing, and really, she was a grownup. Compliments shouldn't put her in such a state.

Compromise.

She shifted her eyes, looked over his shoulder at the iron light fixtures all in a row behind him. "I love this place."

"You haven't eaten anything yet."

"I love it anyway."

"I know you wanted cottage pie, but you might try the stew."

"I guess you come here a lot?"

"I do. My brother owns it." He waggled his thumb toward the entrance. "The hostess is my sister-in-law. Thus the wisecrack about the chef getting cocky."

"The chef is your brother?"

He nodded. "They opened about five months ago. The first month, I gained ten pounds."

Aha. That explained his beefier build. "I did notice you looked a little different since the last time I saw you. I like beefcake Tim."

That got her a lightning-quick smile. He leaned forward, resting his elbows on the table. "Thanks. I figured I could choose to not eat my brother's phenomenal cooking, or I could go to the gym and turn that fat into muscle. It wasn't a hard choice."

He'd definitely made the correct choice. Definitely.

"When we're done," he said. "I'll take you to the kitchen and you can meet him. He's not as charming as I am."

She certainly hoped not. "I guess I'll try the stew from the not-as-charming brother." She placed the menu at the edge of the table, set her hands in her lap. "So, here we are. The mob princess and the Irish cop. Who'd have thunk it?"

"Is that how you think of yourself? The mob princess?"

"No. I think of myself as a woman with a Master's degree who got downsized out of corporate America and started her own business. Everyone else in this city sees me as the mob princess."

He shrugged. "I don't. We can't control who our parents are or what they do."

God, she liked this guy. He was wrong for her in so many ways—the first being she was still in love with Frankie—but how refreshing to share company with someone who didn't flinch over her lineage. And a cop no less.

"Thank you for saying that." A tiny bit of tension in her shoulders eased. "I've spent most of my adult life trying to rise above the mob thing. A fancy job at a big investment firm downtown. Moved into my own place and thought I had it made. Now here I am, back in my parents' home. It's been humbling. But I think it's okay. I'm figuring out how to be Lucia Rizzo, business owner, rather than Lucie Rizzo, mob princess. I like it."

"As we get older, there's some self-acceptance that comes with it."

"Wise man. How old are you?"

"Thirty-four."

Eight years on her. It didn't feel like it. He just felt...comfortable. Easy.

"Huh," she said. "You're practically an old man to my twenty-six."

"Huh," he shot back. "You're practically a baby to my thirty-four."

"Touché, Detective."

He laughed. "Does it bother you? The eight years?"

"You keep telling me I'm hot and it won't."

Oh. Boy. Where did that come from? *Go, Lucie.*

The good detective apparently liked the sound of that

because the side of his mouth lifted into a devastating smile. "Don't you worry about that, Lucie. I'm all over you, babe."

Which might be nice. *Eh-hem.* A waitress came by, took their order and, before leaving, spent a solid three minutes catching up on the restaurant gossip with Tim. All in all, it was a productive few minutes. One of the busboys had stormed out in a snit leaving them shorthanded. On a Friday night. The new waitress was sleeping with the sous chef, making Tim's brother extremely unhappy, and his mother and father had just left an hour ago. Somehow, Lucie was glad to not have met the parents on the first date.

Talk about pressure.

The waitress moved on and Lucie shook her head. This place had more drama than Petey's and the Rizzo household combined. "So, I guess you know everyone here?"

He shrugged. "My family is in and out constantly."

"How many of there are you?"

"Five kids. I have two brothers and two sisters. I'm number four." He pointed toward the street. "My folks live five blocks west of here. They're here a lot. They get their exercise by walking over."

"You're a close bunch then?"

"Oh, yeah. I don't take a bathroom break without someone in my family finding out."

Part of her understood that. As much as her relationship with her father had been strained, he was constantly—even from his cell—up in her business. Part of it came from protective instincts. The other part was simply his sense of control. Something her father craved, but serving time— being *locked up*—had destroyed.

Lucie studied Tim. Checking for the tell; how he felt about his family being so involved in his life. One thing she didn't need was another man who allowed his loyalties to divide them.

"Do you mind that?" she asked.

"Nah. I can handle it."

"What do your parents do?"

"My dad is retired. He was a high school English teacher. My mom used to run a daycare out of the house. She still watches a couple of kids in a pinch, but she's mostly retired too."

Lawdy, compared to her crew, Tim O'Brien's family should have been in a Rockwell painting. What would his parents think of their all-American boy being on a date with Lucie Rizzo?

Just that fast, years of embarrassment came rushing back, turning her stomach to a brick. She'd fought so hard to become her own person, to ignore the snickering about her family. And she'd done it mostly. Until now. When she'd taken a chance on dating someone other than Frankie. Someone outside the life.

Sometimes every step forward turned into a step back.

Tim tilted his head, then leaned in, his big shoulders moving with such ease that her seizing stomach relaxed. He had that way about him. A presence that shattered tension.

Before tonight, it would have made her nervous. Now? She wasn't sure what it made her. Aside from someone who liked being around him.

Dangerous as it might be considering who he was and who she was and, well, the fact that she loved Frankie.

"Lucie? Did I say something wrong?"

She smiled up at him. "No. It's me. Just thinking."

"About?"

"About your normal life and what your parents would think of you being on a date with me."

"Are you a nice person who treats people well?"

She gawked. "I would hope so."

"Then I don't care what they think. I care about what you think and what I think. If we're happy and treat each other right, everyone else needs to get on board. If they don't, it's their problem. Not mine or yours."

If Lucie could have melted into her seat, she'd have done it. Just turned into a puddle of goo right there. Tim O'Brien, in three seconds, had summed up everything she'd wanted to hear from Frankie these last few years.

I'm in trouble.

But one little statement couldn't define her relationship with Frankie. Could it? They had history. Good history where they laughed and loved and understood each other. That meant something. Something solid and pure.

Something she couldn't just toss aside.

"Okay, Tim O'Brien, why does it sound like you've experienced your family not liking the people you date?"

He sat back again, rested his arms on the armrests and glanced around the restaurant. One big swoop before coming back to her. "Very perceptive, Ms. Rizzo. I was engaged once. We broke up four years ago."

"I'm sorry."

"Don't be. There was a reason we dated five years before getting engaged. She dumped me for someone she works with. Said she couldn't deal with being married to a cop. I don't know what she thought for the six years we were together. I'd been a cop that whole time."

"Yeesh."

"Yeah. Making it worse was the fact that my family didn't like her. Not one of them. Now every time I go out with someone, I get the same round of questions."

"What questions?"

He flicked his index finger up. "Is she a nice girl?" Another finger went up. "Do you know what you're doing?" Another finger. "Are you happy?" After that, assuming my answers are all yes, they move on and leave me alone."

"What if your answers are no?"

He set his elbows on the table and leaned closer. Close enough where, if she wanted to, she could edge a wee-bit forward and...

He focused on her lips, smiled at her as she drew closer. "Lucie, if my answers are no, my family never knows she exists. And in case you're wondering, I'd definitely not be bringing her to my brother's restaurant."

He met her gaze and the intensity in his green eyes, the focus, sent an explosion straight from her core. Lawdy, lawdy, the man might make her come apart.

Needing distance, she broke the eye contact, fiddled with her fork, and checked her other utensils for water spots —because that's what normal people did, right?

Across from her, Tim grinned. "Sorry I embarrassed you. Tell me about your day."

Her day? Why would he be asking that? He couldn't have known about the road trip. Could he? She flicked a glance at him then moved to studying her knife. No spots. Clean as a whistle.

"Um, it was fine. Why do you ask?"

He puckered his lips for a second, raised his eyebrows. "Generally when people are having dinner, they talk. Maybe about their day."

What was wrong with her? This dating thing was strange. "Right. Of course. Good. Good day. How about yours?"

He scanned the restaurant, his eyes darting over the occupied tables for a few seconds before he came back to her. "Same old thing. Coupla robberies. I did close one case. Been working on that a few months. Finally got the SA's office to file charges."

Careers. Finally, something they could discuss without her nerves disintegrating. "That must be rewarding. To see your work come together like that."

"You know it. I like to think I'm goal oriented, so, yeah, every case closed is a goal reached."

"Do you like being a detective?"

The man's face lit up, every fair-skinned inch. "I love it. There's always something different. I didn't like being a beat cop so much. Investigations are different. I like the puzzle."

Interesting way to look at police work. Given her current circumstances, she understood that need to connect all the pieces, put them in order to reveal the bigger picture.

She sat forward and propped her chin in her hand. "How much of what you do is skill versus instinct?"

"Both. Absolutely. I never discount my instincts. Sometimes it's the difference between a case going cold and solving it. Even if a lead feels nutty, I follow it."

"Huh."

Maybe this obsession she had with the could-be-fake painting might be her instincts kicking in, urging her to move forward. Really, her life in general could use a good dose of following her instincts rather than always plotting every aspect of her existence. Goals were one thing, but typically, reality always set in and she'd be forced to adjust her plan. Not be so glued to a list. Four years ago, she imagined she'd be married by now—to Frankie—and making millions as one of Chicago's hot-shot investment bankers.

"You look perplexed, Lucie."

She shook off her errant thoughts. "No. Just thinking."

"About?"

"Instincts." She circled her hands around her head. "I tend to think a lot. I wrote a life plan for myself when I was in grad school. I thought it would keep me motivated. And it did. Until I got laid off. Now I wonder if I've been too rigid. Too dialed in."

An older couple from the next table got up to leave, and Tim's gaze swept over them. Head to toe, scrutinizing their movements. Had to be a cop thing.

The couple moved on and he brought his attention back to her. "There's nothing wrong with being ambitious."

"No. But sometimes I second guess myself."

Like when I wonder if my client is a thief.

"Then stop doing that. What's the worst that will happen?"

"I'd be wrong."

"Last I checked, being wrong wasn't a crime." He rested his elbows on the table. "You're a smart, attractive, no-nonsense woman. Give yourself a break. Trust yourself. You might like what you find. God knows I do."

At that, she smiled. "Thank you, Tim O'Brien. You're a good man."

One she might need to spend more time with.

After dinner and meeting Tim's brother, who—*hello*—made a wicked Irish stew, Lucie followed Tim back through the restaurant to the street where dusk quickly faded to darkness. He placed his hand on her lower back, guiding her around the other pedestrians as they moved toward the parking garage on the corner.

Humid lake air surrounded them and Lucie inhaled. She loved this city and any time spent here reminded her how much she'd missed living downtown.

A cabbie honked at a slower car and a slew of curses followed. Another Friday night in Chicago, land of the insane drivers.

All of it somehow comforting to a girl whose life hadn't quite turned out the way she'd planned.

Yet.

At the corner, they waited for the light to turn, giving them half a chance to survive crossing the street.

Tim pointed east, toward the lake. "It's a nice night. What do you say we head up to the lake? Take a walk and grab some dessert somewhere?"

Wow. The man could eat. "Seriously? You want dessert after that meal?"

And a walk on the lakefront. If the man had a Lucie textbook, he couldn't have aced this test any better. When she lived downtown, she'd drag Frankie out to the lakefront for picnics and walks. She had loved the anonymity of it, the being able to walk outside without nosey people staring at them or pointing as often happened in Franklin.

"One thing about me, Lucie. My appetite doesn't quit. Total warrior. And if it means keeping you a while longer, I'm bucking up."

She looked up at him, a big-butt smile on her face because the cute guy liked her. High school much? She tugged on his shirt. "I'd like that. I'll skip dessert, but coffee would be fine."

The light changed and Tim stepped off the curb, hesitating a moment until Lucie did the same, and once again, he set his hand on her back, just a light touch. Not possessive. More protective. She sensed that in him. That protective nature. She liked it. Liked the way his big hand—so new and different—felt on her body. Everything about Tim was different from Frankie. His height, his big shoulders, his fair skin. His attitude toward people nosing around in his life.

They walked the two blocks to the lakefront and Lucie focused on enjoying every breath. That amazing feeling of clean, moist air moving through her lungs. If she were blindfolded, she'd know the second she got within half a mile of the lake. The moisture gave it away and her body responded, took refuge in it. Being here, despite the city noise and traffic, relaxed her.

"Lucie?"

"Yes?"

He dropped his arm over her shoulder, gave a little squeeze. "This is fun."

"Yes it is."

"I'd like to do this again."

"Why do I think there's a but?"

Tim stopped and gently pulled her to the side of the lake path next to a bench. "It's not a but so much. More of a question."

A biker hollered out to the folks walking and Tim nudged Lucie farther off the path.

"Fire away, Detective."

"You and Frank Falcone. I know you have a history."

"That we do."

"A lot of splitting up and reconciling. From what I've heard."

"Your sources are good."

"Yeah, they are."

He shoved his hands in his pockets as if he needed somewhere to put them. *On me.* Her hormones were a naughty bunch tonight. Particularly since the current topic was her relationship with Frankie. Something she didn't want to think about. Tonight she was plain old Lucie—not Lucie Rizzo, mob princess—out on a date with a nice guy.

"Which leads to my question."

"Okay."

"This current breakup with Frankie. Is it permanent? Because I'm not a guy who wants to get in the middle of something. It's not my style."

All she could do was be honest. Each time she and Frankie had broken up, there'd been a feeling that it wouldn't last. They were magnets in the same force field. This time, she honestly wasn't sure.

She reached out and touched his arm because it felt right and easy and she wanted the connection.

"Tim, all I can do is tell you what I know right now. Frankie and I have been apart three months. There's something different this time. Something I can't figure out. I do know I really like spending time with you. It feels new and fun and... freeing. And I like that."

He smiled at her, that lightning-quick one that sent her hormones all a-flutter. "Good enough." He turned, slid his hands from his pockets, threw his arm over her shoulder again and started walking. "Lucie Rizzo, let's see where this goes. I have a feeling it's going to be a great ride."

LUCIE STROLLED UP THE WALKWAY TOWARD HER PARENTS' front door with Tim just behind her. As she walked, she tilted her head up to enjoy the kaleidoscope of stars on a perfect summer evening. She breathed in, let it out slowly, and tried to forget her mother was sleeping upstairs. Living with one's parents might be the best birth control going. Not that she'd sleep with him. Hunky as he was, she wasn't ready for that. Not a chance. She'd slept with three men in her lifetime and Frankie had been the only one in four years. Casual sex may have worked for some, but she couldn't do it. She needed the emotional attachment and commitment that came with making love.

The hormones would have to deal.

When she reached the stoop, the porch light flicked on. Ah, the joy of motion sensors. Couldn't get away with a thing. And if it weren't nearly midnight, Lucie knew the neighbors would have their noses pressed up against the glass to see why the light flipped on. Everyone in this town was fascinated with the Rizzo family.

She reached the top step and turned. Tim was still two steps lower and she was nearly eye-to-eye with him. Tall man. Big man.

Oh.

Boy.

"I had fun tonight. Thank you."

He nodded. "Me too. I'll call you this weekend. Maybe we can get together on Sunday for a while? If it's nice, we can go to the beach."

With his fair skin, he wanted to go to the beach? "I love the beach." She twisted her lips. "We'll need five gallons of sunscreen for you."

"Six," he corrected.

And, oh my, how she loved a man who could poke fun at himself. She shook her head. "I'll say this for you, Tim O'Brien, you know how to make a girl swoon."

Under the glare of the porch light, Lucie's gaze moved to Tim's mouth and that perfect lower lip. His mouth had a fullness to it. So sexy.

After a second, those lips slid into a knowing grin and heat stormed Lucie's cheeks for what had to be the millionth time tonight.

Her thoughts were just plain wicked!

"I do my best," he said, still grinning.

And then, finally, he did it, what she'd been waiting all night for, he moved closer. She knew what this was. Yes. *Bring me those lips, baby!* She wanted those lips.

"Hey."

Gah! Lucie jumped backward, her arms flying as she almost fell flat on her butt on the stoop. Tim grabbed hold before she went over.

Here she was about to lip-lock with the hunky detective and up walks Joey Big Ears.

"Hi," Lucie chirped, guilt flying off her like spurting blood.

Tim grinned, clearly amused that they'd been busted. But, ace that he was, he turned, waited for Joey to step closer, and held out his hand. "Tim O'Brien."

Joey slid a hard glare at Lucie then went back to Tim, grudgingly shaking his hand. "Joey Rizzo."

The two had quasi met a few months back when O'Brien had been investigating Lucie's dognappings. She didn't recall any words actually being exchanged, but there'd been a load of posturing on her brother's part. All she remembered was Joey doing the silent don't-screw-with-us routine. Total charmer, her brother.

But hey, at least this time he'd shaken Tim's hand and actually said something. Progress. Even if it was only two words.

"Where were you?" Lucie asked.

"I... uh...out."

Yoi. Probably making collections at the bar. Something he couldn't readily admit in front of law enforcement. "Okay, then. Great." Lucie jerked her head. "You can go on inside now. I'll be there in a minute."

"Good to meet you," Tim said.

"Right. You too."

Excellent progress!

Joey moved past them and let the screen door smack behind him—a sure sign of rebellion over the fact that Lucie had been out with the enemy.

But Tim was unfazed. He stood, broad shoulders comfortably back, with a big ole grin on his face.

"Nice guy," he said. "I think we'll get along well."

Lucie snorted. Down deep, her love for Joey had grown over these last few months. As annoying as he could be, he'd been there for her. Helping her with the dogs, lugging supplies, and yes, saddling up to get his baby sister out of trouble

"He's a good guy," Lucie said. "Protective of the women in his family. He'd be that way with any man."

Aside from Frankie.

"I'm sure it doesn't help that I'm a cop."

"Ya think?"

The only cops, outside of Tim, who had ever set foot on Rizzo property were the federal agents keeping tabs on her father and Joey and the goings on in the Rizzo world. Her brother's only crime, to Lucie's knowledge, was running his bookmaking business. From childhood, their father had warned him off life as a mobster, and Joey was too terrified to go against his wishes. And whether he wanted to admit it or not, Lucie didn't truly believe her brother had the stomach for mob life.

The porch light flashed off then back on again and Lucie rolled her eyes.

"That would be my cue to go inside and kill my brother. Since you're a detective, you might not want to be here for that."

"Homicide isn't my area anyway."

Ha. Good one. After years of being so serious about every damned thing, Tim O'Brien brought a lightness to her.

"Thank you again," she said. "You have no idea how much I needed a fun night."

He leaned forward and the porch light flipped on and off again. Three times. Now she'd had it. She half turned to the door. "Joey! Quit it! Go to bed, you animal."

Her temper didn't fire that often, but when it did, look out. And more often than not, Joey was the cause.

"Hokay," O'Brien said after her outburst. "I'm gonna go."

She shifted back. "I'm sorry."

He cracked up and ran his hand down one side of his face. "You guys are a riot."

Quickly, before the light could flip off, he kissed her. On the cheek.

Dammit, Joey! She wouldn't have minded a little smooch from the hunky detective.

Right now she had bigger issues.

Leaving Tim standing at the base of the stoop, she slipped through the front door, and feeling a little wistful after a nice evening, offered up a little finger wave before closing it.

Now the war will start.

She wheeled around, found Joey the Snoop—formerly known as Joey Big Ears—standing near the steps. She jabbed her finger at him. "Are you insane? What am I five? Don't you ever pull that stunt again. How humiliating."

"He's a cop!"

"So what?"

That knocked him back a step and his jaw flopped open. "Seriously? What don't you get about this cluster?"

"Yes. Seriously. He's a nice guy. We get along. And, hey, I *like* him."

"What about Frankie?"

"He dumped me."

Joey waved both hands. "You'll get back together."

Historically speaking, maybe. Now, who knew? "You don't know that."

"You're giving up on Frankie for a cop? Dad will shit himself."

"Well, I'm sure you'll get your fun telling both Dad and Frankie about this. Enjoy it while you can."

"You think I'm gonna tell them? You're crazier than I thought. Nuh-uh, baby, that's on you. I'll just sit and watch the action."

She slid her purse off her shoulder and waved it around. "I knew if you saw him you'd be a jerk about this. I should have met him somewhere."

And how fair was that? Now she couldn't bring a friend over? This life. Total killer.

"Wait," Joey said, his eyes shooting crazy wide. "Just hang on one second. You wacky broads cooked up that whole thing with Roseanne earlier, didn't you?"

"Oh, just stop it."

Joey gritted his teeth and jerked his head. "I can't believe it. Witches. I'll give you props though. When I got there, that lunatic had her foot stuck in a hole in her front yard."

That's a good friend. Ro had actually dug a hole and shoved her foot in there.

"I had to dig her out with a garden spade. What an actress! All to get me out of the house. And I find this out now, after..."

He broke off. Gritted his teeth.

"What?"

Not for anything, but Joey was taking this way too hard. All they'd wanted was to get him out of the house. Really not that big of a deal. At least she didn't think so.

"Nothing," he said. "It just *sucks* that you two cooked this up and lied to me."

Oh, please. Lucie flapped her arms, waved them like the crazy person she might be. "Because I knew this is how you'd behave."

"Hel-*lo*." This from Mom marching down the stairs in

her robe, her chestnut hair plastered down on one side. "Do I need to remind you that it's midnight and I happened to be sleeping? At least until the two of you started screaming."

"Ma! Your daughter is dating a cop."

Mom frowned as she hit the bottom step and came eye-to-eye with Joey. "How is that your business?"

Go. Mom.

"Yeah, *Joey.*" *Very mature, Luce. Very mature.*

Joey threw his arms up. "Sure. Take her side. You're both nuts. You know what? I'm goin' to bed. I'm the only one around here with enough sense to see what a train wreck this is."

On his way by their mother, despite his comment about her being nuts, he smacked a kiss on her cheek. Total mama's boy.

"Sorry we woke you. I love you."

"I love you too, Joseph. Good night."

Mom waited until Joey slammed his bedroom door and turned back to Lucie. "A police officer? You're kidding?"

Lucie grinned. "It gets worse."

"Oh, Lord. Tell me he's involved in investigating your father."

"No. He's Irish."

"Well, that should make for interesting Sunday dinners."

THE FOLLOWING MORNING, LUCIE WALKED ALONG THE sidewalk in front of the Bart Owens Gallery with a dopey smile on her face. For the first time in months she felt...decent. Happy, even. Her cell phone rang. Ro. "Good morning, my soon-to-be Academy Award-winning girlfriend."

"Hey, girl, I do what I can. Where are you? I've got samples to show you for our new headquarters."

Samples. Oh. Yay. Sometimes, Lucie just wanted Ro to do it. Not involve her. This would be one of those times. How many variations of one color could she look at? "I told Bart I'd walk Oscar for him."

"It's Saturday."

"I know, but Bart is out of town today. It's not a big deal. I'm doing the morning walk and Lauren's handling this afternoon. I should be done by nine-thirty. Want to meet at the store?"

"Sounds good. That'll give me time to get my fabulous on."

"I'll look forward to that."

"You know it. How'd it go last night? Did you get lucky?"

"Yes. But not in the way you're implying. You have a filthy mind, my friend."

"Oh, come on. I'm divorcing my husband. I'm entitled to a little filth as a distraction. Do tell."

"What's to tell? He's a nice guy. He's..."

What?

Cute. Sexy. Funny. Said all things that made her think about a panty drop? Check. Check. Check and, oh, yes, *check*. "He's different."

"As in, he's not Frankie?"

For sure that. "Definitely not Frankie. He makes me feel...comfortable."

The second the words left her mouth, Lucie winced.

"Bah!" Ro said. "Comfortable. What the hell does that even mean? Listen, honey, I married the comfortable guy, and I just busted him banging a stripper."

"All I meant was he's easy to talk to. There's no judgment. He just listens and then gives his opinion. And it's kind of nice to have a conversation and not have everything I say be used as a weapon."

Wow. That was an interesting reveal. But apparently those feelings had been making a run for it because they shot free pretty easily.

"You like him," Ro said. "Good God, Luce. He's a cop."

"I know. I don't care. I think we're getting together tomorrow."

Ro sighed. Lucie knew how she felt. A little conflicted and confused. "Well, if it's what you want, then enjoy it. Just be happy."

Who knew what she wanted? All she knew was she didn't want to fight anymore, and for one night, Tim O'Brien gave her that. "We'll see. It's early yet. By the way, Joey is not happy with us."

"Ooohhh-weeee, don't I know it. He sent me a *wicked* text last night. That thing should have fried my phone."

Lucie gasped. "Did he really? I'm so sorry."

"Please. I told him to get over it because he was only proving your theory that he'd be an idiot about the cop."

"He must have loved that."

"He swore at me. Via text." Ro giggled. Giggled? "He's straight up nuts, but he makes me laugh."

Eww. With a divorce imminent, the idea of Ro and Joey... just eww. "Um..."

"What?"

Not my business. "Nothing."

"Then I'll meet you at the store around 9:30 and we'll look at samples."

"Thanks, Ro. For everything. I love you."

"Back at ya, babe. Later."

Stowing her phone, Lucie cut down the alley to the back door leading to the gallery's office. She unlocked the door and readied herself for the requisite leg humping from Oscar the kink. Imagine if the dog hadn't been neutered?

Once inside, she spotted the gallery door open—odd, considering Oscar wasn't allowed in the gallery without Bart present. Where the heck was this dog?

"Oscar?" she called. "Here boy."

The tippity-tap of nails echoed in the gallery. Oh, darn it. That dog would be toast now. Bart must have forgotten to secure the door.

"Lucie?"

Bart's voice. She cocked her head. Had she mixed up the date? On the one morning she wouldn't have minded staying in bed a little longer. Sheesh.

And yep, Bart swung around the stairway and headed straight for her with Oscar the perv scooting around him. Lucie bent at the waist, held her palm out low. "No humping, Oscar."

The dog came to a stop, gave her a sniff and planted his butt. "Good boy. Stay."

She pointed at him, made sure he knew she meant business, then straightened up and faced Bart. "Hi. Did I mix up the date? I thought you were gone today."

He smacked himself on the head. "I'm so sorry, Lucie. I forgot to tell you my plans changed. I don't know where my mind is lately. I won't need you today. Obviously, I'll pay you for your time."

At least she hadn't been the one to make the mistake. All in all, not a big deal. She waved the suggestion away. "Thank you, but that's not necessary. I needed to be up anyway to review some samples for my new office."

"Wonderful. How's that going?"

Oscar came out of his sit/stay and sniffed her shoe. If he

made a move toward her leg, she'd lose it. "It's going well. I'm excited. It should be ready in a couple of weeks."

"Congratulations. Your business is taking off. It has to feel good."

"Yep. After being downsized, I took a good bounce."

Bart sat behind his desk, grabbed a stack of folders from his inbox and rifled through them. "A bounce you made happen. And my offer still stands. If you have any other clients needing artwork, I'd be happy to offer you a commission."

The prior night's conversation with Tim, the one about how he always followed his gut, came back to her. Concern over the Bart situation had been nagging her, making her wonder if he was into something not-quite-legal.

And bringing her in on it.

Can't have that. Not with her business growing. No risks to her reputation could be taken.

"Thank you, Bart. I appreciate that. The extra money will come in handy for my business. I've worked hard to become my own person. To separate myself from my father's lifestyle."

Bart cocked his head and smiled in a greasy salesman sort of way that made the hairs on the back of her neck dance. He went back to the folders pulling one from the bottom of the stack and then scooted to the lateral filing cabinet behind him. A key stuck out of the lock on the cabinet and he twisted it, opened the drawer, filed the folder, and relocked the cabinet before turning back to her. "Lucie, you're such a dear. It has to be difficult dealing with your father's troubles. I completely understand. Whatever I can do to help. Just let me know."

"Thank you. I appreciate that."

Oscar, having had enough of all the talk and no action,

climbed on top of her foot, wrapped his front paws around her calf and rode her like a wild mustang that needed breaking.

At least someone was getting a little excitement.

"Oh, Oscar," she said. "You're such a perv."

Bart snapped his fingers. "Off, Oscar!"

A second later, Oscar dismounted.

"Good boy," Bart said. "Lucie, again, sorry about the confusion this morning. We'll see you Monday, yes?"

"I'll be here."

With bells on. Because something about this conversation just didn't sit right and she needed to find out why.

8

————

Lucie pushed through the glass door leading into Carlucci's—er, the new Coco Barknell—and found Ro lining up tile samples in a row on the floor. Next to each tile, she'd placed oversized paint chips.

Lucie contemplated the mighty nice and mighty expensive-looking tile.

Before she could comment, Ro slashed the air with her hand. "Don't get your panties in a bunch. It's porcelain. Not travertine. And all of them are remnant, so we can get them cheap."

Phew. "You scared me for a second there."

"You know I always take care of you."

Yes, she did. Always. Lucie tossed her messenger bag on the desk next to Ro's purse and a spiral notebook. Funny thing about Ro. She loved the finer things, but when it came to taking notes, she went for simplicity. No fancy leather portfolios. Just a plain, old-fashioned spiral notebook. Go figure. "You do always take care of me. I love you, my friend."

"Yeah, yeah. Ditto."

Ro tried to blow that off and be the tough, street-wise

girl everyone thought she was, but Lucie knew better. Everyone needed to hear they were loved. Including Ro. But, she'd let it go and not embarrass her friend. Her best friend. Her sister. "So, I'm sorry Joey is mad at you."

Continuing to study the tile, Ro waggled her hand, then squatted to switch out paint chips. "He'll live. He just likes the drama."

Speaking of... "I just came from the gallery."

"I know. You're early. What happened?"

"Bart screwed up the schedule and forgot to tell me. Anyway, I made sure to tell him I don't want to be associated with my father's business. Or criminal activity."

Ro stopped arranging tile, just froze right where she was and looked up at Lucie. "*Really.*"

"Yep."

"And?"

"He sort of...put me off. Gave me some line about how difficult it must be."

"*Really.*"

Wow. Two *reallys* in a matter of seconds. Lucie moved closer to the samples and picked one up. Too much brown. She set it back down. "If I hadn't grown up in the life like I did, maybe I'd have bought it. But the whole thing just didn't sit right with me."

With that, Ro stood, set her hands on her hips. "I don't trust this guy. What do you want to do? Your new boyfriend *is* a cop. You could talk to him about it."

Her boyfriend? *I don't think so.* What a mess that would be for Sunday dinner. *Dad, welcome home from jail. Meet my new boyfriend, Detective Tim O'Brien.* Amusing as the thought was, she couldn't go there. Not until she figured out what she and Frankie were doing. "He's not my boyfriend."

"Blah, blah."

"And, no, I'm not talking to him about it. If this Lutz thing turns out bad, I'll look like the scam artist I've tried so hard not to be. A thief. A *criminal.*"

"Oh, the theatrics." Ro rested her hand against her forehead and threw her head back, sending her hair flying. "I may need to sit down."

"Go ahead and laugh. You're not the one people are waiting to see fall off her perch." Lucie shook her head. "We're getting distracted here. I think we should call that attorney who handles private sales for the Gomez family. We'll tell him we want to buy *My Darkest Night.* If the family still has it, we'll know Lutz has a fake. If the family doesn't have it, we can find out who they sold it to."

"He may not tell us."

Lucie sighed. "I know. It's worth a try though. We'll tell him you're willing to pay big bucks for it. Heck, we've promised to compensate everyone else, might as well tell him the same thing. Lawyers like money too."

"I'm up for it. Do you have his number?"

Lucie dug through the inside zipper of her messenger bag for the number. "Right here. I think it's his office number. He's probably not there on a Saturday, but we can leave a message."

Ro went back to arranging the tiles while Lucie dialed. Thinking like a true detective, she punched in the code that would mark her number as private so Mr. Isby, the lawyer, couldn't identify her by caller ID. She'd learned that little trick two years ago from Joey. Sometimes having family members who knew this stuff came in handy.

While waiting for the call to connect, she pointed at the second tile from the left. "I think I like that blue one."

Ro nudged it with her toe. "I like it too, but I'm worried about the footprints. Might need something more neutral."

Roger Isby's phone rang as Lucie studied the other sample tiles. That blue one kept dragging her back though. How bad could the footprints be? She stepped on it to see if her sneaker left an imprint, but before she could lift her foot, Roger Isby answered.

"Hello?"

Tile forgotten, Lucie perked up. "Hello. Is this Roger?"

If so, kind of a funny way to answer his office line. But there was music playing in the background. Van Halen. How fascinating. Or maybe not. She supposed lawyers were allowed to like classic rock.

"Yes. This is Roger Isby."

As Frankie would say, *score!* "Hi, Roger. My name is..."

"Delilah," Ro whispered, her mouth opening wide as she enunciated each syllable.

"Delilah Stone."

Dear Lord, she'd just given herself a porn star name.

"How can I help you, Miss Stone?"

The music on the other end went silent. "I was given your number by Carlton at the Montrose Gallery. I'm actually surprised I caught you working on a Saturday."

"I'm not working. This is my cell. He must have given you the wrong number."

"Oh, I'm sorry! I thought... Well... if you'd rather we speak on Monday, that would be fine."

Please say no, please say no.

Beside her, Ro whipped her hands in mid-air and the nearly psychotic movement made Lucie a little dizzy. She turned away and received an exaggerated sigh.

"This is fine," Mr. Isby said. "Depending on what you need. I'm not in my office and don't have access to my files."

Lucie spun back to Ro, gave her a thumbs up. "Oh, I don't think that will be necessary. My employer is interested in purchasing an Arturo Gomez painting. *My Darkest Night* is the title. Carlton said he doesn't have it in his inventory, but suggested I contact you."

"I see. Would this be for a private collection?"

"Yes, sir. My employer is an avid collector. She would like to purchase it for her husband."

"The stripper-banger." Ro rolled her eyes so hard it should have knocked her sideways.

Lucie gave her a full-on grin.

"Ms. Stone, I'm not sure where that painting is. I can contact the family and check its status. I can't promise anything."

Really getting into her acting, Lucie hesitated, pretended to absorb this information while she formulated a response. "I understand. We would certainly appreciate any help you could give us. Of course, we'd be happy to compensate you for your time."

They'd offered to buy off everyone else, why not a lawyer?

"That won't be necessary. This is what I do for the Gomez family. Let me call them and see what I can find out. Can I call you back?"

Lucie rattled off her number and disconnected. She'd just have to remember to answer as Delilah when he called back.

Ro pointed at the floor. "You left a footprint on the blue one."

Lucie glanced down and a small wave of disappointment hit her. One footstep left a dusty imprint. Imagine what people in and out all day would do to that. "Well, shoot."

"I like the blue and this lighter brown one with the flecks in it. The brown one will hide the dirt."

Fine. Whatever. If she couldn't have the blue, Ro could just pick. "Let's go with the brown then."

Ro jotted a note in her notebook. "What'd the lawyer say?"

"He'll get back to us."

"Then we'll wait." She gathered up the samples. "I'll head over now and order the tile and paint. I think we can get it all done early next week."

"*That* would be awesome."

Ro set the discarded tiles on the desk and shoved the one they'd chosen into her tote. "It'll give you another week to move all the stuff in here before your dad comes home." She gestured to the back room. "We need to deal with that disaster back there. No idea what all is in those boxes."

Ugh. Those boxes. Who knew what could be in there? With her luck, Lucie would find a dismembered body. Lovely thought. She checked the time on her phone. Not even 10:30. Plenty of day left. Might as well uncover that body sooner rather than later.

At that, she laughed. Dead bodies. *I'm losing it.* "I'll go through some of it now. I'll start a garbage pile and have Joey get rid of it. Once he's done being mad at us."

"He's a big baby. He means well though."

Ro gave Lucie a hug and sailed out the door. Time to at least begin tackling the storage room. Lucie supposed she could call Mrs. Carlucci and tell her to get her stuff out, but saddling an eighty-five-year-old woman with all the junk was just plain mean.

She pushed open the swinging saloon doors—those had to go—and took in the stacks and stacks of battered boxes. Sunlight poured through the glass door, illuminating the multitude of dust particles floating in the air.

She flipped the switch on the wall, swarming the place

with fluorescent light that could fry an egg. That fixture would have to be changed. She'd add an electrician to Joey's to-do list. In this town, there had to be at least one electrician who might want the opportunity to work off his gambling debts.

Hypocrite. That's what she was.

"Dammit."

This life. So complicated. She should find someone on her own. Just jump on the Internet and find a local electrician. One who would probably overcharge.

Still, she could say she'd handled it. By herself.

She grabbed hold of a square banker's box and opened it. Paper work. She scanned the first few pages. Vendor invoices from 1985.

"Garbage."

Easy.

She grabbed another box stacked on top of a taller box the size of a dishwasher. Hang on. That bigger box looked newer. Not like the rest of the dust-covered ones with tattered edges and the funky pukish color of old cardboard. And she didn't remember seeing it back here before.

She dragged it out and found another identical one behind it. And another. Then another.

Five in all.

On the last box, a white label had been torn off the front, but a corner with a date—six months ago—still remained. Six months. Mrs. Carlucci said she hadn't been in the space in almost a year.

A snaking feeling curled around Lucie's neck and moved straight up into her skull. Someone had put these boxes in here recently. Hopefully it had been Ro storing fabric samples or something.

But Ro had already told her she wouldn't deal with this

mess. And she wouldn't have buried the boxes under the older ones.

Nope. Without a doubt, someone didn't want Lucie to see them.

Joey.

At least she wouldn't find a dead body in the boxes. Even pain-in-the-butt Joey couldn't commit murder. But he might agree to help hide stolen merchandise for one of their father's cronies.

"Please, Lord. Don't let him have done this to me."

He wouldn't. Not after they'd been getting along so well. He knew what Coco Barknell meant to her and wouldn't risk her business. Would he?

She flipped the top of the box and—gah!—the horror. Inside were the ugliest velour tracksuits—red, green, black, navy—she'd ever set eyes on.

Resting her head back, she stared at the ceiling where a watermark would need to be repaired. More issues. Great. She squeezed her eyes closed and fought the swirling panic ricocheting around her head. *Damn him.*

"No, no, no. He did *not* do this to me."

She glanced back at the box and reached in, sliding her hand along the edge as far down as she could go. She went through the next box, rifling through the contents. More tracksuits.

Next box.

More tracksuits.

After sifting through all five boxes, she stood tall and set her hands on her hips.

Five boxes of the ugliest velour tracksuits money could buy.

"I won't just kill him," she said. "I'll bury him in one of these ugly suits. I'll make our mother see him in this thing."

That alone would destroy Joey.

Storming back to the front room, she snatched her phone off the desk and dialed the soon-to-be dead man.

"What's up?" Joey said, his voice slightly hoarse.

She'd woken him up. Good.

"I'm going to bury your giant butt in one of these tracksuits." And then her barely contained temper broke loose, tearing up her flesh like a band saw. "How could you do this to me? I trusted you."

"Ho!" he hollered. "What bug crawled up your ass?"

"I just found your little stash in the storage room at Carlucci's."

" I don't know what the hell you're talking about."

Oh, now he wanted to play dumb and pretend these boxes hadn't fallen off a truck somewhere. That he hadn't stored—or perhaps let someone store—stolen items in her workplace? Idiot.

"You're trying to tell me you don't know anything about these ugly velour tracksuits hidden in my storage room? Only three people have keys to this place. Me, Ro and you. And Ro wouldn't be caught dead in the same ZIP code as these suits. So you get down here and get rid of them."

From Joey's end of the phone, something squeaked. Probably his bedroom door.

"First of all," he said, "I don't know squat about any tracksuits."

Another noise came through the phone. Water running maybe. No, more of a direct stream.

Oh. My. God.

The last bit of her control let loose and roared, filling her brain with swear words she'd never in her life uttered.

"You're peeing!"

God, he was such a pig.

"Hey, you woke me up. I had to go."

Forget killing him. *I'll bury him alive in one of those suits.*

"Get your butt down to Carlucci's and get these boxes out of here."

"They're not my boxes!"

The swooshing of the toilet flushing came through the phone and Lucie fought a sudden sickness in her empty stomach. "Make sure you wash your hands."

"Luce?"

"What?"

"I'm wiping my hand all over my phone. While I'm talking to you."

Ew. Just gross. She'd never touch his phone again.

"Ass!"

Her brother laughed, and a second later, she heard running water. "You are so flipping easy. But back to your stolen track suits. I'm pissed that you think I'd do that to you. Seriously?"

The hot stab of guilt wasn't his style, but it was most definitely effective. She'd totally let her emotions run amok.

No, he wouldn't do that to her. Five months ago, she'd done the same thing and jumped to conclusions when she'd found that diamond stored in her craft supplies. He'd been innocent then too.

She sucked a huge breath, then let a good dose of guilt sink in. "I'm sorry. I just... We're the only ones who have keys."

"You haven't changed the locks yet, dummy. How do you know who has keys? Those locks are forty friggin' years old. Plus, they're so cheap any novice could pick them."

He had a point there. Another load of guilt piled on. She had to stop thinking the worst of her brother. Needling her was his favorite hobby, but as far as she knew, he'd never expose her to any trouble.

"I'm coming down there," he said. "Give me fifteen minutes to shower."

"What are you going to do?"

"You know what I'm gonna do. I'm gonna find out who has big enough balls to store that crap in your place. If they're hot, Dad will lose his mind and we don't need that right before he comes home. He'll wind up violating parole and be in a jackpot again."

"Dad can't know about this, Joey. You know how he gets about me starting a new business."

"Be real, Luce. Even if I don't tell him, someone knows they're there. And my guess is if they're dumbass enough to put them there, they're dumbass enough to tell someone."

Unfortunately, all true. In Lucie's limited experience, her father's cronies liked to gossip. On most days, Petey's was an all-out gossip-fest, which was one of the reasons Frankie liked going in there. One-stop shopping. Lunch plus all the crime family dirt.

But she couldn't think about Frankie now. She needed to get rid of these suspect tracksuits. Fast.

Stolen or not, she wanted no part of it.

And as soon as Joey got here, they'd deal with it. For now, she'd set all five boxes right next to the back door so they could load them into their cars and dump them. She just wanted them gone. Disposed of immediately.

Outside, sirens blared. From the sound, they were coming closer. Nothing new, considering Petey's was only a few doors down. Someone was always getting arrested over there. As long as the cops stayed at Petey's and didn't wander the block looking for velour tracksuits, she'd be fine.

What a thought.

The sirens grew louder then went quiet. Close. Really close. Had to be Petey's.

She shoved one box against the back wall, then dragged the others over. The last box still had the flaps open.

"Hi, Lucie."

Whoa. She spun around and came face-to-face with Brock Lang, an old schoolmate of Frankie and Joey's. He now stood in front of her in his Franklin P.D. uniform.

Casually, she shifted right, stood in front of one of the open boxes.

"Hey, Brock."

Much like Tim the night before, Brock scanned the room then settled his gaze on Lucie doing a crummy job of trying to hide the tracksuits.

"What's up?"

"We got a tip about some stolen merchandise stored here." He peeked over Lucie's shoulder. "Tracksuits. Just like those."

9

IN THE THREE SECONDS IT TOOK BROCK TO STEP AROUND HER, Lucie's stomach curled, nearly doubling her over from the cramping. No. *Nuh, nuh, nuh, nuh, nuh.*

He reached for the box, his movements steady and efficient, but in Lucie's mind, everything had gone into super slow motion. Her hands shook furiously at her sides, but her feet stayed put. *Don't move.* She'd seen enough with her father to know that if she made any attempt to stop Brock, she'd be in handcuffs.

Brock set one of his hands on the edge of the box and smirked. In high school he'd been a skinny, pencil-necked—the slutty girls called another part of his anatomy a pencil—weasel who'd done everything he could to cause trouble for other students. She wouldn't go as far as to say he was the most hated kid in school, but his sneaky, deceiving ways hadn't earned him many friends.

From what she'd heard, nothing had changed, and the fact that he now wore a uniform only made him worse. The uniform equaled a massive dose of attitude on steroids.

A 'roided weasel.

Terrific.

She pointed at the box. "Brock, you may not believe this, but those aren't mine."

"You're right," he said. "I don't believe it. This is your place. If they're not yours, who do they belong to?"

"I...don't know."

Lamest excuse ever, but hey, it was true. Even if no one would believe it.

"And I suppose you don't have a bill of sale for them?"

Uh, hello? If she didn't know who they belonged to, why would she have a bill of sale? At this point, as her father had taught her, she should probably just shut up. Stop talking.

Now.

But darn it, the pencil-necked weasel obviously thought she'd turned out just like her father. The one thing she'd fought so hard against.

Brock strode to the door where she had lined up the other boxes. Slowly, he opened the top flaps on each box and peeked in.

Every nerve Lucie possessed fired, urged her to deny, deny, deny. But would that make her look guiltier?

Brock reached for the radio fastened at his shoulder. "This is unit 29. I need assistance transporting large boxes. Evidence. SUV would do it."

Evidence. Was he kidding?

"Brock, please. There's a mix-up. I honestly don't know who they belong to."

"Yeah, well, tell it to a judge, Lucie."

Lucie lunged backward, held her hands in front of her. "Wait. What?"

Meeting her gaze with those hateful, smug eyes, he slipped handcuffs from his utility belt and held them up. "Hands behind your back. You're under arrest."

Nothing had changed. Old Brock was still that weasel who took joy in watching other people in turmoil.

"Luce?" Joey hollered from the front of the store.

Finally. "Back here. Joey, I'm being *arrested*!"

Two seconds later, Joey pushed through the saloon doors, nearly smacking her in the face. Those damned doors had to go.

He spotted Lucie with her hands cuffed and pulled a face. "What the hell? Brock, you dumbass, take those cuffs off her."

"Yeah," Lucie said. "Not the dumbass part. The handcuff part. Please."

The weasel didn't look convinced. He grabbed Lucie by the elbow, his grip hardly gentle. He held out his arm to shove Joey aside. "I'm taking her in."

Being a good five inches taller and thirty pounds heavier than Brock, Joey folded his arms and turned himself into a wall blocking the path. "For what?"

Brock jerked his thumb toward the boxes. "We got a tip about stolen tracksuits. Five boxes from a robbery a few months back—and guess what?"

"I don't need to guess. This is stupid. You're arresting *Lucie*? She won't go thirty-six in a thirty-five zone because she's afraid she'll get locked up."

Brock the pencil-necked weasel grinned. "I guess you don't know your sister so well. You Rizzos are keeping it all in the family. Let's go, Lucie."

Oh and didn't that just make her skin burn.

Using way more force than necessary, he gripped her arm and pushed her forward. And one thing Joey never tolerated was someone threatening or manhandling his sister. Considering her lineage, not that many people had actually ever *put* their hands on her. *Leave it to the weasel.*

Joey stepped forward and got right into Brock's space. "Take your hands off my sister. Now."

"Screw off, Joey. She's going to jail."

But Brock hesitated, probably thought better of making an enemy out of any member of the Rizzo clan, and let out a long breath. "I'm just doing my job."

He nudged her forward, a little gentler this time, and held his other arm out to angle around Joey.

Panic mixed with Lucie's burning anger and she dug her feet in. Heck no, she wasn't going to jail. "I... They're not mine. I swear."

"Yeah, I know," Brock said. "Move it."

He led her past Joey, whose eyes turned vicious, absolutely hateful, as he stared down the weasel. She whipped her head back. "Joey, please, help me. What do I do?"

He held up his giant hands, all calm and cool as if he'd done this time and again. "Relax. I'll take care of it. I'll have you out pronto. Trust me."

"I need a lawyer."

Already, he was scrolling on his phone. "I'm on it. I'll get you Dad's guy. He's on retainer anyway."

Great. A criminal defense attorney on retainer. If it got her out of the clink before anyone found out about this, she'd never comment on it again.

How humiliating.

"Thank you, Joey."

Brock pushed open the main door. Harsh sunlight blinded her and she blinked a couple of times to adjust her eyes. On the sidewalk, a small crowd had gathered and the low murmur of voices scraped against Lucie's already pulverized nerves. Pretty soon the entire town would know. Her poor mother.

Relax. Concentrate. She swallowed back a lump in her

throat and lifted her head a little higher. And she certainly wouldn't cry. Rizzos didn't cry. Any sign of weakness made for great gossip.

Jimmy Two-Toes, one of her dad's cronies from Petey's, shoved through the small crowd with Lemon, another of Dad's crew, on his heels.

"What's this now?" Jimmy said. "Brock, you dickhead, you got nothing better to do than harass innocent people?"

"Yeah," Lemon said. "Leave her alone."

The men she'd spent years despising were now defending her. But they shouldn't be speaking to an officer that way. Even if it was true. If they kept this up, Brock would arrest them too and her father would lose his mind.

She needed to shut them up. "It's all right, guys. Please."

"No," Lemon said. "You're a good girl. Everyone knows that."

One more time she glanced back, found Joey right behind her, lowering his phone from his ear. "I'm on it," he said. "We'll get her out."

Brock opened the rear door of the patrol car, set his weasel hand on top of her head, and guided her in. Her butt landed on hot leather, stinging the backs of her legs. She wiggled back, trying to keep her shorts from riding up, but no luck.

Gently, she leaned back, let her shoulders slump forward to ease the pressure. Outside the window, a dozen sets of eyes watched her. Mrs. Overmeijer snapped a photo with her phone and Lucie nearly lost that tight hold on her control.

Head high, she turned away from the window, aimed her gaze at a jagged rip in the headrest in front of her. She'd just concentrate on that tear, imagine all the ways it could have gotten there and the number of people who would have sat in this very spot staring at it. Her mind zeroed in and slowly, the roaring panic, the skin frying anger, dissipated.

"I'm okay," she muttered. "Just a mix-up."

But in the back of her mind, she understood all too well that she was in the one place she'd never wanted to be.

On her way to jail.

LUCIE SAT ON THE BENCH IN THE HOLDING CELL, KNEES together, elbows glued to her side because—heaven help her—who knew what kind of germs might be in residence. She refused to let her bare skin touch anything. Anything!

But all in all, the cell was nicer than she'd expected. Well lit with concrete walls painted a pale beige, it didn't have that dank dungeony feel she'd expected.

On the bench bolted to the far wall sat Fusion—hopefully not her real name. Fusion had been arrested that morning for prostitution. Or as she called it, providing services down at the Love-Thy-Neighbor-Here place on Janes Avenue. The place was legendary in Franklin for all the wrong reasons. Reasons that included Lucie's not-so-saintly mother committing adultery there twenty years earlier. One thing about Franklin, the landmarks saw a lot of action. Literally and figuratively.

Lucie sighed.

What a life.

The door at the end of the hallway slammed. She perked up, hoping that maybe—*please, please, please*—her lawyer might be the one strolling the corridor. Did lawyers even come back here? Wow, she was criminally bad—pun intended—at being a jailbird.

She scooted to the end of the bench, ever hopeful she

might get sprung. Seconds later, Tim appeared on the other side of the bars.

And the humiliation grows...

Being his day off, he wore cargo shorts with his badge hooked on the waistband and a T-shirt tight enough to display his chiseled shoulders. Hands in pockets, he studied her with pursed lips.

"Hey, handsome," Fusion said. "You looking for me? I'll treat you right."

Lucie rolled her eyes. Fusion needed shock therapy. Who tried to pick up a cop while locked in a cell? Unbelievable. Or maybe that's the way things were done in here. How would Lucie know?

Tim shook his head, but a lilting, mischievous smile played on his lips. "Lucie, Lucie, Lucie. I thought I gave up my bad girl phase in college."

Oh, hardy, har. She drew a breath, tried to smile. She appreciated his attempt to lighten the mood, but—God—this was mortifying. A burst of air caught in her throat and pressure built behind her eyes. She inhaled through her nose. The stale smell of old sweat and dirty bodies traveled down her throat and she choked out a breath.

"Lucie?"

Dammit. No crying. She grabbed onto the bars and gripped them—no crying—but... She couldn't do it. Couldn't contain them and tears spilled over. Humiliation complete. "I'm so sorry."

Tim set his big hands over hers and squeezed. "Hey, hey, hey. It was a joke."

"I know. It's not that. We were just out together last night and here I am in jail. I swear to you I didn't know those boxes were there. I just found them this morning. As soon as I found them, I called Joey to see if he knew where they came from. Check my phone. You'll see."

"Shhh," he said, keeping his voice low. "I talked to Joey. He got you your father's lawyer. They're on their way."

Still blinking back tears, she nodded. Lawyer. "Okay. That's good." She glanced back at Fusion still giving Tim the once-over. Prostitutes. Go figure. She faced Tim again. "How'd you know I was here?"

"Well, sweetness, I happened to call you and Joey picked up. He grabbed your phone for you, by the way."

"Joey told you I'd gotten *arrested*?"

She'd kill him. One date and her brother tells Tim—a detective!—she'd been arrested. Way to kill a girl's chances.

Tim shrugged. "Don't get pissy. He figured I could help. I made a few calls. Maybe it'll get you outta here fast."

Ignoring the germs, she rested her head against the bars. "Thank you. I can't believe this."

"You'll be okay, Lucie."

She lifted her head. "Just so you know. I've never been arrested before. I don't have a rap sheet."

He ran his finger over her knuckle, just a gentle, supportive touch. "Rap sheet. That's funny."

"I'm just saying."

The door at the end of the hallway opened again and Tim stepped back.

"Rizzo," the uniformed officer yelled. "You're going home."

Oh, thank God. She met Tim's gaze, knowing her speedy release probably had more to do with him and less to do with the top-notch lawyer her father kept on retainer. "Thank you," she said.

"Don't thank me. Joey did most of the work."

How crazy was it that *Joey* had bailed *her* out? This was a nightmare she'd never anticipated. The ribbing would be endless. Particularly since he'd managed to never get arrested.

Lucie Rizzo.

Jailbird.

She sucked in a breath and held it for a few long seconds.

Tim stepped back as the officer unlocked the cell door and waved Lucie out. Soon she'd be standing on the sidewalk in the sunshine and fresh air. Something she had a whole new appreciation for. For two years, this had been her father's life. She couldn't fathom that.

After collecting the brown paper bag containing her belongings, she walked to the front of the building. From behind her, Tim pushed open the glass door leading to the lobby where Joey, her ape of a ball-busting brother, stood waiting.

In none other than a velour tracksuit.

At least it didn't look like the ones seized at the store.

With Tim beside her, she halted and blinked a couple of times to make sure this wasn't some twisted nightmare.

"I'll kill him where he stands."

"Wouldn't blame you if you did," Tim said, "But that'll definitely get you jail time."

"Luuuuce," Joey drawled, "how ya doin'?"

"Shut it, Joey."

He held up his hands in his classic *who me?* gesture. "Just making sure you're okay."

The desk sergeant grunted and she shot him an apologetic look. Joey would never learn. This was why people didn't like them. This...this indifference toward the law.

I'll kill him later.

But he'd gotten to her fast—faster than she'd imagined.

For that, she'd love him forever. Well, as much of a pain in the butt as he was, she'd love him forever anyway because he was her brother. Underneath all the nonsense, he was a sweet guy who always took care of his family.

But the track suit? She could have lived without that little jab.

Regardless, she went up on tiptoes and kissed his cheek. "I can't believe you walked in here wearing that getup."

"Classic, right? I had it in the back of my closet. The sergeant almost crapped himself."

That made her smile. Just a little. "Thank you for getting me out."

He patted her back. "No sweat. Even if I harass you over it, you shouldn't be in here."

She turned to Willie, her father's lawyer, as usual dressed in a custom-tailored suit. She shook his hand. "Thank you for getting here so quickly."

He nodded his bald head and hit her with the slick smile that matched the slick suit and cocky demeanor. "Of course. I'm always available to Joe's family."

Considering his retainer, she supposed that was true. It probably should have been a comfort, but... nah. Normal people, upstanding, law-abiding citizens shouldn't have a defense lawyer on retainer. Simple fact.

"Let's get out of here," Joey said. "I'm gettin' a rash."

The four of them piled out of the police station into the glory of late afternoon sunshine and the fresh air she'd craved minutes ago. The station stood on a corner lot nestled in between row houses on each block. A few cars cruised the street, but otherwise, traffic was light.

Willie said something about calling the prosecutor. Something about a deal. All of it was goo in her mind. Later, she'd ask Joey or Tim about it. Now? Exhaustion had set in.

At the parking area, a space so small she couldn't call it a lot, Willie slid into his Jaguar and waved goodbye. On to his next client.

Joey swung his key ring on his finger. "Who you riding with?"

"I can take you," Tim said.

He wanted to take her. Another burst of relief. He wasn't dumping her. At least not yet. "Are you sure? You've already done enough."

He set one of his big hands on her shoulder and gave it an affectionate squeeze. Joey didn't just flinch, his whole body spasmed. Being so close to Frankie, seeing her with someone else couldn't have been easy.

"It's okay," Tim said. "I don't mind."

Joey dug Lucie's phone from the front pocket of the ugly velour track pants and handed it over.

"Thanks," she said.

"Sure." He hit the button on his key ring and stomped to the car. "I'll see you at home at some point."

"Okay. Does Mom know about this?"

"Oh, she knows. The minute you got hauled away, The Franklin Press went into action."

The Franklin Press. Otherwise known as the gossip mill.

Lucie winced. "Is she mad?"

"At you? No. But she's pissed. And she's working the neighborhood, trying to figure out who did this to you. She's no slouch either, you know."

Yes. She did know. Mom was practically a landmark in this town. Nobody crossed her.

"Quit worrying about Mom and focus on Dad. He'll find out soon enough."

Her father with his jailhouse snitches. The man got

information faster than the Internet. "I will. Thanks again, Joey."

"Later, Luce. Love ya."

Oh, now Lucie knew, without a doubt, she'd stepped into someone else's life. Jail and her brother saying he loved her? Too much.

They watched Joey wheel out of the lot. Almost dreading it, she faced Tim, staring up into his pretty green eyes. "Guessing you're ready to dump me about now. Not that we were an item or anything, but this sort of throws a kink in you spending time with me."

"Is that what you think?"

"It's true, isn't it?"

"Actually, no." He puffed out his cheeks. "You, on the other hand, seem really bothered by the fact I'm a cop. If you want to end this, just say so. No harm, no foul. We go back to being two people who sort of know each other."

Was that what she wanted? To force him away. To relieve herself of the headache of dating a cop. Even if she really liked that cop. If she did that, her father's notoriety would once again influence how she lived her life, and she'd fought too hard for that *not* to happen.

Nope. She enjoyed Tim O'Brien's company. If they decided not to see each other, it wouldn't be because he was a cop and she was Joe Rizzo's kid.

"I don't want that. Not at all. I was giving you the out."

"Well, I don't want it."

What a guy. He didn't care what people thought. He was on her side. The thing she'd always wanted from Frankie, but couldn't quite get him to be one-hundred percent, without fail, on board with.

"Good," Lucie said. "Thank you for supporting me today."

He dropped his arm over her shoulder, turned her

toward his car. "You bet. Now tell me how the hell you think those hot tracksuits got into your storage room."

Who knew dating Lucie Rizzo would bring this kind of action?

Tim sat in the living room of Joe Rizzo's house, something that amused him on several levels. As he listened, Lucie basically vomited some wacked-out story about a "maybe-fake" painting.

He leaned forward, rested his elbows on his knees and clasped his hands together. "Let me see if I've got this straight. Your art history major, dog walker got you riled up about a painting you brokered a deal on and now you think it might be a fake Gomez. Whoever he is. *And* you overheard a shady conversation with the art dealer you brokered this deal with. Do I have that right?"

"Yes."

Not bad tracking on his part. "By the way, you could have mentioned this last night when I asked about your day."

"I didn't want to involve you. I didn't know what to do."

He held his hand up. "We're gonna chalk it up to us getting to know each other's hot buttons. Future reference, full disclosure is preferred."

She rolled her bottom lip out, blinked those big blue eyes and something inside him came unhinged. This girl might do him in. "Damn, you're cute, Lucie."

"I'm just trying to do the right thing and I don't want to put you in an uncomfortable position."

"I'm a big boy. I'll let you know when I'm sideways about something. Got it?"

"Yes."

Excellent. Lucie Rizzo and her looney family were a handful, but she couldn't help who her father was. Why walk away from what appeared to be a great girl because of her family tree? Didn't seem right.

"Good," he said. "Now back to what we know. After your trip to Michigan, you contacted the lawyer to see if you could track the origin of the maybe-fake painting."

"Yes."

"And then you found the tracksuits in your storage room."

"Yes."

"Were they there yesterday?"

She wrinkled her nose. "I can't be sure, but I don't think so. Those bigger boxes kind of stood out and I was back there on Thursday and didn't see them. Do you think the boxes are related to the maybe-fake painting?"

"Don't know. Could be a coincidence."

She flopped back into the chair, ran her bottom lip against her teeth, and nibbled. "Either way, I'm in trouble for keeping stolen merchandise in my shop."

"Not if we can prove you didn't know they were there."

"I don't even know where they came from!"

"I know where they came from."

She eyed him. "Where?"

"The back of a truck."

JUST STOP IT. "SERIOUSLY," LUCIE SAID. "A TRUCK? YOU'RE telling me they literally fell off of a truck?"

For years in this neighborhood whenever Lucie inquired about merchandise with a dubious origin—meaning they were stolen—she was told "It fell off the truck."

As if it were an accident that four cases of cigarettes or CDs suddenly rolled out of the cargo space of an eighteen-wheeler.

Tim snorted. "Not exactly. A few months back, a truck was being unloaded in an alley behind a privately owned boutique. Two men pulled up, held the driver at gunpoint, and took as many boxes as would fit in their SUV."

"Five boxes, right?"

"Six, but who's counting?"

"Me, Tim. I'm counting." She huffed out a breath and waved her hands. "Whoever stole those boxes has been hanging on to them for months and now they suddenly show up in my shop?"

"Appears that way. And, just so you know, the back window of the store was unlocked."

"It was?"

"Yeah. Joey told me. After they arrested you, he went back inside to make sure the cops only took those five boxes. He spotted the unlocked window while he was on overwatch."

Now this was news. Had she ever even bothered to check the windows? She thought back over the last week. Nope. Never checked them. She'd made sure to always double-check the locks, but never once considered the windows. Why would she? She hadn't opened them and just assumed they were secure.

Shame on me. "So, someone could have climbed in the window, unlocked the door and hid the boxes."

"Yep. Have you had a beef with anyone? Someone mad at you?"

At this, she rolled her eyes. Tim was a sweetie, but he had zero experience dating a criminal's daughter. "You do remember my last name, don't you? Half this state has a beef with my father. And everyone around here knows how protective he is of me."

"Huh."

"Don't sound so shocked. My father is a lot of things, but he's not a man who doesn't protect his loved ones. No one messes with his family. He's a maniac about it. Everyone knows to leave me—and Joey to a certain extent—alone. And someone storing stolen merchandise in my store would not sit well."

Tim relaxed back, drummed his fingers on his thighs. "Someone could have set you up to flip your father off."

Score one for the cute detective. Lucie snatched her cell phone off the coffee table and punched the screen. "This is one for Joey."

She pressed the speakerphone button and waited. On the second ring, Joey picked up.

"Hey. Did you see Mom yet?"

"You're on speaker. Just so you know. I haven't seen Mom. She left a note. She's out with Delores. Probably shaking people down, wanting to know who set me up."

Joey groaned. "Jeez, that Delores. She's a tiger. She grabbed my ass this morning. What am I supposed to do with that?"

Tim burst out laughing.

"Who's that? O'Brien?"

"Yes. It's him," Lucie said. "Joey, listen up. Tim just told me those track suits came off the back of a truck."

"Sure they did."

"No. Literally. The truck was being unloaded and two guys robbed it."

Her brother, being her brother, laughed.

Such an ass. "It is *not* funny!"

At her raised voice, Tim's eyebrows hitched up. She

wasn't allowed to raise her voice? Nice, petite girls some-times came with tempers. Even if it didn't come out often, she was most definitely one of those girls.

"Okay, Luce. It's not funny. Why are you calling me?"

"We need to know who stole those boxes."

"I'm working on it. Nobody is talking. I think this is one for Dad."

Without a doubt, he'd lost his mind. Just left it in the street somewhere. "Are you insane?"

"You just figured that out? If you want answers, Dad's the guy. Besides, he was just moaning that you haven't gotten your skinny butt up to see him."

"That's because he's mad about..."

Frankie. She met Tim's gaze and held it. He cocked his head and studied her with those deep green eyes, clearly wondering what she didn't want to say in front of him.

But some things needed to stay unsaid. Telling a man, a potential love interest, that her father expected another man to be his son-in-law wouldn't do anyone any good.

"Yeah, I know." This from Joey, who obviously under-stood what she didn't want voiced. "But if you want fast answers, Dad's the guy. Whoever is involved with this is not gonna tell *me* where those boxes came from."

"Okay."

"Okay? That's it? No argument?"

"No. No argument. For once, I'll agree with you. Don't do anything. I'll call you back."

She poked at the screen and slouched back in her chair, hands on top of her head. Stuck. That's what she was. Without her father's help, they might never figure out where those ugly tracksuits came from. Which meant, not only visiting her father, but telling him about her arrest. Oh, that would not be good.

Maybe she'd just call him with this information.

Chicken.

Tim touched her knee. "What are you thinking?"

"I'm thinking I need to get on the list to visit my father. And won't that be fun?"

A triple-staccato knock sounded at the front door and Lucie bolted upright in her chair. *Oh. My. God.* That distinctive knock belonged to one person and one person only and a surge of panic had her contemplating sprinting out the back door.

She sat for what had to be a good thirty seconds just staring at Tim until Frankie knocked again.

Tim pointed at the door. "Uh, you want me to get that?"

Lawdy, no.

She shook her head, but didn't move.

"Luce!" Frankie called. "You okay? Joey said you were coming home."

Tim's gaze shot to the door and then back to her and something in those luscious green eyes sparked. Yes, handsome man, that would be my boyfriend—ex-boyfriend. Whatever! Damned Joey! Why would he tell Frankie that? Now she had to answer the door. She hopped up, pulling away from Tim because—sweet, baby Jesus—she never imagined this scenario.

"I'm... uh...just going to get that. Be right back."

He spread his hands wide. "Guessing that's Frankie. Should I go?"

"No!"

Absolutely not. The next few minutes would be awkward, but it wasn't like Frankie found them naked and swinging from the chandelier. And wow, that was a vision. And definitely something she might like to try. With Tim. *Whew.*

Lucie swung the door open, found Frankie just about to bang on it again. "Hi. Sorry."

He pushed by her and stepped in. "No problem. What's this about you being arrested? Whoa."

He skidded to a stop just as Tim stood and for a second the air in the room disappeared. Whammo. Gone. The good news was they might all suffocate and die and she wouldn't have to figure a way out of this little love triangle.

Frankie held his hand out to Tim. "You're the CPD detective who handled the dognappings, right?"

"Yeah. Tim O'Brien."

The two men shook hands and suddenly Lucie had to pee. Badly. Flop-peeing again. Terrific.

Frankie let go of Tim's hand, turned back to Lucie, and shifted his eyes left in a way that screamed why-is-this-guy-here?

"Is everything okay?" he asked.

And, yep, just a wee-bit awkward. How would she explain this? Why would Tim even be here? Aside from the fact that she'd gone out with him and this wasn't necessarily a meeting related to her arrest.

The two men stared down at her. What? Was she supposed to say something? Other than announcing she really had to pee? She crossed one foot over the other and wobbled a little. Frankie and Tim each grabbed one of her arms to keep her from falling and all that bottled panic revealed itself in a burst of hysterical laughter. *Please let me die right here.*

Frankie's gaze stayed glued to Tim's hand a second and then—uh-oh—slowly crawled up her arm to her face. He knew. Just standing there, the tension so thick it could crack someone's skull, Frankie had figured out Tim was probably not here on police business.

"Luce," Frankie said, "am I interrupting something?"

How the hell would she answer that? If she said no, she'd insult Tim, who'd done nothing but help her and make her feel things she hadn't felt in way too long. If she said yes, she'd be telling Frankie, in the most inconsiderate way, that she and Tim were... What? She didn't know what they were. Not yet anyway. And if she didn't understand it herself, how would Frankie?

Total pickle.

Tim let go of her arm and stepped back. "No," he said. "I was just leaving. I heard about Lucie's arrest and thought it might be related to a case I'm working."

And, yes! *Tim O'Brien, you are an amazing man.*

"And is it?" Frankie asked.

Tim shook his head. "No." He turned to Lucie. "Thank you though."

No, Detective. Thank *you.* "Of course," she said. "Thank you for coming by. I'll let you know if I hear anything else."

Tim strode out and Frankie dropped onto his favorite chair. The winged-back one. "What case is he working that involves you?"

If she sensed suspicion in his tone, she couldn't quite blame him. Then again, Frankie was a worrier, so he could have been just obsessing over her arrest. "It's nothing." She patted his shoulder. "Thanks for coming by. I'll fill you in on the morning's events, but right now, I need to use the bathroom."

Damned flop-peeing. Forget the flop-peeing. What about this sudden love triangle? This had been a humdinger of a day so far. And something told her, now that Frankie had seen her and Tim together, that things would only get worse.

Eventually, she and Frankie needed to decide what they were doing. For both their sakes.

Eventually.

Not today. Today, she needed to figure out where those tracksuits came from.

10

ON SUNDAY MORNING, LUCIE MARCHED THROUGH THE visitor's entrance of the Bruce Correctional Facility, a medium-security prison just over the Wisconsin border. In terms of a weekend commute, it wasn't horrible. Still, the idea of her father being locked up like some sort of animal sickened her. The main reason she didn't visit often. Was it fair to her father? Probably not. But walking through those doors, being searched, and having her belongings X-rayed wasn't fair to her, either. His lifestyle, not hers, had put him in this place.

Harsh thinking perhaps, but the Rizzos were accustomed to harsh realities.

"Morning," the guard said, waving her through. "You're good."

She clipped her visitor's pass to the collar of her baggy shirt. One lesson she'd learned early on: no tight or revealing clothing. Provocative dress could send the prisoners, many of whom had a definite lack of female visitors, into a frenzy. *No thanks.*

A guard escorted her into the visitation area, a large

cement-walled room that resembled a high school gym more than a prison. The smell certainly fit. Stale yet antiseptic.

How Dad stood it, she'd never know. But she reminded herself, he'd be out of here soon and would have all the fresh air he wanted. If only she'd managed not to have to come back here for another two weeks. This couldn't wait though. And she'd admit part of her, down deep, still wanted to be Daddy's little girl and make him happy.

She sat at the corner table because, according to Dad, it backed against a wall with only one other beside it where people could eavesdrop. *The good table.* Lucie blew out a breath and shook her head. *I hate this place.*

Her father entered the room with two other prisoners. He found her and the side of his mouth lifted. As usual, he wore orange prison scrubs that hung on his lean frame. Hopefully when he got out and enjoyed Mom's cooking again, he'd regain the twenty pounds he'd lost. He could also stand to give up the buzz cut that made him appear down-right skeletal. Before prison he'd had an amazing head of thick, salt-and-pepper hair.

Really, what she wanted was her father back. Flaws and all. The man moving toward her dressed like an orange Popsicle wasn't him.

"Hi, Dad."

He slid onto the bench across from her. By now, she knew not to try and touch him. Contact with the prisoners was forbidden. Every now and again, because her Dad was —believe it or not—an affectionate man, he touched her hand, but it always earned him a glare from the guard. Over-all, he'd been a model prisoner. The guards treated him with respect, looked him in the eye when they spoke, and he did the same.

"Hi, baby girl."

Baby girl. Her childhood nickname. And one he rarely called her anymore. Another testament to their strained relationship. With him coming home, they needed a truce. Even with Joey moving to Frankie's, it would be close quarters. For her mother's sake, she didn't want them at war.

"I can't wait to get out of here, Lucie. First thing, I'm gonna grab your mother and we're going out to the lake. I need sun and fresh air."

Lucie nodded. When it came to being by the water, she and Dad were of the same mind. "She'd like that I think."

"I'm glad you came today. Didn't expect to see you until I got home."

"I know. And honestly, that was my plan. I hate seeing you in this place." She held up her hands. "But I don't want to argue over it."

He shrugged. "Then there's a reason you're here."

"There is."

"Frankie?"

Oh, Lord! Once again everything revolved around Frankie—Mr. Perfect in her dad's eyes—and whether they'd ever get married. "No, Dad. We're still on the outs. Sorry."

"He's a good—"

"Yes. I know he's a good boy. This time it was his doing, so save the lecture."

Dad's lips bowed down as he took that in. "That's...surprising."

"Yep." She'd forego telling him about the Irish cop. One thing at a time. "There is a reason I'm here. You know I rented Carlucci's for my new Coco Barknell headquarters, right?"

"Yeah. Joey mentioned something about it when he was here the other day."

Joey, bless his devoted heart, visited their dad three times a week. Without fail. Mom didn't even come that often.

"He's helping me with the contractors. We've been getting along. He's actually helping me run the dog walking side of the business."

"Ah, that's good. It's the way it should be."

"I know, Dad. Anyway, I had a problem at the store yesterday and we thought—Joey and I"—throwing Joey's name in there couldn't hurt—"that I should tell you in person."

Dad's frown came back. He leaned forward and dipped his head. "What happened? Someone robbed the place?" He bit down. "Rogue sons of bitches. I'll knock their lights out."

"No. Not that." Thank goodness. What a mess that would be. "Someone stored stolen merchandise in the storage room. Tracksuits."

As usual, her father sat still. The man wasn't one for big drama. When faced with a problem, he typically kept his body movements to a minimum. Lucie always thought he did it to keep people a little off balance, make them wonder, like now, what exactly went on in his mind.

"Sons of bitches. They know I don't want my kids involved."

"It gets worse. Someone tipped off the police... Well..." She dropped her chin to her chest, closed her eyes and fought the increasing tightness in her throat.

Risking the guard's wrath, Dad touched her hand then slid it away. "What happened? Whatever it is, I'll fix it."

This was the daddy she loved. No matter what, when it came to his family, he did what needed to be done. She raised her head, met her father's gaze and held it. "I got arrested."

Boom. He leaned back, gritted his teeth, and slammed a fist on the table, sending the bang of metal echoing off the cement walls. "I'll kill them."

And holy cow, Lucie flinched hard enough to almost tip her right out of her chair. Not only the unexpected physical reaction from her father, but the threatening outburst where a guard most definitely heard him.

"Hey," the guard warned from his spot by the door, "take it easy."

Dad shifted sideways, faced the guard, and raised one hand in a mea culpa. "Sorry."

The guard nodded and Dad came back to Lucie, closed his eyes for half a second, and breathed. Prison Zen moment?

He opened his eyes. "You were locked up?"

She nodded. "Only for a few hours. Joey called Willie and they bailed me out."

Best to hold off on Tim's involvement. Her father wasn't exactly a young man and the combination of his straight-laced daughter being arrested then being aided by a cop might give him a heart attack.

"Willie said he'd talk to the prosecutor, but basically, we have to prove I had no knowledge of this. If we don't, I'll have a criminal record."

"You'd never work for a bank again."

Being stubborn, Dad still saw Coco Barknell as a side job until she went back to investment banking. Right now, she didn't have it in her to remind him her intention was to grow her side job into a Fortune 500 company.

Dad drilled his finger into the tabletop. "That's not gonna happen. We'll find the one who did this. Believe me, whoever it is will go to the cops and clear this up. All charges will dropped. *Believe* me."

On Monday morning, Lucie was beginning to feel—odd as it was considering her current circumstances—lighter. A casual dinner with Tim the night before might be part of her mood. Something about him took the pressure off, let her feel at ease and not so tightly wound.

And, best of all, there was no arguing over distancing themselves from *the life*. As much as she loved Frankie, the issues in their relationship revolved around their families. And no matter how they tried, they always wound up in the same ugly place.

With Tim all the baggage went away. She could simply be a twenty-six-year-old woman finding her way in the world. One who wanted to kiss a cute detective, but whose nosy brother wouldn't stop interrupting long enough for that kiss to happen. Damned Joey.

But right now, she had a job to do on an August day so hot her lips weren't just dry, they were shedding.

Nugget, an adorable tan and white Beagle, pranced alongside Lucie, scoping out the next patch of grass to fall victim to his urine stream. On walks, Nugget didn't mess around. He was all business, all the time. The fact that Lucie slipped him a treat when they got back to the house probably didn't hurt, but this dog was a dog walker's dream.

"One thing, Lauren," Lucie said to her trainee. "Nugget always gets a treat when we're done. It's part of his routine. Don't forget, okay?"

Lauren jotted a note in her trainee book. Being a stickler for details, Lucie had created a handbook with the Coco Barknell logo on the front and Lauren dutifully took notes on each pet. Regardless of who walked the dogs on any given day, the transition between walkers needed to be smooth.

Joey, of course, was the wild card. Chances were he completely blew off her instructions and did his own thing. She'd like to set up some kind of surveillance to see. Hmm...a doggie cam. That might have some merit. She'd have to work out the logistics.

Lucie and Lauren trekked back to Nugget's house, a renovated brownstone that, in this neighborhood, went for at least three million. The Horvaths had moved in over a year ago, but the house still looked newly remodeled. Mrs. H. apparently had OCD tendencies because the counters always sparkled—quite a feat with black marble—and the floors held not one scuffmark. Nada.

On her best day, Lucie couldn't manage avoiding footprints on the hand-scraped floors and always wound up cleaning them before she left. Luckily, she never had to go farther than the mudroom.

Once through the back door, Nugget immediately plopped his furry butt in front of the treat cabinet.

"He's so cute," Lauren said.

Bending low, Lucie gave Nugget a scratch and a nuzzle. "Yes, he is." She kissed the side of his head and handed him a treat. "Good, baby. Lucie loves you."

"You're so good with the dogs, Lucie. The owners must be crazy about you."

Lucie shrugged. "We had a dog growing up. He died when I was in college. Some day I'll have another one."

Some day when she lived in her own place again. And was allowed pets. Her apartment downtown hadn't allowed animals, and Mom certainly had no interest. She had her hands full with Joey.

And Dad.

She snorted. A dog would probably be easier to control than those two.

Lauren scooped up Nugget's water bowl. "He's out of water. Poor guy. I'll fill it."

"Okay. The kitchen is right through there." Lucie pointed then checked the time on her phone. "We're a few minutes behind, so let's make this quick. Grab some paper towels while you're in there. We might have to clean the footprints."

"We will?"

"Client is a neat freak. Can't blame her. The place is stunning."

Lauren headed into the kitchen with Nugget's bowl while Lucie stowed his leash.

"Lucie?" Lauren called. "Do you think I could use the bathroom?"

Now she had to pee? Before this was over, they'd be scrubbing every inch of flooring on the first level. But they'd been moving for two hours and Lauren had slammed two cups of coffee. As an employer, Lucie couldn't very well limit her intake of liquids.

Or her need to pee.

"Sure. The Horvaths don't mind. Down the hall on the right."

"Great. Thanks."

She set the bowl on the counter and scooted down the hall. "Oh, that's cool."

"What?"

"Have you seen this painting?"

Here we go again. "Lauren, go pee. Focus."

"I know, but it's right here on the wall across from the bathroom. You've gotta see it. I think it might be a Nodai."

Lucie would have to inventory which clients were art collectors and not assign Lauren to those homes. A passion for art was enviable, but not when they had a schedule to keep.

"We have to go." Lucie squatted to gather some of Nugget's toys. "Here you go, baby."

"It's just so beautiful. I've never seen a real one."

A real one. *Oh no.* Two months ago, she'd passed Bart Owens's card to Mrs. Horvath. Sculptures and paintings throughout the first floor were obvious indicators that they liked art, so Lucie, thinking of her loose agreement with Bart regarding commissions, had told Mrs. Horvath about the gallery.

But that had been the last of it. She'd never been notified of a sale, and she certainly never asked. She'd simply trusted Bart would let her know. Or hand over a check.

Lucie shot to her feet. Disregarding the fear of footprints, she hustled to where Lauren wistfully admired a giant painting spanning the four-foot wall across from the powder room.

Eeee-gads. Lucie slapped her hand over her eyes. *What the hell is that?* Could it be what she thought? Nah. No one would put that across from their powder room where guests and children would see it.

Had to be a mistake. Lucie cracked two fingers for a peek and—*hello, fella.*

In the painting, maybe something from the Renaissance period based on the color and appearance, a naked woman sat backward on top of an equally naked and—*eh-hem*—extremely endowed man.

In a half-buried wheelbarrow.

A wheelbarrow!

Lucie dropped her hand from her eyes and took it all in. Every perverted and yet entirely fascinating inch. Every inch. "Wow."

"I know, right?"

"What is this? Early European porn?"

"No," Lauren spat, her outrage obvious. "It's the earliest form of erotic art. Look at the lines, Lucie. It's amazing."

She tipped her head sideways. Too much. Quite literally. The man's... uh... *member,* or rather the size of it, damn near terrified her. She glanced down at her crotch, then back to the man in the painting. No way that thing fits. No way.

What sane woman would let... She couldn't even *think* about it. *God, the agony.* She closed her eyes and scrunched her face. "I almost can't look at it."

Lauren laughed. "Trust me. If this is a Nodai, and I think it is, it's a classic. Worth millions."

If that were the case, Lucie should invite an artist into Frankie's bedroom when he did his magic on her. They'd be billionaires. Just thinking about Frankie and his zest for lovemaking—and the lack of it in her life—made her cheeks hot. Now what? She was some kind of nymphomaniac from looking at a painting?

"Are you sure?" she asked, still not believing this painting was on display across from the bathroom. "Millions?"

"Yes! What makes them so valuable is they're part of a series. Twelve in all, if I remember. They all show different sexual positions. I'd have to look this one up to see what number it is. I wonder if it's labeled anywhere."

Lauren reached for the frame and Lucie locked on to her wrist. "No you don't. If this thing is worth millions, you can't touch it. Not when you're on Coco Barknell's time. If you damage it, I get sued. Nuh-uh."

The company's insurance premiums would skyrocket.

Lauren snatched her hand back. "Sorry. But I'm so curious. Lucie, these paintings are rare. I think most of them were destroyed in a fire in the 1800s. I'd love to know where they got it."

So would Lucie. Because a deal was a deal, and if this painting was worth millions, Bart Owens owed her a good chunk of cash. But considering how rare Lauren said the paintings were, it could be a copy.

Or Bart sold the Horvaths a fake. After Lucie vouched for him.

A sick feeling tumbled inside her and a vision of the cell she'd been locked in on Saturday flashed in her mind. *Here we go again.*

"I don't know where they got it."

But she'd find out. Somehow, she'd find out.

At home that evening, Lucie sat at the dining room table with her laptop and her favorite Notre Dame glass. The glass held diet pop, but she might be switching to something stronger if Bart Owens turned out to be, as Ro would say, a lying, scheming rat bastard.

She took in the stacked plastic bins in the corner and the bolts of fabric propped against grandma's breakfront. As soon as the renovations on Carlucci's—she had to start thinking of it as Coco Barknell—were complete, all these supplies would be moved over and her mother would have her dining room back.

In time for her father's return.

Timing was essential. Mainly because she had no interest in her father carrying on about how his dining room looked like a storage closet. Much less the idea that Mom was now working almost thirty-hours per week as a seamstress. Oh, boy, *that* would be interesting. No wonder Joey wanted to move out.

The front door flew open and smacked against the wall. Seriously, Ro was going to put a hole in the wall if she kept that up. Lucie's best friend strolled in on five-inch heels that made her already long legs look like skyscrapers.

She came to a stop at the end of the table and cocked one hip. "Sorry it took so long to get here. I came as soon as I got your message. What's up?"

"We're on a mission."

Ready for action, Ro did a fast clap and immediately slid into the chair next to Lucie. "I love missions. What is it?"

"We have to verify if a painting I saw at the Horvath's today is a fake."

"Another painting? What is it with you?"

"I know. I can't help it. Lauren spotted this one when we walked Nugget today. According to her, if it's real, it's worth millions."

Ro puckered and blew air through her lips. "Is this one you brokered for Owens?"

"Not sure. That's part of the mission. I did pass along Bart's name to Mrs. Horvath, and I know the painting is probably new because it wasn't there last week. But Bart didn't tell me if he sold her the painting."

"Okay. I gotcha. You want to see if the thing is real first in case Owens makes a habit of selling knockoffs. And if it is, you can ask him if he's been a rat bastard and cheated you out of your cut?"

Ah, Ro. How well Lucie knew her. "Simply put, yes. I started researching the entire series of paintings. Most of them were destroyed in a gallery fire in 1821. I was just starting to look up each individual piece to find the Horvath's."

Ro smacked her hands together then flicked them out. "I'm on it. What do you need me to do?"

"There are a lot of paintings in the series. We're double teaming it. I'll show you a photo of the Horvath's painting and then we need to figure out if it was one of the ones destroyed. If it wasn't, we figure out where the real one is. Who knows if the Internet can tell us all that, but it's worth a try."

Lucie picked up the tablet she used when she didn't feel like lugging her laptop around and handed it to Ro. "Here you go."

"Thank you."

"You're welcome. Now, I'm going to show you the painting. Try to refrain from any sarcastic comments."

"This sounds juicy."

"You really have no idea."

Anticipating something exciting, Ro scooted closer. "Is it porn?"

How did she know that? "Why would your mind automatically go there?"

"It's porn? Really?" Ro hooted. "You're kind of a prude, so I went straight to porn."

A prude. Of course there were worse things, but somehow it felt like an insult. Whatever. "Lauren says they're classics of early European erotic art. It's meant to titillate."

"I always loved that word. Titillate. It sounds so dirty."

Focus. Focus. Focus. "Remember. No sarcasm."

"Blah, blah."

Lucie swiped at the pad on her laptop and the image of the painting filled the screen. For the first time—ever—Ro might have been struck mute. She leaned in, craning closer to the screen. "Well, well, well. Mister, where have *you* been all my life? And is that a *wheelbarrow*?"

Unbelievable. Totally off-point here. "What did I just say?"

Ro slouched back, resting her hand on her forehead. "I know, but, Luce, you can't put that in front of me and not expect it." She dropped her hand and straightened up again. "I don't know why this surprises me. Even four hundred years ago men had one-track minds. And frankly, not that this matters, but I think the logistics on that wheelbarrow thing are a little suspect."

Lucie laughed. She couldn't help it. She had the most incredibly twisted inner circle. But God, she loved them. "You're right. And if you're done ogling, can we get back to business here? We need to figure out if this painting was destroyed in that fire. Hopefully, it wasn't and it's hanging on the Horvath's wall."

"Okay. We've got this. Show me the rest so I'll be able to tell which ones were destroyed."

Please. As if Lucie believed that. "You just want to look at them."

Fighting a grin, Ro set the tips of her fingers over her mouth and giggled. "I'm so naughty."

"Fine. Be naughty. Just find that damned painting."

"Okay. But I'm writing down the name of this website."

***

TIM SAT AT HIS DESK, CLEARING OUT SOME REPORTS WHEN HIS cell phone rang. After starting the day with two hours of paperwork, he welcomed the distraction and seeing adorable Lucie Rizzo's name lifted his mood considerably. He hit the button. "Hey, pretty lady."

"Hi. And thank you."

"For what?"

"For telling me I'm pretty."

"I only speak the truth."

"And for saving my butt with Frankie. That was awkward."

"I know. For me, too. It was easier all around for me to just handle it. At least for now."

He was a nice guy, but that only took him so far and if things progressed between he and Lucie, she'd need to make a decision. Him or Frankie. End of it. Tim didn't share. Ever.

His lieutenant walked by the desk and dropped a file without even slowing down. "Take a look at that before court this afternoon."

At two o'clock, Tim would testify for the prosecution on a home invasion from eight months ago. The suspect was pretty much screwed, but Tim never went into court unprepared. "Uh, sure." He went back to Lucie. "Sorry. My boss. So what's up?"

"I'm sorry. You're busy. I'll call you later."

Again with the apologizing. Lucie Rizzo apologized a lot. For things she shouldn't be apologizing for. He'd break her of that if it killed him. "No, Lucie. We're good."

She hesitated for a few seconds and Tim glanced at the phone's screen to make sure the call hadn't dropped. Not uncommon in the precinct with all the cement walls.

Nope. Plenty of bars. He'd wait her out.

"Okay," she finally said. "Could I ask your advice on something? Not personal. Business. Sort of. Well, it's kind of both."

Tim smiled. Dang, he *sort of* loved this girl. Definitely a worrier. But there was more. Way more. Ambition maybe. And the drive to make sure the world knew she was more than a mob guy's kid. "Sure."

"Great. Can I buy you lunch?"

He stared down at the folder Lou had just dropped on his desk. Between what he already had on his desk and that file, his day had gone to hell pretty quick. "Today?"

"Yes. I know it's short notice, but I'll be seeing the client it involves this afternoon."

"Is this a legal issue?"

Again she hesitated and Tim's shit meter went off.

"Well, I guess I'm not sure."

"Which is why you want to ask me about it?"

"Yes."

He checked his watch. "Can you do it early. Maybe 11:30? I have to be in court this afternoon."

"Absolutely. 11:30. I'll text you the address. Thank you."

As if it were a hardship seeing her in the middle of the day. "No. Thank *you*. This might be the best part of my day."

And who said cops couldn't be charming? Frank Falcone better be on notice that Tim wanted his girl.

Ninety minutes later, he walked into Rizzo's Italian Beef, got a laugh out of her inviting him to lunch at her mobbed-up father's restaurant, and found Lucie sitting at a table by the window. He walked over, hung his suit jacket on the back of one of the empty chairs, slipped off his tie, and rolled it.

If he had to eat at Rizzo's, he was having a beef sandwich and they were tricky bastards. By the end of the meal, he'd be sure to have sandwich juice dripped down the front of him. As it was, he'd have to be careful with the shirt.

"Hi," he said to Lucie, who watched him shove the tie into the inside pocket of his jacket. "Court hearing today. I don't want to mess up my clothes."

"Smart, Detective. Is that the voice of experience?"

"Yep. Want to order before I sit?"

"Sure."

He stepped behind her, scooted her chair from under her, and held out his hand. The early lunch crowd trickled in, and roughly half of the fifty tables were occupied, the voices all melding together and bouncing off the brick walls. As restaurants went, Rizzo's appeared to do a healthy business. The food was good and the owner's reputation didn't hurt in terms of tourists. Everyone wanted a look at one of Joe Rizzo's joints.

Tim followed Lucie to the counter, where they ordered and were handed a number for the table. While waiting for their food, Tim took the empty seat beside her and decided, once again, that he liked looking at Lucie.

"Thanks for meeting me," she said.

"Thanks for calling. What's up? Problem with a client?"

"I'm not sure."

Lucie gave him the short version of her problem and finished just as a tray of food landed on their table.

Tim dove into his sandwich and the flavor of the beef, a little peppery but not too much, exploded in his mouth. Damn that was good. He set the sandwich down, wiped his mouth and decided he'd have to visit Rizzo's more often. Being a cop, he hadn't wanted to support a business connected to organized crime, but hell, this was a damned good sandwich.

And then there was Lucie...

"Back to your problem," he said. "Are you afraid this painting is another fake and your client bought it from Owens?"

"Exactly."

Again with the Owens guy. Something was up with this dude. "I'm gonna look into Owens. Quietly. See if anything pops."

"That's not why I asked you here, but thanks. What I need to find out is if the original painting was destroyed in the fire. Ro and I did some research last night, but I can't find anything on this particular painting. Do you have any idea how I find out if it's the original?"

He didn't, but the guys who worked fraud probably would. "Let me talk to a few people who handle fraud cases. They might know. Which painting is it?"

Tim took another bite of his sandwich.

"It's called *Position Seven*."

He stopped chewing and swallowed. "Come again?"

"That's the title. *Position Seven*."

"Kind of a generic title. Do you have a picture of it so I know what I'm looking for?"

"Um..."

"What?"

She stared at him a second, a pinched look on her face. Eventually, she grabbed her backpack from the chair beside her. "Nothing. It's just... nothing. I'll show it to you." She hit him with a fast, toothy smile. "Free Wi-Fi at Rizzo's."

Nervous. Whatever this painting was, it had her rattled. "Lucie, I've been a cop twelve years." He wiped his hands on his napkin. "Nothing shocks me. Show me the painting."

She tapped the screen of the tablet and nodded. "It's a Renaissance. Same as the Lutz's painting. Lauren says it's a classic. If it's the real deal, it's worth millions."

After tapping the screen a couple more times, Lucie held out the tablet, but then snatched it back. "No snarky comments."

He laughed. "Give me the damned tablet."

"Fine. Just remember what I said."

Too damned cute. He took the tablet and—*whoa*. He might have to take back that line about nothing shocking him. And crap on a cracker, he suddenly had a vision of Lucie sitting backward and bare-butt naked on top of him. *Day-am.* He cleared his throat, kept his eyes glued to the tablet and not on Lucie's lovely and ample chest, willing his body to remain unaffected. Definitely not an easy task. "All righty, then. Is that a wheelbarrow?"

"What is it with people and the wheelbarrow?"

"It's a legitimate question. I mean, I know it's buried, so it's stable, but that has to be uncomfortable. Not to mention a challenge."

A woman squeezed behind him and he held the tablet against him. Didn't need the general population thinking he was a pig. He smiled up at the woman, waited for her to clear the area, and got back to business. He turned the tablet sideways for a better view and whistled. Across from him, Lucie shifted and he glanced up, meeting her gaze for a solid thirty seconds, hopefully letting her know that, yes, his mind had definitely gone to the gutter and it was all about her. Her cheeks fired and the very real possibility existed that he might have fallen in love. *I'm so going down.*

He handed the tablet back, then reached into his jacket pocket for his notepad.

"What are you doing?"

"Writing down the website. If I'm going to find this painting, I'll need specifics." Yeah, he'd definitely be reviewing that website on his own time.

"Oh, boy."

Damned. Cute.

"Relax. It's art. Not a big deal." He leaned over, ran his hand over the back of her chair, and got right up to her ear. "But if you ever want to try that wheelbarrow thing, I'm your guy."

11

———

Lucie parked her scooter in the alley behind the Horvath's house and unclipped her helmet. From inside, Nugget heard her pull up and went into his barking frenzy, anticipating her arrival and his afternoon walk.

"I'm coming," she said, "keep your shorts on."

The back door opened and Lucie flinched as sharp warning tingles shot up her arms and down her legs. The Horvaths both worked. *Burglar.* Instinctively she reached for her messenger bag and the pepper-spray she kept handy. At times, she even carried a stun gun. After the dognappings five months earlier, she'd become her own special cross-breed of Wonder Woman and the Terminator.

Mr. Horvath—thank goodness—slid into the open doorway. "Hi, Lucie."

Lucie removed her helmet, hung it on the handle bar of the scooter, and blew out a heavy breath. The tingles on her arms and legs peeled away as the adrenaline dump tapered off. After the last few days, her nerves were dust. What kind of paranoia drives a person to want to pepper spray their own client?

As usual, Mr. Horvath's short, dark hair was combed and gelled into businessman mode. She guessed his age to be around forty, but thought maybe he enjoyed a little Botox every now and again. The few wrinkles he did have strategically accentuated his crystal blue eyes. He wore a grey suit, but the jacket and tie had been discarded. Lunch break or half day. She didn't care which.

"Hi, Mr. Horvath."

"Sorry if I startled you. I took a couple of hours off this afternoon. I should have warned you."

Lucie closed the flap on her messenger bag and adjusted it on her hip. "Good for you. Is Nugget ready for his walk?"

"You know he is. He's been sitting by the door waiting for you. But, I'm glad you're here. I wanted to show you something."

Huh?

A client had never said *that* to her. And truth be told, it scared her a little. Well, maybe not scared, but she definitely had a moment's hesitation.

Whatever it was, he sensed it and shot his hands up. "I bought a painting from Bart. Wanted you to see it."

Oh, God. She'd have to look at the guy with the tree-sized member while standing next to her client. Her very male client. And, hellooooo, he'd just inadvertently answered her question about where he'd acquired this latest acquisition. Assuming, of course, that was the painting he referred to.

She breathed in, set her shoulders, and prepared herself to act surprised. Please be another painting. Please.

Behind Mr. Horvath, Nugget barked and he stepped aside, letting the dog charge out to see Lucie. She bent low, got her usual lick on the chin and gave Nugget the snuggles he'd grown used to. Great dog. Such a love bug.

"That dog," Mr. Horvath said. "You'd think he never got any attention."

Offering up one more good rub, Lucie stood. "Nah. He just likes his Lucie love."

"Come on in."

Please don't take me to that hallway. But, nope, Mr. Horvath led her into the kitchen straight to the hallway. *Doggone it.* She could barely look at that painting the first time with Lauren. Now she had to do it with a man. A handsome one to boot.

Just don't look at the penis. If she could do that, she'd be fine. *No penis.*

Mr. Horvath swooped his arm. "Here it is. We're just thrilled. It nearly broke the bank, but Bart says we got a steal on it and it'll triple in value in a couple of years. It's a Nodai."

Lucie braced herself, then tore her eyes from Mr. Horvath to look at the painting. Yep, same tree-like member.

"The wheelbarrow is a kick, isn't it?"

God help me.

"It certainly is. Wow! It's so...big."

Ach.

"The painting," she said.

Oh, that just made it worse. Now he'd know she was thinking about the member.

Mr. Horvath laughed. "I know. It's crazy. It's part of a series. Twelve in all. Most of them got toasted in a fire, but Bart managed to snag one of the last remaining ones. I think someone in Europe had it."

Okay. She couldn't look at it anymore. The penis was too much. Burned her eyes like acid. She faced Mr. H. "That's terrific. I'm glad it worked out between you two."

But the rat bastard never paid me.

Mr. Horvath unglued his gaze from the painting and

faced her. "It did. I'm actually thinking about investing in another painting with him. Another undervalued Renaissance Bart thinks might go up in value in the next few years."

Interesting. She'd probably get screwed out of that commission also. "It's sort of like flipping houses, only with paintings."

"Exactly. If all goes well, it'll be tremendously profitable."

"I could see that. I guess you have to make sure you have all the documentation in order if you're going to flip them."

"Oh absolutely. In the art world it's called provenance. If the provenance is good, there's no question regarding the work's authenticity."

Thank you so much for that info. "So what's considered good provenance?"

"It could be a signed certificate or some other statement from an expert on the artist. What Bart gave me was a receipt from the gallery."

If Mr. Horvath had the receipt, the painting must have been real. And she'd definitely gotten burned out of her finder's fee. Now she'd have to have a conversation with Bart. One that might cost her a client. But if this painting was worth millions, even if the Horvaths didn't pay that much, her commission alone would set her up for the next year.

Nugget nudged Lucie's leg and she glanced down at him. "I'm sorry, baby." She rubbed the underside of his chin. "Let's get this show on the road."

Before I commit a homicide.

On her way home, Lucie stopped off at the shop to make

sure everything was locked. Her new routine since her arrest. From now on, the place would be locked up tight.

By the newly installed locks.

At this point, she'd adopted Joey's favorite saying: Fool me once, shame on you, fool me twice, I'll kill you where you stand.

She double-checked the front door, giving it a good tug before turning toward her car parked across the street. The fading afternoon sun did nothing to alleviate the suffocating heat and humidity, but she tipped her face up and took a second to simply breathe and be thankful she wouldn't be stuck in an office for another four hours. Banker's hours.

Not anymore.

Her phone rang, then did a quick double vibrate in her back pocket. Always a thrill, that. At least for a girl who'd spent most of her evenings the last three months solo. The vibrating stopped—maybe she'd start calling her own phone for a fix. Or maybe she just needed a vibrator. Eh. Why bother?

She slipped the phone from her pocket. Tim O'Brien. *Hi there, handsome.* No wonder her mind went straight to the lack of sex in her life. She had the hottie detective buzzing her butt.

She tapped the screen. "Hi."

"Hi to you. Are you home?"

"Not yet. On my way. I detoured to make sure the store is locked. What's up?"

"I talked to my fraud guy. Your painting," he continued, "is alive and well. My guy did some digging. He said it's in a gallery in Italy."

Okay. So maybe Bart wasn't a lying, scheming rat bastard. "Huh. Bart could have bought it then."

"Could have. It's worth three million."

Lucie froze, just stopped right in the middle of the side-walk, and a kid on a bike swerved around her, nearly taking her down and plowing into a lamppost himself.

"Watch it, lady!"

Any number of comebacks sprang to mind, but somehow the words wouldn't pass through her lips. Three million *dollars*?

Wha...*gulp*. "Three," she choked out. "*Million*?"

"According to my guy."

She knew the Horvaths had money—well, appeared to have money, simply based on the home they lived in. But three million on a painting?

"Wow."

"Of course, that doesn't mean the one hanging on your client's wall isn't a copy."

She leaned against the lamppost the kid almost clob-bered, but leaped forward when the hot metal scalded her back right through her shirt. Yowzer!

"If it's a copy, he's pretending it's not. I saw him today and had to stand there while he gushed over his new acqui-sition. Do you know how embarrassing that was? I mean"—she waved her hand—"with the erotic nature of the thing. The painting. Not the..." Dear God, her mouth had suddenly figured out how to work and now she couldn't stop the flow. She closed her eyes. *Stay on point.*

From his side of the conversation, Tim cleared his throat. Probably hiding a laugh.

She opened her eyes again and stared straight ahead at the dry cleaners across the street. "Go ahead, Detective. Laugh all you want. He's my client for God's sakes and he's got that...that...*member*...hanging on the wall. Anyway, he told me Bart gave him paperwork authenticating the paint-ing. So, it must be real."

"You never know. The art world is hinky. Art dealers fake that stuff all the time."

Great. Mr. Devil's advocate. "So, I'm back where I started?"

"Unless I can come up with probable cause and have someone review the documentation, pretty much. Hang on." A muffled sound hit her ear. He must have put his hand over the phone. "Lucie?"

"I'm here."

"I gotta go. I'll call you later."

She disconnected and shoved her phone back into her pocket, hoping for another buzz at some point. The plight of a single girl.

Ro's Escalade came to a stop in a fire zone in front of the store. A second later, Lucie's BFF hopped out and the rear hatch of the vehicle came open. Dropping something off maybe.

Lucie wandered over while pondering her lack of probable cause.

With her father's history, she knew all about what law enforcement could and couldn't do without probable cause. Probable cause—PC—protected citizens from unreasonable searches by law enforcement. Right now, Tim or any police officer had no PC to search Bart's premises. Nothing.

That didn't keep Lucie from wondering if Mr. Horvath's paperwork was legit.

What she needed was a copy of that receipt.

Ro reached into her SUV, hefted an oversized tote on her shoulder, and glanced down at her stretchy V-neck blouse that clung to her curves like Oscar the Perv working Lucie's leg. Ro adjusted the front of her shirt, gave her boob a little adjustment to maximize the cleavage and Lucie knew exactly how she'd get a copy of that receipt.

Two hours later, Lucie and Ro marched down the sidewalk to the Owens Gallery. The early evening sun had turned a rich, burnt orange and Lucie wanted to be on a beach somewhere, watching that sun drop away. Soon, she'd treat herself to a vacation. She and Ro maybe. A girls' trip.

Ro came to a stop and faced Lucie. "How do I look?"

Lucie did a perfunctory scan of the wrap dress that really needed a cami under it, but for this, Ro had pulled out the stops.

Or the boobs, as the case might be. "Well," Lucie said, "your boobs are definitely on overtime."

"You said you needed me for a mission. I assumed that meant full-cleavage. Soooo, I went full-cleave."

Lucie held up a finger. "I said I needed your help. That's all."

"Which, hello, usually involves me utilizing my assets. Where did I go wrong?"

Got me there. "Okay. But just so you know, I love you for more than your boobs. You know that, right?"

"Pfft. Of course. What's your problem?"

Good old Ro. "No problem. Just making sure. Anyway, here's the deal. I called Bart and told him I had a friend interested in buying some art. When we get inside, you distract him and I'll go into the office to say hello to Oscar. Hopefully, the filing cabinet will be unlocked and I can have a peek."

"Easy," Ro said. "I'll keep him away from the office."

"If the cabinet drawer is locked, I'll text you. That'll be your cue to tell him you'd like to see the provenance for whatever painting you're looking at."

"Provenance?"

"Yes. It's documentation that the painting is legit. He'll come into the office, see me playing with Oscar, and unlock the drawer so he can get whatever he needs. Hopefully, he'll leave the cabinet unlocked when he returns to you. Got it?"

"Ten-four. Roger that. But holy hell, sister, there's a lot of hopefullys happening with this mission."

Lucie sighed. "I know. But it's the only option."

And asking for help from Joey or Tim was out of the question. Joey would have a cow if he knew they were up to this. Plus, Tim might not approve. But he was the cop, not her. Probable cause wasn't her issue. She just needed a look at that receipt. Then she'd snap a photo with her phone and call the gallery where it was purchased. If anything about the transaction seemed fishy, she'd turn the photo over to Tim and that should give them their probable cause. At least in her mind.

Time to get to work.

Ro and Lucie strolled through the front door of the gallery. The bells on the door did their little jangle and Bart entered the room from his office, closing the door behind him so Oscar couldn't run out. Lucie turned her head away and whispered, "That's the office."

Ro immediately offered up one of her sexy girl smiles and waved. "Un-huh. Got it," she said without moving her mouth.

Seriously. How did she *do* that?

"Hello, Lucie," Bart said. "Thank you for coming in."

Lucie set her hand on Ro's arm. "Hi, Bart. This is my friend Ro. She's the one I called you about. She's interested in possibly starting an art collection."

Bart shifted his attention to Ro. To his credit, he lingered on her face for at least two-point-five seconds then his gaze... *Come on, fella, come to mama...* traveled lower and—bam— darted right back to Ro's face.

Just. Hold on. Here.

What happened to the whole moth to a flame theory? Huh. Leave it to them to find the one man completely uninterested in Ro's assets.

"Well," Bart said, "you've come to the right place. Do you have a particular style in mind?"

Ro made a non-committal humming noise. "Not really. I'm new at all this. Maybe you could show me different styles?"

Bart gestured to the wall. "Of course. Right this way."

Ro angled right, toward the wall at the front of the gallery and pointed. "Let's start there."

Excellent. As far from the office as possible.

Lucie swung her thumb to the back of the building. "Is Oscar in the office?"

"He is," Bart said. "He's a rascal today. All he wants to do is play."

"Do you mind if I head back there and say hello? I missed him today."

"Be my guest. Just be prepared. You know how he gets with you."

Oh, she knew. The minute she stepped into his sight, the dog would pounce on her and give her a hump worthy of Olympic competition.

"Thanks for the warning."

"Have fun, Luce," Ro called, giving her a finger wave.

Despite Bart's lack of interest in the boobage, could this operation be going any better? She'd just close the door behind her, give Oscar a quick pat, and snoop in the files. If they were arranged alphabetically by client and not in some CIA-worthy filing system, even better.

She opened the door, and as expected, the second Oscar smelled her, he charged. She quickly shut the door and braced herself against it, holding her hand in a stop. "Be good, Oscar."

But this darned dog was so cute with his tail flicking back and forth she could barely stand it. Lucie squatted to give him a rub. "No humping." She nuzzled his neck. "I have important business back here."

Oscar slapped a couple of licks across her cheek, and sensing him getting wound up for action, she stood, moving sideways around the desk to the cabinet.

The key wasn't in the lock—not necessarily a bad sign— and she grasped the handle. Shoot. Should have worn gloves. "Ach. What kind of detective are you?"

Too late now. She'd just wipe it clean when she left. Then again, someone had told her that didn't work, but she couldn't remember why. Something about DNA maybe. She didn't know.

Gah.

Just as she wrapped her fingers around the handle, Oscar mounted her. "Off!"

Damned horny dog. But he was apparently in mission mode as well. He wrapped his front paws around her calf and went to work. She reached down, nudged him away and held him with one hand while yanking on the drawer. Nothing.

Locked.

God! Should have known—Oscar and the boob rejecting notwithstanding—things were moving along too well. Whenever that happened in her life, it meant a spectacular screw- up would ensue. She breathed deep. Went to plan B. Yes, she had a plan B because that's what A-type personalities did.

They planned.

Forced to let go of Oscar, she dug her phone from her

pocket and put her fingers to work texting her accomplice. In all caps so she'd understand the urgency.

LOCKED. GO TO GUNS.

Lucie shoved the phone back and squatted once again, pushing Oscar off and holding him at bay while giving him a scratch. If Ro had initiated plan B, any second now, Bart would come through the door and see Lucie on the floor with Oscar.

"Let's do this, Perv."

Oscar gave her another lick and she nuzzled him again. Stupid dog. She simply couldn't stay mad at him.

And sure enough, the door opened, and in stepped Bart, grinning from ear to ear at the Lucie-Oscar lovefest.

"Well, look at you two," he said.

"Yep. Just me and the love machine. Everything okay?"

"Oh, sure. Roseanne would like to see the provenance on one of the paintings."

"Provenance?"

Oh, I'm good! She might join the Screen Actors Guild after this performance.

"Yes." Bart scooted behind her. "It confirms the painting's authenticity."

Pretending to ignore him, Lucie rubbed noses with Oscar and scratched behind his ears. "You're a sweet, sweet baby," she said, baby talk in full swing. "Yes, you are."

Bart retrieved a file from the cabinet, slipped a document out and kneed the drawer closed.

Please don't lock it.

"You know, Lucie, you don't have to sit in here with him. He'll be fine."

To add a little insurance to that no locking thing, Lucie stood, stepped back a foot to give herself leg room and shook out her legs. All while moving in front of the cabinet so Bart couldn't flick that lock.

"Oh, I know." Lucie stuck one leg out, gave it a good stretch. Good, long, lock-blocking stretch. "I just like playing with him."

Bart drew his eyebrows together and maybe, perhaps, she'd gone a little too far on that stretch. "Stiff legs. Sorry. All that walking."

"All right." He held up the file. "Back to work. Just come out when you're ready."

"I sure will."

After I get done rummaging through your files.

The second the door closed, Lucie lunged to the cabinet. Oscar followed suit by lunging on Lucie. Perv.

"You're a sick pig, Oscar." She couldn't waste time shoving him off and just let him have his way with her.

Hump, hump, hump. She ran her fingers over the folders and slowed when she reached G. *Hump, hump, hump.* Perusing the names, they appeared to be alpha by client. Yes! She got to H and flipped through. Horvath. There.

Thank you for being a normal filing person.

Go to work.

Hump, hump, hump. Crazy dog.

She tugged the file out, flipped it open, and spread the pages. Door. *Check it.* She glanced over. Nothing. She dug her phone out. Thank God for the miracle of cell phone cameras. *Snap, snap, snap.* One each of a client information sheet, a bill of sale and an invoice—holy mother of God— for nine-hundred-thousand-dollars. Even as an investment banker, she'd been awed by sums of money that large. Tim had told her the original was worth three million. If that were true, the Horvaths did indeed get a deal.

If what they had was the original.

Sweat bubbled on the back of her neck, tickling her. In an attempt to dislodge the moisture, she rolled her shoulders. No good. Forget it.

She set the three pages aside and spread the remaining two out. Snap, snap. Done. She slapped the file closed.

"Hold on one second, Roseanne."

Bart's voice.

From just on the other side of the door.

Yikes! A shot of panic raced straight up into her shoulders, stabbed at her neck. She steadied herself on trembling arms. Locked her nerves down. No time for panic. *Close the drawer, close the drawer.*

Lucie's phone buzzed and she glanced down. Ro. No time. Fingers spazzing, she shoved the folder back. Was that the right spot? Who knew?

Lawdy!

"No," Bart said, his voice even closer.

Right spot or not, she'd have to go with it. Hip-checking the drawer, she shoved Oscar off and dropped to her knees. Thinking it was playtime, Oscar lunged, knocking her off balance and back against the desk. She clocked her head on the top of the cabinet and a sharp jab radiated from the back of her head clear around the front. This was one dangerous mission. Mounting a full frontal assault, Oscar straddled her leg, trapping it against the floor and *hump, hump, humped* his way to heaven.

Seriously, this dog needed to get laid.

The door came open and Bart's gaze zoomed to Lucie rubbing her head and Oscar having his way with her.

"What happened?"

"Well," she said, "you were right about him being playful today. He just knocked me right into your desk, the little devil."

And thankfully, Oscar didn't speak human. He'd totally throw her under the bus. Totally.

Bart kneeled beside her, locked his gaze on hers. "Are you okay? Any blurry vision?"

So, Lucie, how did you get that concussion? Well, you see, one of my clients humped me into a desk.

The horrors of this job were sometimes plentiful. "Oh," she said, "I'm fine. But I think it's time for me to leave Mr. Oscar be. I don't want him too wound up." She pointed to the door. "I'll just head out."

She shoved the perv off, got to all fours, and slowly rose to her feet. No whirling room. No swaying. No nausea. Okay. Good.

Bart held out a steadying arm, but Lucie ignored it, set her shoulders back. "I'm okay. Thank you, though."

She headed toward the door.

"I just need to file this and I'll be out there." He waggled his eyebrows. "We may have a winner, Lucie. And a hefty commission for you."

Oh, they'd see about that, wouldn't they?

Lucie strolled out of Bart's office, her gaze glued to Ro. Suddenly, she had to pee. Sometimes that happened at the worst moments. Flop-sweating had nothing on flop-peeing.

Ro squinted and cocked her head.

Lucie smiled all big, bright and cheery. "I'm back. You about done here?"

They probably shouldn't rush out, but at this point, Lucie didn't want to be in the gallery a second longer than she had to be.

"Yes."

Ro motioned to one of the paintings. A rather dark contemporary with harsh splashes of red and black that Lucie surmised might be indicative of Ro's current emotional situation.

"I like this one. Once the divorce is final, I may treat myself."

Unsure whether Ro was still method acting or really intended on buying the painting, Lucie nodded. "Good for you."

Bart entered the room, shutting the door behind him so Oscar the Perv couldn't hump anyone. That dog was almost a menace. Almost?

"Is there anything else I can show you?" Bart asked.

"I think I'm good," Ro said. "I do like this one. I can't swing it right now though. If you still have it when I'm ready, I'll be back."

She stared at the painting, her normally bright eyes a little droopy and with a wistful longing Lucie had ever only seen on her once before. And that was during a conversation about—if one could believe it—Joey.

Blech.

Ro wanted that painting. For whatever reason, it spoke to her. Depending on the cost, if they had a good month with accessories sales, Lucie could give Ro a much-deserved bonus. A bonus that would get her a painting. Without Ro, that first lucrative Frampton's order, even if it had irritated Lucie at the time because they weren't equipped for such a large undertaking, would never have happened. Their success had been a complete team effort and Ro had led the charge.

Bart did a weird little bow that had Lucie quirking an eyebrow. Kinda creepy.

She held her hand toward the door. "We'll get out of your way. Have a good night."

Once on the walkway, surrounded by that same off-the-scale humidity, Ro nudged her with her elbow. "Did you find anything?"

To be sure they weren't being surveilled, Lucie glanced behind her. Even if Bart were watching them from inside, it wasn't as if he could hear them. Unless he'd planted a bug or something.

Lawdy, this was an epic level of paranoia.

"I did. I took pictures of everything in the Horvath's file." She patted her back pocket where her phone was safely stored. "There was a receipt inside from a gallery. They paid nine hundred thousand for porn."

Ro whistled and clicked the key fob to unlock the car. "Big bucks."

"He bought it from the Contessa Gallery. In Rome. All I have to do is find the phone number, slip into my Delilah alter ego and tell them I'm interested in buying the *Position Seven* painting."

"It's late over there now. The gallery is probably closed."

Lucie shrugged. "So, I'll try first thing tomorrow. If they tell me the painting was sold, then maybe I can weasel out of them who they sold it to."

"And if they still have it?"

Lucie stopped near the front tire of the car, cocked her head, and stared at Ro over the hood. "Then, my best buddy, we know the Horvaths have a fake."

12

———

THE FOLLOWING MORNING, LUCIE WENT INTO MISSION-critical mode. If her clients were being swindled, she needed to know and deal with it. Straight away.

She sat at the princess vanity table that had been in her childhood bedroom since her twelfth birthday. Next to the desk, she'd set up a card table with a printer and a monitor she could plug her laptop into. All of it packed into her micro bedroom.

She'd already printed the photos she'd taken of Bart's files and now had them set out in front of her as she dialed the number on the Contessa Gallery's receipt.

"Whoopsie."

She'd forgotten to add the digits that would mark the call as a private caller. Subterfuge. So many details to fuss over. She stabbed at the screen to clear the number just as Joey's big head appeared in her doorway. Only eight o'clock and he was dressed and moving already. What was that about?

"Why are you awake?"

"I gotta run over to the apartment. The painters are coming by to give me an estimate."

Her brother was serious about moving into Frankie's house. She'd hoped it was a phase. "You're painting in there?"

"Bet your ass. That yellow isn't exactly my style."

Oh. Right. The last tenant had been a woman. "Do you need a hand with picking out colors? I could get Ro over there."

"Nah. I'm good. Thanks though."

"Sure. I'll see you later."

Joey left and Lucie dialed Rome again, this time making sure to punch in the privacy code. After two rings, a woman answered. "Pronto?"

Oh, jeepers. Lucie's Italian was more than a little rusty.

"Buon giorno. Parla inglese?"

"Yes," the woman said in a peppy British accent.

Calling Italy and getting a Brit. Fun. "Good morning," Lucie said. "My name is Delilah. I'm calling from the United States and hoping you can help me locate a painting."

"Oh, of course, mum. From the States, you say?"

"Yes. My boss is looking for a particular painting. *Position Seven* by Nodai. I researched it and discovered you might have it at your gallery."

The woman sighed. "It *is* a classic. And quite lovely."

A snapshot of the painting flooded Lucie's already seared brain. God, that thing. She opened her mouth, silently gagging. Obviously, she'd never make it as an art critic. "Yes, it is. Which is why I'm hoping you'll tell me you still have it."

In actuality, she didn't want them to have it. That would mean Mr. Horvath might have the real painting and Lucie wouldn't be in bed with a scheming swindler.

"Allow me to check. Can you hold one moment?"

For good news, she'd hold for ten moments. Lucie sat back in her desk chair.

"Hello?" the woman with the British accent said.

Lucie sat up, tapped her fingers on the desk, and said a silent Hail Mary. At this point, she needed whatever help she could get. "Yes. I'm here."

"I've just checked the computer. It appears we still have the painting."

An obscene—absolutely filthy—level of panic set in.

Please no. Lucie lurched in her chair and her shoulder blade smacked against the wood frame sending a sharp stick of pain straight down her spine. "You... uh...have it?" she stammered.

Please say no. That it was all a big mistake. Wrong painting. Had to be.

"Yes, mum. *Position Seven,* correct?"

Dammit. *Here I am, officer, slap on the cuffs.* Even Tim O'Brien couldn't get her out of this one. Nor would she want him to. Why should he risk his career trying to help her? The mob guy's daughter. This was just a fabulous capper to the whole getting arrested thing.

"Mum?"

"Yes. I'm here. I'm just...stunned." No lie there. "My boss will be thrilled. I will have to speak with her and call you back. Thank you so much for your time."

Even though you've just sentenced me to twenty years in prison.

Could she get that much for art fraud? A small cry sounded in her throat, all that spewing panic probably. She disconnected and sat back, breathing in a few times, then flexing her fingers and rolling her shoulders and neck.

"I can do this."

No problem. After all, it wasn't her fault, right? She hadn't known Bart was a con artist. How could she? She'd just call Tim and tell him what she knew. That's all. He was in the loop—more or less—on this whole thing. He'd understand.

She hoped.

"Hi, it's me," she said when Tim picked up. "Uh... Lucie."

They were far from the level where he should be required to recognize, immediately, without hesitation the voice attached to the "it's me" statement.

"I know who you are, Lucie."

Huh. How about that? Maybe she'd misconstrued their level of familiarity.

"Plus," he said, "there's this cool new thing you may have heard of. Caller ID."

She rolled her eyes, found herself smiling in spite of her soon-to-happen arrest for art fraud. "Oh, hardy-har, Detective."

He laughed and the husky tone, the pleasure, immediately lifted her mood. *I really like you, Tim O'Brien.* Which would be a total problem when Frankie decided he wanted to come back to her. Assuming that would happen. With each day, she wondered.

"What's up?" Tim said "I bet you miss me."

As a matter of fact... "Oh, the charm. It's almost too much to handle."

"I know. It's a curse."

Now it was her turn to laugh. Something she'd cherish after the anxiety of the last few minutes. This guy had a way of making impossible situations seem not so impossible. "You know, Tim O'Brien, I really like you."

"That's good. Because I really like you, Lucie Rizzo."

Most definitely, this would be a problem if Frankie

changed his mind. How she felt about that, she wasn't sure. With Tim, everything was shiny and new and fun. No baggage. But Frankie? She had history with him and that history clung to her. Truly, a lifetime of memories.

The Falcones had been in her life since she could remember. And the idea of a life without Frankie in it darn near devastated her. Left a gaping hole. But was that because she was simply used to his presence? The other half of Frankie and Lucie.

The bookend.

The problem with bookends was they usually spent most of their time apart.

But back to art fraud. "Soooo," Lucie said. "I think I need to share some information with you."

Of course, Tim might not approve of her super-sleuthing techniques. Still, she'd gotten the information she needed and might possibly have enough evidence to launch an investigation into Bart Owens.

"Can I come by and see you?"

"Yeah. I'm at the precinct. You coming now?"

"I can be there in thirty minutes."

EXACTLY TWENTY-EIGHT MINUTES LATER, LUCIE MARCHED into the police station, where a woman manned the phone at a desk behind the glass-walled lobby. Two patrons sat in the reception area. The middle-aged woman read a maga-zine while a younger guy messed with his phone. Lucie stepped up to the window's built-in speaker and told the woman Detective O'Brien was expecting her. Two minutes later—*voila*—a door at the side of the room opened. There stood Tim. A mighty handsome Tim in navy slacks—again without the jacket—a crisp, white shirt, tie perfectly knotted. How she loved a man who knew how to knot a tie.

His usual flirty smile appeared. "Good morning, Ms. Rizzo. Come in."

I so need to jump this guy. Whew. What the heck was wrong with her these days? Even with her current stress level, she couldn't be within feet of this man without thinking about sex. With him.

Loneliness. Had to be. Or stress release. Right?

Right.

"Good morning, Detective."

He stepped back, holding the door open for her, his gaze on her the whole time. Once again, she was made aware of a certain level of chemistry between them. Chemistry that didn't quite crackle, but simmered long and slow and left her a little tingly. She liked this man. And she wouldn't feel guilty about it.

Not anymore.

Once through the door, careful not to touch her, Tim held his arm out and motioned her down a long corridor. A minute later, they stepped into an interview room similar to the one she'd been confined to after being arrested four days ago.

Then she'd been terrified. More than a little shell-shocked and not completely absorbing how she'd wound up in that bit of nastiness.

Today?

Still terrified.

But oddly calm. Almost resigned. At least now she grasped what had happened and how she wound up here. Different day, different experience. Today, she was here to possibly blow the whistle on a fraudster.

Which in some ways made her a squealer—a rat—and

heaven knew her father hated rats. But Bart could be a thief. He may have swindled her right along with her clients. Rat or no rat, she wouldn't tolerate being taken advantage of.

Tim pulled out a chair for her—how sweet was that?—and then took the spot across from her. He squared his shoulders and rested his hands on his thighs. Casual but commanding at the same time. The man had a way about him. A very good way.

"What's going on, Lucie?"

Now or never. "Ro and I did a little sleuthing."

His body remained still, but something in his eyes changed. More direct, maybe a little suspicion thrown in.

"Sleuthing."

"Yes. On Bart Owens." She pulled the large envelope with the photos from her tote and slapped it on the table.

He glanced down at the envelope, a small grin playing on his lips. "This, I can't wait to hear."

"*Position Seven.*"

"The wheelbarrow?"

"Again with the wheelbarrow?"

He hit her with a slow-moving smile that definitely stirred dormant parts of her anatomy. The heavy eye contact didn't hurt.

"Fine. The *wheelbarrow*." She slid the photo of the receipt out of the envelope and showed it to him. "This is the receipt for the sale of the painting."

He picked up the photo and scanned it. "How'd you get it?"

This is where it could get sticky. Technically, she wasn't sure if her snooping would be considered trespassing. Or some other legal term.

She held up a hand. "Full disclosure. Just as you asked."

"Full disclosure."

"I snooped in Bart's files."

His head dropped forward. "You snooped?"

"Yes. When I walk Oscar, I pick him up in Bart's office. It's in the rear of the gallery. He keeps a filing cabinet in there. Ro and I went to the gallery last night."

"Why?"

"I needed someone to keep Bart busy so I could snoop. Ro can be...uh...distracting."

"Holy crap," Tim said. "You girls are evil."

"I think that's a bit of an exaggeration, Detective. It's not my fault men are idiots and drool at the sight of Ro's cleavage."

Immediately, Tim's eyes went to Lucie's chest. *Idiot*. She sighed.

He held up a finger. "For the record, I don't drool at the sight of Ro's cleavage. Yours on the other hand—"

As usual, Lucie's cheeks fired. Flop-peeing and flop-blushing. Terrific. She couldn't look at him. Couldn't do it. If she did, she knew what she'd see. She'd see heat and lust and an opportunity to haul herself over this table and plant one on him.

No hauling or planting. Time to be serious here and stay out of prison.

Instead, she studied the envelope, analyzed the side seams for a solid ten seconds. Finally, hormones relatively under control, she raised her gaze, found the handsome detective with a slightly amused half-smile. "So. Okay." She waggled her hand. "While Ro kept Bart busy looking at art, I went in to say hello to Oscar the Perv."

"Oscar the Perv?"

"He humps my leg."

"Lucky bastard."

Lucie burst out laughing, picked up the envelope, and

smacked his forearm. Five minutes ago, she'd walked in here half a wreck, wondering if she'd get locked up before she had a chance to explain herself. Now, she wondered if she'd get locked up before jumping a cute detective.

"Hey," he said, "I can't help it if I have a jealous streak."

"Tim! I'm being serious."

"So was I."

Lucie shook her head, scrunched her nose and tried to put a little mean into her stare-down.

He grinned again. Apparently, her mean stare needed work.

"I couldn't resist." He rolled his hand. "Continue."

"Thank you. Yeesh!"

It took all of two minutes to fill him in on the covert mission and phone call to Rome.

After Lucie carefully outlined the details of her investigation, Tim picked up the photos, scanned them again and stuffed the pages back in the envelope. He secured the flap, his fingers deftly handling the doo-hickey clasp. The man had some long fingers. His hands overall were large. She thought back to the night on the lake when she'd walked beside him with her much smaller fingers wrapped in his. Nice feeling. All around a good night.

She cleared her throat. "What are you going to do with those?"

He tapped the edge of the envelope on the table. "Call Rome and talk to the owner of the gallery. See what he has to say about this receipt you just gave me. If it's one of theirs, it'll tie back to something. If it's not"—Tim shrugged—"we'll know Bart forged it."

AFTER FINISHING WITH TIM, LUCIE TREKKED BACK TO Franklin and—lucky her—found a parking spot right in front of her store. Two doors down, Petey's hopped with double-parked Caddies and Lincolns. Must be a meeting of the minds this morning.

Frankie's father, no doubt, would be there. His entire crew spent an inordinate amount of time at their corner table, reading the newspaper, talking smack, and generally killing time in between their activities. Whatever those activities might be.

And here she was, opening an office just feet away as her father was about to be released from prison.

If her father took to hanging at Petey's again, she'd go insane. Full-blown commitment-worthy insanity. He'd be popping in and out on her all day. And then he'd bring his cronies with him. All while she tried to run a business.

Maybe one of his parole restrictions would be to stay out of Petey's.

That's all she could hope for.

Her voicemail chimed as she got out of the car. She must have missed a call. On the sidewalk, she paused to enjoy the decidedly not-suffocating warmth—finally the humidity gave mercy—while she checked the call log. Two calls missed. One being Frankie.

An instant quasi excitement-slash-panic flooded her. As usual, she wondered if this would be it. *The* call. The one where he'd say he was ready to try again. That he missed her and their life together.

That he wanted her back.

Her stomach pinched. Squeezed like a tight fist inside her. A week ago, she'd have been overjoyed at the prospect of a reunion. Now, suddenly, it gave her stomach cramps.

Confused.

That's all she was. The super-cute Irish cop had gotten her all hot and bothered with his charm and humor and...well...*newness*. But she had history with Frankie. He knew her inside and out. He fit every curve and nuance. He understood her.

And he'd just called her. A week ago, she'd have run straight to him. Now, thinking back on all the nights alone—and spending time with Tim—she didn't know.

Don't think about it.

She tapped the voicemail button. One voicemail. Not Frankie. The plumber Joey had hired couldn't start the job today.

"I should have hired someone myself."

She scrolled her phone for Joey and waited for the call to connect. No answer. He said he'd be at Frankie's, just a few blocks away, working with the painters. Since she suddenly had time on her hands, she'd swing over there and let him know his plumber crapped out on them. And wow, that term was appropriate in so many ways.

She headed east toward Frankie's. Depending on his schedule, he might be at work and she wouldn't have to see him. After just seeing Tim—and experiencing the lightness and fun that always came with him—she didn't want to squash it by worrying over the current status of the Frankie situation.

Soon, they'd have to decide what they were doing. Not today. But soon.

Her phone rang. Probably Joey calling back. Strange number and definitely not Joey's. Wait. A Michigan area code. *Ooh.* Roger Isby. The Gomez family lawyer. *Ooh, ooh, ooh.*

She tapped the screen. "Hello? This is L...Delilah."

Close one. Almost catastrophic since Mr. Isby only knew her as Delilah, the overworked assistant.

"Hello, Delilah. This is Roger Isby."

"Yes. Hi, Mr. Isby."

At the corner, Lucie turned left and ran into Mrs. Delvin, a retired teacher from her grammar school days.

"Good morning, Lucie," she said.

Ach! All she needed was her cover being blown by her third grade teacher. *Get rid of her.* Not wanting to be rude to either Mr. Isby or Mrs. Delvin, Lucie smiled and waved at the woman and then pointed to her phone while mouthing an "I'm sorry."

Mrs. Delvin nodded, patted Lucie's shoulder, and moved on toward the center of town.

"Delilah," Mr. Isby said, "I spoke to the family regarding your interest in the painting."

Uh-oh. This didn't sound positive. Or maybe the lawyer always had that flat tone. "Thank you. Hopefully it's good news."

"I'm afraid not."

"Oh?"

"The family is retaining the painting for their private collection."

Lucie halted in the middle of the sidewalk. Her vision did a loop-the-loop and she swayed a little, put her free hand out for balance. No good. She fell back a step, literally blown backward by the lawyer's announcement that the Gomez family still had control of the original painting.

That swindling Bart. *Thief.*

"They still own it?"

"Yes. Arturo's younger sister has it in her home. She is quite attached to it and doesn't intend on selling."

Which meant Mr. Lutz had a copy. Or a forgery. At this

point, was there a difference? Probably not because, either way, Mr. Lutz was under the impression he had the original.

And he didn't.

As just confirmed by the Gomez family lawyer.

Deal with it. That's all. Being a Rizzo, she'd had bigger problems than this. She straightened up and set her shoulders like the good little soldier she'd been taught to be.

"Delilah?"

"Yes," she said. "I'm here. Just thinking."

"I'm sorry to disappoint you."

The guilt set in. Darn it. This man thought they wanted to buy that painting when all along, they'd been lying. Tricking him into telling them if the family still owned the original. *Bless me, Father, for I have sinned.*

Between the guilt over lying and the guilt over setting Mr. Lutz up with a swindler and the guilt over enjoying Tim's company, could this morning get any worse?

But seriously, she needed to buck up here. She was Joe Rizzo's kid and this was a blip. Mere nonsense.

She breathed in, shook her head, and wrangled her self-control. *You can do this, Luce.*

She started walking again, away from the storefront, away from Petey's and all her father's friends, who were no doubt holding court. *Just get away.* She waved at a passing car—no idea whose—when the driver honked.

"Oh, Mr. Isby, that's all right. I know my boss wanted that painting, but I completely understand. It's a family heirloom. I wouldn't part with it, either."

"Thank you for understanding. There are other paintings available if your employer is interested."

"I'll tell her. And thank you."

She disconnected and immediately bent at the waist, resting her hands on her thighs. She needed help. Someone who could make things happen. Someone who could sort through information and come to a logical conclusion.

You know.

Yes, she did. She stood tall, took another long pull of the mercifully not-as-humid August air and dialed Tim.

Three rings in, his voicemail came on, and his deep voice nearly crawled right through the phone line, wrapping her in that odd comfort she always took from him.

"Hi. It's me. Lucie. The lawyer from Michigan just called about the Gomez painting. The family still has the original painting and it's definitely not for sale. Mr. Lutz has a copy and that makes two-for-two on the fake painting scale. I'm freaking out. Please, Tim. I need your help."

13

———

Not knowing what else to do until Tim returned her call, Lucie kept moving to Frankie's. She needed to accomplish something right now, and the plumber issue gave her a distraction. Something she could deal with and maybe actually manage to figure out. Unlike her forged paintings dilemma.

As long as this trip to Joey's new apartment didn't include running into Frankie, she'd be fine. She checked the time on her phone. Not even lunch time. And that meant the very real possibility of running into Frankie since he worked evenings at the newspaper. His stories needed to be filed right after the evening games, so he typically didn't get home until after midnight.

But maybe she'd get a break today, because right now, their romantic situation had no teeth in comparison to being someone's prison bitch.

"No way. *Nobody's* bitch."

Lucie quietly opened the outer door of Frankie's three-flat and the faint smell of his cologne, some fancy stuff he bought at Neiman's, permeated the hallway. Every instinct, the sheer muscle memory, drew her gaze left. The door leading to his apartment.

Habit or not, her body would have to get used to heading upstairs to see Joey. Her brain understood the concept. She just couldn't get the rest of her to fall in line.

She set her hand on the banister and squeezed. *Upstairs.*

Stepping softly, she darted up the stairs, checking Frankie's door every few feet just to make sure he didn't come out. She cleared the second floor landing.

Made it.

Either Frankie hadn't heard the front door open or he wasn't home. Which, of course, made her wonder where he might be. *Upstairs. Keep moving.*

Lucie stopped again at the third floor landing, knocked lightly and waited. No answer. Joey had said he'd be here with the painters all morning. They could've been in the back part of the house and didn't hear her knock. She checked the knob. Unlocked. Maybe she shouldn't be walking into her brother's apartment, but he hadn't moved in yet, so it wasn't like she'd catch him running around commando.

Besides, it wouldn't be the first time she'd seen that disgusting sight since moving back to Chateau Rizzo. The man walked around in his boxers as if she and her mother weren't even there.

She pushed open the door, checked right where the room led to a short hallway to the kitchen at the back of the house. She glanced down the hall, didn't see anyone. Hmm...

"I'm telling you," Joey said from the front room, "I've got the picture right here and you don't have it."

"Are you insane? I'm good, but not that good."

Ro's voice. At Joey's. And what were they talking about?

Probably something about decorating. Her brother was no dummy and probably recruited Ro to help with paint colors and furniture placement. Lucie stepped around the short wall separating the entry from the living room.

"Guys," she said, "what are you arguing about?"

"Ohmygod."

The panic in Ro's voice, that slight break, should have been the first clue, but no. The second clue was the important one. The clue Lucie saw rather than heard. Joey flat on his back on the bare hardwood floor, cell phone in hand, while he studied the screen. Sitting on top of him, facing his feet—*my eyes*—Ro inhaled hard enough to make her extremely naked boobs bounce.

Lucie scanned her best friend's bare legs straddling Joey's hips. Slowly, as if taking in a bad wreck, she shifted her gaze up. To the dark, swirling hair on Joey's chest and then, still taking in that horrendous wreck, she followed the flash of bare skin to where Joey's hip met Ro's leg.

Too much. Gah! *My eyes.*

Lucie started screaming. A blood curdling, axe-murderer-is-chasing-me scream that bounced off the stripped walls and echoed through the empty apartment.

Ro scrambled to lift herself off of Joey, but he locked his fingers around her waist, squeezing with enough force that the veins in his hands popped.

"Don't get up," he said. "I'm naked here!"

And Lucie screamed louder, threw her hands over eyes that had to be bleeding. Had to be.

"Luce!" Ro said, "Stop that yelling. The whole neighborhood can hear you. Joey, hand me that shirt."

"God's sakes, Luce," he said. "Turn around."

And still Lucie screamed. Too much. All of it. No woman should have to see her brother naked.

Ever.

Somewhere behind her, Ro laughed, but it wasn't a ha-ha laugh. Nervous, not typical of anything Lucie ever heard from her BFF.

"I'm afraid to look." Lucie poked at her closed eyes. "It's like tiny daggers shooting into me."

"What the hell's the screaming?"

Frankie's voice. Huffy. As if he'd sprinted up all three flights. With all the screaming, he probably had.

Lucie opened her eyes, found Frankie in the doorway, his chest indeed heaving. She threw her hands out. "Don't look!"

Last thing she needed was Frankie seeing Ro naked. If he saw that perfection, she'd be doomed. She'd never feel comfortable *au natural* in front of him again.

And yet, he leaned left to peek around her. "What's wrong?"

She shifted to block his view. "Please don't look. It's a nightmare."

"Is someone dead?"

"Not yet. But Joey could be soon."

Again Ro laughed, but this time it wasn't so panicked. "Usually, I'm the drama queen."

Frankie's jaw didn't just drop, it plummeted. "Ro?"

Again, he tried to peep around Lucie. Again, Lucie blocked his view. She tapped her fingers over her eye sockets. "Are my eyes bleeding? They have to be."

Frankie snorted. "No. You're fine. What's wrong?"

"Lucie," Ro said, "don't be mad. It's not what you think."

Oh, *that* was priceless. What she'd just witnessed could only be a few limited things. And she was damned sure it was what she thought it was.

"Not what I think? I just walked in on you and Joey,

apparently re-enacting the wheelbarrow and you're telling me it's not what I think? What the hell *else* could it be?"

"Ooh," Frankie said. "I missed something good. What wheelbarrow?"

"Shut it, Frankie," Joey barked. "Ro, grab my damn pants."

Ach. *My eyes.*

Fighting a laugh, Frankie bit his bottom lip and Lucie's head nearly exploded. She stabbed him in the chest with her finger. "Don't you dare laugh. I might be traumatized by what I just saw."

"Trust me, honey," Ro cracked, "you didn't see the best part."

And Lucie started screaming again. This nightmare wouldn't end.

Frankie reached for her, squeezed her arms. "Sshhh. It's okay. You're fine."

Not fine. Totally not fine.

"Luce," Joey said, his voice calm. As if she hadn't just walked in on him and her best friend experimenting with early European porn. "Quit that goddamn screaming. We're dressed. You can look."

Finally, she turned and spotted Joey tucking his shirt into his shorts. Basketball shorts. Ones that left no doubt the wheelbarrow scene had not been as they say, fully consummated. Lucie spun back to Frankie. "I can't look at him in that condition. And he's lucky—so lucky—because right now I could beat him with a shovel. To death." She faced her brother, but kept her gaze above his shoulders. "The fact that she's my best friend is bad enough. Given the history, I could live with that. But, cripes, Joey, she's still *married*. She's vulnerable right now."

He screwed up his lips. "Ro has never been vulnerable a day in her life."

"The two of you, shut up." This from the married one. "Luce, it's not like I'm cheating on a saintly husband. He was screwing a stripper. And hello, he's moved out and the divorce is in the works. Besides, you can't blame Joey for this. It takes two people."

Ignoring the horror of Joey's expanded crotch, Lucie dragged her eyes to Ro. "When did this all start up again?"

"The other night was the first time. I swear."

"When the other night?"

"The O'Br..."

Ro stopped talking, flicked her eyes to Frankie. *The O'Brien night.* Thank goodness she didn't let that fly. Lucie nodded. "The night Joey went over to your house?"

"Yes."

She thought back to that night, back to Joey busting her on the porch with Tim. Keeping her eyes above his shoulders, she pointed at Joey. "That's where you were coming from that night?"

"Yeah. But I'm not talking to you about this. It's not your business. I don't talk to you about Frankie."

Lucie opened her mouth. Shut it again. He was right. All these years, he'd never once butted into her relationship with Frankie.

"He's right, Luce," Frankie said.

Ro moved in front of her, drawing her full attention and Lucie got a whiff of Joey's soap, musky stuff that wasn't half bad. But it was on Ro's skin. This would take some getting used to.

Ro grabbed her hands and squeezed, refocused her.

"Luce, I'm okay. All of this is okay. He's always been good to me. I promise."

She knew that. Mostly. Joey always treated the women he dated with respect. Never talked about their sexual proclivities or badmouthed them to his friends. He just never wanted to grow up and commit and eventually the women moved on. No hard feelings. Her brother was a master at no-hard-feelings.

But this was Ro and they all had a lot to lose. Ro hadn't let go of her hand yet, so Lucie gave it a gentle squeeze back. "I just don't want you to get hurt."

"Sometimes, sweetie, that's just inevitable. Who thought Tommy would wind up being a cheating bastard? He was supposed to be the safe bet."

Yes, he was. Tommy was the rebound after Ro had dumped Joey.

Lucie glanced back at Frankie. For Lucie, he'd been the holy grail of jackpots. With him she had love *and* the safe guy. The one who would never hurt or betray her.

And yet, they couldn't figure out how to make their relationship work.

Obviously thinking she wanted his opinion, he held his hands out. "You gotta stay out of it, Luce."

Yeah. She did.

Whatever this was—lust, love, or anything in between—Joey and Ro would have to figure it out. Hopefully, they wouldn't kill each other in the process.

Ro and Joey. Together. This town might not survive.

She went back to them. This time meeting Joey's gaze, making sure he knew she wasn't messing around. "Ground rules." She held one finger up. "I don't want any of the gory sexual details. From either of you."

"Jeez. Even I wouldn't do that."

She turned to Ro. "That goes double for you. I don't need to know how you feel about"—somehow, God help her, her gaze went to Joey's crotch and she slammed her hands over her eyes—"his parts."

Joey threw his arms up. "Luce!"

"I'm sorry. But she likes to talk about stuff like that and I don't want to hear it."

"You guys talk about that?" Frankie wanted to know.

"Don't worry, Charm Pants," Ro said. "She gave you an A rating."

Cripes. Lucie bared her teeth. "Ignore her, Frankie."

"Don't I always?"

Point there. Whatever. Back to business here. "Second..." Lucie held up another finger. "If you have a fight, I will not take sides. Unless, of course, one of you does something completely stupid. In which case, I will kill you because I don't need that kind of stupidity around me. Got it?"

They both nodded.

"Third."

"That's a lot of rules, Luce," Joey said.

"This is my last one. I never, ever, want to walk in on what I just walked in on. Locks were made for a reason. Lock. The damned. *Door*." She flapped her arms. "Do you have any idea what it'll take to wash that image out of my head? I might need counseling after this."

Joey waved her off. "Who invited you here? I told you I'd be busy."

"Because you had painters here! I figured you were looking at paint samples. I certainly wouldn't have shown up if I'd known you two were reenacting early European porn."

Frankie stepped forward and raised his hands. "I wanna know what this wheelbarrow thing is."

"Dude," Joey said, "you won't believe it. I'll give you the website."

"Sshhh!" Lucie hissed. She spun toward the door, started to leave and stopped. "I came here to tell you that plumber you hired blew me off."

"That son of a bitch. I'll call him."

"Fine. Whatever. I'm out. I may need Valium after this."

FRANKIE HELD THE DOOR OPEN FOR LUCIE AND SHE BREEZED out into the hallway. The sharp smell of polished wood reminded her of the pride Frankie took in taking care of the house. Every weekend he cleaned three stories of oak rails and spindles until they gleamed. From the day he'd bought this house, he'd done the same routine. Sometimes she'd even helped him and found the task so tedious she'd thought she'd throw herself over the railing.

From the third floor.

Where Joey and Ro just did the nasty.

Blech.

Even more reason to go over the railing. Frankie though? He'd told her cleaning the rails was his therapy. He'd put his headphones on and zone out. If she didn't think too hard about the tediousness of the task, she could see where the repetition and the quiet would be relaxing.

She hit the first step and made her way down. "You called me this morning. What's up?"

"Uh, nothing. We can talk about it later."

She knew that tone. That not-quite-confident edge his voice took on when he had something—not necessarily good—to share.

Terrific.

She paused on the stairs, turned back, and Frankie halted on the step above her. His dark eyes were shadowed, something she'd just now noticed. She wondered if he'd worked late last night. But this wasn't the normal Frankie-is-tired look. This was more than that, and her fingers suddenly turned to icicles. She flexed them in and out to get the blood moving and work away some of the tension curling up her arms.

What now? They were already broken up so that wasn't it. What if he was sick?

"Frankie, I know you. What is it?"

"It's not important."

"If you called me, I would think it is."

He paddled his hand, motioning her forward. "Let's—uh—go into my apartment."

"Is this bad news?"

"Luce, please. I'm not gonna stand on the steps and talk to you."

She moved down the stairs, her pace quicker than it had been a minute ago. "This can't be good," she muttered.

At the first floor, she swung around the banister and headed into Frankie's apartment.

"Have a seat," he said.

This is bad. She lowered herself to the leather, hand-me-down sofa she'd sat on thousands of times, yet none of it seemed normal. Or comfortable. Maybe she just didn't want to be in Frankie's space unless they were a couple. She missed him too much and being here reminded her of their failures.

Lately, everything about Frankie brought sadness and fear and...questions.

And, God, she didn't want this heaviness anymore. This always thinking and wondering and hoping. What the hell had happened to them that they'd forgotten to have fun?

Frankie sat in the matching chair across from her and

leaned forward, resting his elbows on his knees. "I don't know how to do this."

It's bad. Maybe he was sick. Cancer. Please. Not that.

"Whatever it is, just say it."

He nodded, ran his hands together, slowly rubbing. Finally, he looked up at her, met her gaze. "I got a job in New York. At ESPN."

It hit her like a bomb blast, rocking her upper body, forcing her to squeeze every muscle to stay upright and not sink back.

New York. ESPN.

Did he really just say that? After years of begging him to move out of Franklin, possibly to New York where he could work as a sportswriter and she on Wall Street. After all those conversations when he'd told her—definitively—he would *not* leave his parents.

For her, he wouldn't leave his parents.

For ESPN?

Sure. Why not?

Talk about cutting to the bone.

"New York," she said, desperately trying to keep her voice level and contain the frustration and—yes—the flat-out anger consuming her.

He sat back, held up his hands. "I know. I know. I'm a shit. We had countless fights over moving and I never would. I'm sorry."

Lucie swallowed, blinked a couple of times, but couldn't manage one word. Not a single word. After all they'd been through together. Nothing.

"Luce, it's a good offer. It'll get me closer to being on air."

His dream. Being a television announcer. Well, really, his dream had been to play professional baseball, but chronic concussions had destroyed the hand-eye coordination that had made him such a good ball player. Instead, he'd studied journalism and had been working as a columnist, but really, his goal was to be in front of a microphone.

"I see."

But, really, no, she didn't. *I asked him for this a thousand times.* And each time he'd told her no.

"What would you think," he said, "about going with me?"

Oh. Six months ago, she'd have dropped to her knees and thanked the stars above. Now? Now it set something off in her so wild and cold she clutched the sofa cushion with both hands, her fingernails ripping right into the leather. After all the debating, arguing and breaking up, he wanted her to shut down her growing business, just put a halt to her life to go with him to New York.

And oh, right, they were broken up.

She shook her head, cleared the surging disappointment. This was Frankie, always trying to find a work-around to make her happy. Somewhere in his twisted mind, he thought finally giving her the thing she'd been begging for would make her not mad at him.

Well, wrong. She wasn't about to pick up her life to relieve his guilt.

Particularly when she wasn't even sure he still wanted her. The three months of being apart certainly didn't indicate that.

She looked down at the floor, at his sock-clad feet. "Well, I guess I should say congratulations on the job."

You rat-effing-bastard.

This was Frankie. Never had she considered referring to him in that way, but what was it with the safe guys lately? Ro's safe guy turned into a stripper-banger and now Frankie —steady, reasonable Frankie—had lost his damned mind and expected her to give up everything without the promise of a future together.

"Thank you," he said. "I know it's a shock."

She laughed, but the lack of humor should have bludgeoned him. "That's one way to put it."

"I'm sorry."

"For what? For doing something you would never do for me, but now suddenly expect me to give up a growing business to follow you across the country when—oh, hang on—you *broke up* with me." She dug her fingers into her forehead. "God, even saying it out loud it sounds insane."

"I thought maybe we could start over."

Brilliant plan. "Again? What will be different this time? Other than the fact that I will once again be without a job and starting over while you get to chase your dream. If we were still together, if we were engaged or married, I wouldn't hesitate. But we're not together right now. You can't expect me to give up my life for a maybe."

"Luce, I'm trying. I don't want to lose you."

"Frankie! You broke up with me three months ago. I've been sitting around, waiting for you to decide what you wanted. Now, it seems, you've decided New York is what you want. Fine. Great. Good for you for making a decision."

"I had to do something. This tension with my father is killing me. And my mom keeps asking why I don't come around as often. I feel guilty as hell over that, but I'm not about to tell her what he did. Nuh-unh. I don't see why her life has to be torn apart just for me to make a point."

Of course he didn't. This was the problem. His parents came first. Always. Even when he was mad at his father. And now, he was doing it all over again. Running away from the situation because he didn't want to disappoint anyone or upset his mother. Good old, Frankie, still trying to stay loyal.

At Lucie's expense.

A crushing weight landed on her shoulders, bowing her body. She slumped back into the sofa. *I'm so tired of this.*

Everything hurt. Her body, her mind, all of it.

She closed her eyes, drew air through her nose, and let it out. She didn't have the energy for this. After all these years of loving him, a love she'd probably always cherish, she couldn't do it anymore. Couldn't live with this constant drama and carrying the entire Falcone family on her back.

Now, she was done.

She stood, stared down at her sneakers, and blinked back the moisture filling her eyes. So many tears she'd unleashed over the years and it all came down to Frankie doing the thing she'd always wanted. Leaving Franklin. Only he was doing it alone.

She lifted her head, walked to where he sat and put her hand on his shoulder. "I can't, Frankie. I'm sorry." She looked up at the ceiling, let out a sarcastic laugh. "Ironic, isn't it? You're moving to New York and I'm staying in Franklin. Who'd have guessed that one?"

But Frankie stood, grabbed onto both her arms, and held tight. "Don't decide now. Give it some thought. I don't leave for two weeks."

Two weeks. "Wow."

"Yeah, they wanted me out there ASAP."

"That's good, Frankie. They're excited to have you."

"Just, please, give it some thought. Okay? Do that for me?"

She reached up, cupped her hands over his cheeks, and kissed him. A slow, lingering kiss that tore something inside her away. This might be it. The last time she'd ever kiss Frankie. Ever taste his lips and run her fingers over his perfect face in that intimate way only lovers understood.

A sob caught in her chest and she broke the kiss, breathed through the ache. "Frankie, I love you. You know that."

"I love you too, Luce."

"I know. And I think that's why this is so hard. We've been on the rollercoaster for years now. Heck, the people in this town take bets on when we'll break up and get back together. It's become a foregone conclusion. A damned habit."

"Luce—"

"Some habits aren't good." She dropped her head, let the tears finally come, and gulped a huge breath. "It's time to be fair to each other." She looked up again, met his gaze, and the look in his eyes, that shattering heartbreak she knew was there because she felt it too.

The dismantling of a life they'd hoped for.

"We have to let each other go." She backed up, held her hands out. "I'm ending this. Right now. Goodbye, Frankie."

14

———

Tim finished dealing with a burglary on the South Side and retrieved Lucie's message. He'd just detour into Franklin and stop by the storefront. Yeah, he could have called. But he was close, and he damned sure didn't like the shaky tone in her voice. He hardly knew Lucie Rizzo well enough to know her signals, but that tone wasn't like anything he'd heard from her. So he'd check on her. Which he'd do for anyone in distress. Cops did that.

All the time.

And, well, well, well, there she was in her cute shorts and a T-shirt that sagged a little on her tiny body but somehow managed to look completely adorable. She quasi-walked-ran down Franklin Avenue toward the store. He honked, but she kept moving, not even glancing up as she raked a hand over her face.

Hang on. Was she... *crying*?

At the next corner, he waited for an oncoming car to cruise through the intersection and he swung a U-turn. He double-parked behind a Cadillac sitting in front of Petey's and locked up before following Lucie into the store.

She was sobbing, sprawled across the crappy desk, her right cheek plastered to its surface. And this wasn't run-of-the-mill crying. This was walls-coming-down, lung-busting wails that echoed through the mostly empty space.

Holy crap. He took three steps closer, then stopped. He probably shouldn't even be here. Had no idea how she'd feel about him invading her space and seeing her come apart. But this kind of turmoil? He couldn't walk away. Besides, she'd called asking for help. And now he was here.

He took the last two steps toward her. "Lucie?"

She jerked up, spotted him. Her mouth flew open, releasing another piercing scream.

Whoa. Not exactly the greeting he'd expected. And, damn, the girl could holler.

He hauled ass, grabbed her arm, pulling her up into a hug. "Honey, what happened? Is it the Lutz thing?"

She gripped the back of his shirt, squeezing so hard, he felt the material bunch in her fist.

"I can't stand it anymore. I just can't."

"What?"

"All of it. I'm just trying to make a living. And deal with my crazy family. I got arrested and I may have brokered an illegal deal. Two illegal deals! And Joey and Ro were doing the wheelbarrow and Frankie is leaving and...and...I don't want to be anyone's bitch!" She reared back, slapped him hard—really hard—on the chest. "And you!"

"Ow."

What the eff? What did *he* do that got him that hard whack?

She smacked him again. "I like you and...and all I keep thinking about is kissing you and the guilt sucks. Sucks!" She inhaled a huge breath. "Oh my *God,* my life sucks."

Dropping her head against him, she continued to sob.

He just let her wail. He hadn't survived crazy sisters without learning a few things. One of those things being that sometimes women just needed to blow off steam.

He held on to her, patting the back of her head. "Let it out. I've got you."

Frankie is leaving? Clearly, whatever that was, she hadn't taken it well. It hurt to see her this way—not to mention the shot to his ego—but Frank Falcone was out of the picture.

I'm a schmuck. That's what he was because, as much as he didn't like seeing Lucie torn up like this, the idea of Frank Falcone gone made Tim a happy guy.

But he wouldn't apologize for wanting her to himself.

"Sshhh," he said, still patting Lucie's head as her tantrum subsided.

Tim fought the urge to speak. Another thing he'd learned from his sisters. Speaking right now could possibly get him in trouble for some obscure reason he wouldn't fully understand. He'd play it safe and wait the whole thing out.

Lucie finally let out a little sigh that should have hit him as exhaustion but somehow made him think of a bed and other reasons she might sigh, and his extremely male body responded. Yeah, total schmuck. But hey, he hadn't seen a ton of action lately and sighing from Lucie—a woman he definitely wanted to see action with—was causing problems.

With her proximity, he needed to not have a physical reaction. One that she would most definitely feel jutting against her hip.

Too late. Definitely happening.

He stepped back, putting distance—plenty of distance—between them. "Are you okay?"

She ran the palms of her hands over her eyes, let them

rest there a second before lowering them. "I'm sorry. What a meltdown."

"Rough few days. And you're under some pressure. All around."

"I think it all just hit me."

"Seems like it." He waved one hand. "Anything you want to talk about?"

Frank Falcone leaving?

"We probably should. I have a lot to update you on."

AFTER THE RECORD-SETTING ENTRY FOR THE MOST humiliating moment, Lucie boosted herself to a sitting position on top of the desk and wiped the last of her tears. Too bad the plumber had bailed on her because she'd love to go into the bathroom and throw some water on her face. Wasn't that her father's cure-all for crying women? "Go on," he'd say. "Wash your face."

If only it were that easy. Oddly enough, it always did make her feel better. Not that she'd ever admit it to him.

Tim grabbed the folding chair Ro had left in the corner and set it in front of the desk. He leaned back, rested his hands on his thighs, most definitely his go-to position when trying to appear casual, and waited.

Bless this man for being smart enough to not react to her complete mind melt.

He looked up at her and his amazing lips lifted into a smile.

"I love your lips," she said.

Why fight it? The situation couldn't get anymore humiliating.

"And," he added, "you stated you'd like to kiss them. Just

so there's no confusion, I'd like that as well. I was giving you space. But now that I've been alerted to this situation, I'll be sure to fulfill any desire you might have. Make that desires. Plural."

Lucie snorted. A big, long one that made him laugh. "Thank you for your willingness to please."

"I do what I can. But first, let's talk about the challenges you're facing. The most important being your legal dilemmas. You should know I have received copies of the Contessa Gallery's invoices from the last six months. They assure me they have the original *Position Seven*. I didn't have a chance to look through everything, but the receipts they sent me have different fonts than the one you have. Horvath's is close, but not the same."

"That jerk faked the receipt?"

"Perhaps. I'm looking into it. Now, on this Lutz thing."

Yes, the Lutz *thing*. The Horvaths she could almost deal with. She didn't have the long-standing friendship with them. The emotional connection. They were clients. Acquaintances. The Lutzses? With them came history, shared respect. If she'd gotten them hooked up with a swindler, she'd never forgive herself.

"Tim, that's freaking me out. The lawyer called this morning and told me the family still has the original painting and they don't intend on selling it. Ever."

"Lutz has a fake then."

"Yes. And he believes it's real. He told me that. Bart paid me a commission on the sale. Can I be charged with conspiracy or something?"

"You didn't know about it, right?"

"Of course not."

He lifted one hand palm up. "Then we'll fix it. By the time I get done with this guy, he'll be standing on his roof screaming you had no knowledge of his fraudulent activities. Bet on it."

"You make it sound so easy."

He shrugged. "I'll take care of it. Do you think Lutz would show you the provenance on the painting? I'd like to get a look at it. If he faked the Horvath's receipt, he probably did the same with Lutz's paperwork. I could ask Lutz myself, but the minute a detective starts asking questions, it'll raise suspicion."

"And Bart will close ranks."

"Or run."

What a mess that would be. If Bart did this, he needed to go to jail. "I could pretend I'm curious and see if Mr. Lutz will show me the provenance. I won't come right out and ask, but I'll frame it so he offers up the paperwork. He might not show me the actual receipt, but if it's some kind of certification. Maybe."

"That'd work. If you feel comfortable with it."

Ha. She didn't feel comfortable with much of anything today.

Lucie swung her legs to let off some energy. Dog walking might be just the therapy she needed. Exercise, fresh air, doggie licks. There might be hope for this day yet. "I'll tell Joey I'll walk Otis this afternoon. Sometimes I run into Mr. or Mrs. Lutz at the house."

"Don't be too pushy about it. Keep it casual."

"I will."

"So if I'm keeping track, that's two issues we've dealt with in the your-life-sucks department."

Tim O'Brien. Great guy.

So far.

Lucie nudged his knee with her foot. "Those are the big ones."

He looked straight at her, his gaze unwavering. "Then there's..."

Lucie knew he wouldn't say it. He'd wait for her to offer it up. As if it violated some sort of man code. Whatever the reason, she'd put him out of his misery. "Frankie leaving."

"Yeah." He scratched the back of his neck, wrinkled his nose. "You, uh, slipped that in there. What's that about?"

"He's moving to New York. A job at ESPN."

Tim continued to study her. No frown, no quirking eyebrows, no narrowed eyes. Nothing. Investigator body language for I-will-give-you-no-hint-of-my-thoughts.

"I see," he said.

"Yep."

"And you're upset about that."

"He asked me to go with him."

"Shit."

Lucie smiled at that. Had to love a man who wasn't afraid to speak his mind. "I said no." The eyebrows finally went up. *Ha.* Surprised him on that one. "Gotcha, Detective."

"You sure did."

"You're surprised I said no?"

He poked his bottom lip out. "I guess I am. After spending years with the guy, you didn't want to think about it?"

What did that say about her? Or her relationship with Frankie? All this time they'd been doing battle, splitting up, reuniting, always coming or going, and now, finally, it appeared to be over and she didn't want to at least consider his offer?

Simple answer. No. Later she'd decide if that made her heartless. She couldn't think about it now. She shook her head. Too many thoughts to contend with.

"When I worked as an investment banker and wanted so

badly to leave behind the mob princess moniker, I begged him—absolutely pleaded with him—to move to New York with me. I had a plan for us."

"And?"

"He wouldn't leave his family. I can't tell you how many arguments we've had over his family and their constant involvement and meddling. He put them before me every time."

Well, all but one time when his father's twenty-year-old jewelry heist put Lucie in danger. At least then Frankie had taken her side. She couldn't tell Tim that. That secret, out of loyalty to Frankie, would go to her grave with her.

"Really."

And the way he said *really* let her know that he understood he'd scored big points on their first date when he'd commented about his family's interference. With him, his family's opinion didn't matter.

The one thing Frankie could never give her.

"Yes, Detective. You won yourself a gold star."

He grinned. "I like gold stars."

"I bet you do."

"You've gotta be upset though. All that time with him and now he's leaving."

She brought her hands up to her head, slowly ran them over her tied-back hair that had to be a mess by now. "I am upset. But he's leaving after he never would for me. That tells me something." She nudged him with her foot again. "And then you come into my life and remind me what fun is and it makes me realize what I've been missing."

He clapped his hands then swung them wide. "Another gold star for the Irish cop. When I'm good, I'm good."

"Yes. And if you get me out of this mess with the paintings, it'll be a hat trick."

He brought his hands back to his thighs and tapped his fingers. "What do I get for that?"

"You'll get something. Don't worry. But—"

"Ach. I hate the 'but'."

"I want to be honest with you. I like you. A lot. I just don't want you to be a rebound. It's not fair to you."

For a second, he didn't respond. Just took that in. "You and Frankie broke up three months ago, correct?"

"Yes."

"I'll take the risk. You're as level-headed as they come, Lucie. You're not gonna jump into anything without knowing what you're doing. I'm in. Whatever you want from me, it's yours."

Lucie hopped off the desk, grabbed Tim by the cheeks, and planted one on him. Just let him have it. Obviously, he didn't mind because he clamped his hands over her backside and pulled her forward and down onto his lap until she straddled him.

In the middle of Carlucci's! Well, Coco Barknell, but still, anyone could walk by. She didn't care. All she cared about were his lips and hers doing this way cool dance. She slid her hands over his shoulders, prayed the folding chair could hold both of them and went to work feasting on him, brushing her lips against his, loving the feel of his minty breath mingling with hers. New and fun and...different. Yes. And she liked different. Liked the way he tentatively touched his tongue to hers, testing, and when she responded, he pulled her closer.

So. Good.

"Sister! What the hell?"

Lucie lurched back, her heart slamming from the sound of Ro's voice. Tim hung on, kept her from going over and crashing to the floor. Lucie whipped her head left to where Ro stood in the doorway, hands on hips and looking fierce.

But Tim. And his amazing lips. *Go with the lips.* She turned back to him, ready to dive right back in.

"Hey," Ro hollered. "You must be crazy. Two doors down from Petey's and you and the hunkmeister are going at it like horndogs. Anybody could walk by and see you. Anybody meaning your father's friends."

From under Lucie, Tim gave a full-on, high-voltage smile and patted her rear. "I've gotta get back anyway. Would love to pick this up later, though."

"You know it, Detective." Lucie waggled her eyebrows. "Maybe you can interrogate me?"

"Oh, honey," Ro said. "You'll also need my help in the dirty talk department."

Who cared? Lucie never claimed to be a grand seductress. All she wanted was fun, and Tim O'Brien, without a doubt, provided that.

"If you're really lucky," Tim said, "I'll even handcuff you."

Tim strolled out of the shop, offering up a quick nod to Ro, who eyeballed him up and down with that *No you didn't* look she performed so well.

With the hunkmeister gone, she whirled on Lucie, who'd moved back to sitting on top of the desk, swinging her legs just for the heck of it because kissing Tim had been a nice distraction. And after the day she'd had so far, she didn't mind that.

"Well," Ro said, "I'm glad to see you're finally getting some, but really, Luce?" She circled her arms. "Here?"

"I don't care who sees me. I'm done caring. How's that?"

"*Bravo.* The one who always makes herself sick over what other people think is going to the dark side. I'm thrilled. Let's just not make this a suicide mission. If one of those nut jobs at Petey's saw you, they'd be talking all kinds of smack. You know that'll get back to Frankie. And your dad. You want that kind of heat?"

As her best friend, Ro knew how to get straight to the issue at hand. Lucie never minded. Ro loved her and that love meant being honest. Under any circumstances.

Everyone should have that kind of friend. Someone who cared enough to say even the most awkward things.

"Of course I don't want that," Lucie said. "But I'm getting tired of worrying about what everyone thinks. For once, I want to have some fun. Ro, do you know how long it's been since I've just had fun?"

"What does *that* mean?"

"Fun. As in not stressing over every decision. Over who will get offended if I do something a certain way or who will leak info to my dad. I'm just done. I can't do it anymore."

"Ah. So the Irish cop is some kind of twisted revenge?"

God no. "No. Not at all. Here's one for you. I like him. A *lot*. Being with him feels new and easy and he doesn't judge me."

"Frankie never judged you."

Lucie gasped. "Of course not. I'm talking about people outside *the life*. They judge me. It makes me wonder if part of what made Frankie and I work was that we understood each other's worlds. It made things simpler. No learning curve."

"Nothing wrong with comfortable." The second Ro said it, she stopped. Shook her head. "Unless comfortable is a stripper-banger. I guess."

"I'm done with comfortable. Besides, it doesn't matter anymore."

"I know."

"You know?"

Ro nodded. "Frankie caught me leaving Joey's. He told me about New York."

"Can you even believe it? After all the times I begged him to leave Franklin?"

"I'd be irritated. But, Luce, are you sure you want to call it quits? I know you love him."

"I do love him." As long as she could remember she'd loved him. "But I have to let him go. Someone has to end this or we'll be forty years old, still living this way, and wondering how we got to that point."

Ro stepped forward and wrapped Lucie in a hug. "Ah, Luce. I'm sorry."

She tipped her chin up, rested it on Ro's shoulder, expecting that any second it would hit her. That she and Frankie were over. But...nothing. All there was now was a hug from her best friend. She wouldn't cry. At least not now. She'd accept what had been coming for so long and embrace it. Follow whatever this new absent-Frankie path would be.

That's what I'll do.

She patted Ro's back. "Yeah. Me too. I'll always love him. I know that. But it's over. Time for both of us to move on."

She backed out of Ro's arms and glanced at the door Tim had just walked through. Whether he'd be the one she'd move on with, she didn't know. All she knew was that suddenly, her body was lighter, as if her chest had opened up and she could breathe again.

Freedom.

15

———

Walking Otis at the end of the day had become Lucie's standard operating procedure. Ending the day with all that doggie love would never be a bad thing. After Otis's late walk, she punched in the code on the Lutz's garage and watched the door go up. Living in Lincoln Park, the Lutzses and their two neighbors had the rare perk of having an attached garage. That's what a teardown and a rebuild bought for their money in this cushy neighborhood.

The Lutz's car was parked next to Lucie's scooter, which Mr. L. stored for her when she wasn't in the city. The car didn't always mean someone was home. To avoid parking woes, the Lutzses often cabbed it around the city. Mr. L. had even been known to take the bus since it stopped right at the corner of his office.

The one Lucie used to work with him in. The place where he'd befriended her and helped her transition out of her corporate job and into picking up doggie accessory clients to make ends meet. Making ends meet turned into Coco Barknell. All because the Lutzses introduced her to a few people after she'd made Otis a fancy dog collar.

Lucie would always be thankful for their support. Always. Getting them hooked up with a swindler wasn't exactly a great way to repay their generosity. *Please let them forgive me.*

Otis, needing to be the man in charge, led her to the inside door. As Coco Barknell grew, she'd had less and less time for dog walking and missed Otis the most. A big lug of an Olde English Bulldogge, he was seventy-five pounds of unconditional love.

"Relax, Otis, you'll get there. If you're lucky, I'll give you a bully stick."

She eased the door open and Otis squeezed through, his nub of a tail whipping—if nubs whipped—back and forth. She dropped the leash and he dashed right to his water bowl on the far side of the mudroom.

She peeked through the open door leading to the kitchen. "Hello?"

No answer. Crud. So much for running late—*wink, wink* —in the hope of finding someone at home.

Lucie unclipped the leash and stowed it in the utility closet. She glanced back at Otis, still drinking, his tail moving into hyper-speed. "I know, boy. You want that bully."

She grabbed one from the stack, bent low and gave him a nuzzle, receiving a sloppy lick for her troubles.

God, she loved this dog. "You're awesome-sauce, Otis."

Something about the love of a good dog always made her a little gooey.

When he plopped his big butt to a sit, she handed over the treat and he took off to his giant doggie bed to enjoy his snack.

"Bye, Otis. See you tomorrow. Love ya, buddy."

Outside the garage, she spun back to hit the button.

"Hi, Lucie. Don't close it."

Mr. L.'s voice. She turned and found him just hitting the tiny driveway. He wore a black suit, a crisp white shirt, and a pink tie. She loved a man in a pink tie. His matching pocket hankie had long since given up the fight and drooped, but still made a sharp contrast to the dark suit.

And better yet, she'd had perfect timing. Maybe her plan wasn't a bust after all.

"Hey there," she said. "The big guy and I just finished our walk. He's inside. I gave him a few extra minutes today since I was running a bit late."

"Great. Thanks. We're heading out tonight so the exercise will wear him out. The wife wanted me home early. Apparently, I always make us late. I'm going inside to prove I'll be ready on time. No distractions."

Lucie glanced back at the door, at her scooter, then to Mr. Lutz again.

Time to get to the bottom of whatever this mess with Bart was.

Putting on a good show, Lucie started down the driveway then snapped her fingers. "Oh, Mr. L., quick question. If you don't mind."

"Sure. What's up?"

"The painting you bought from Bart, my friend is thinking about making a purchase but she's new to buying art. Is there some kind of paperwork she needs for insurance purposes? You know, proof of authenticity or whatever."

And if she did say so herself, that insurance idea was nothing short of genius. Even if it felt crummy lying.

The corners of his mouth dipped down for a second and Lucie reconsidered her brilliance. Maybe she'd overstepped here. But, really, she hadn't asked for his bill of sale for crying out loud. She waved it away. "Don't worry about it. I'll figure it out."

Mr. L. perked up. "No, Lucie, it's fine. What she needs is called provenance. Bart gave me a signed certificate. If you want, I'll pull it and show you a copy when you come back tomorrow. The original is in my safe deposit box, but I have a photocopy here at the house."

Well, that was easy. "Thank you. I'd appreciate it. That way I'll just tell her to ask for that. But don't worry, I won't tell Bart you showed it to me."

Mr. L. shrugged. "I've got nothing to hide. If he has a problem with it, then he's paranoid."

Lucie, not as skilled in her method acting as Ro, let out an awkward laugh. "Paranoid. That's funny."

"Lucie?"

"Yes?"

"Are you okay?"

She'd known Mr. L. since she'd been in grad school. He'd hired her despite her association with the Rizzo crime family. He'd had faith in her. Had always been honest and even helped her find work when she'd been downsized.

And now she harbored the secret that Bart Owens had swindled him. She looked beyond him to the house where Otis was probably still working that bully stick and something inside her detonated, sending a burst of sweat pouring down her back. Just boom.

What the hell was she doing?

This is wrong. If the situation were reversed and she'd gotten ripped off, she'd want to know. She'd want her *friend* to clue her in.

She couldn't do it. Couldn't stand in front of him, this man who'd been so kind to her, and lie to him.

"No," she said. "I'm not okay. I have to tell you something and I feel horrible about it."

Tight-lipped concern flooded his face. "What is it?"

"The Gomez."

"What about it?"

Where should she begin? That blasted piece of crap painting might destroy her relationship with the Lutzses.

And take Otis out of her life.

Just come clean.

"Okay," Lucie said. "Here it is. You won't like it, so brace yourself."

Lucie spent the next few minutes enlightening Mr. Lutz on Lauren's fascination with the painting, Lucie's subsequent research and contacting the family about *My Darkest Night.* Admitting it lightened the load, cooled that detonated burst inside her and just plain felt...right.

Mr. L.—bless him—had barely reacted. His eyebrows had drawn in slightly, but beyond that? Nothing. After a few seconds, he held up his hands. "Y-you're telling me," he stuttered, "that my painting is a fake?"

"Yes, sir. I'm so sorry. I can't believe it. I hope you know I'd never intentionally be involved in criminal activity. I wouldn't want you to think..."

Again he paused, narrowed his eyes and slightly puckered his lips. Back when she'd been his assistant, she'd seen this look many times when he mulled over a difficult situation or investment deal.

She stepped forward, ready to face his wrath. "I'm so sorry."

But Mr. L. shook his head. "This isn't your fault. You were trying to help."

Yes. And look where that got her? She mopped her

hands over her face. "I feel bad. You've been so good to me. You don't deserve this."

"You're sure it's a fake?"

"I spoke with the family's attorney myself. He said they still have the original and they don't intend on selling it. That sounds like proof to me."

Mr. L. jerked his head, pressed his lips together for a second. "I'll talk to Bart. Give him a chance to explain this. I don't know enough about art."

What was to know? She'd just told him he had a fake. Where was the outrage? The horror over being swindled?

"If you'd like, we could do that together. Since I'm the one who busted him."

His gaze shot to hers. "No," he said a little too quickly.

What was up here? Nothing about his reaction seemed right.

Mr. L. circled one hand. "I, uh, don't want him to feel ambushed. I'll take care of it, Lucie. And, thank you."

"All right. Let me know if you need anything. I'm happy to help. Even if you want to go to the police, file a complaint or whatever, I can help. I have a friend who's a detective. He'd help us."

His eyes bulged and his face contorted into stiff lines. Finally, some sort of outrage. She'd have been a maniac by now.

"The police," he said. "I don't know that it's necessary. Not yet. If that painting is fake, Bart Owens is going to make good on it. Believe me."

He rested his hand on her shoulder and she stiffened. Friends touched each other all the time, but this was...odd.

He lifted his hand away and Lucie fought the urge to step back. Maybe the situation had simply made her jittery. A little off her game. Whatever.

She jerked her hand toward the street. "I'm going to, um, head home. Let me know if you need any more information. And again, I'm sorry."

Mr. L. headed into the house and Lucie hotfooted her way down the driveway. She'd gotten lucky and nabbed a parking spot two houses down, a welcome event since her feet were killing her.

She hopped into the car, fired that puppy up, and buckled in. By now, traffic would be miserable, so she mentally prepped herself for an excruciating ride home. She could just add that to her crummy mood. She'd completely blown the plan by telling Mr. Lutz about the fake painting. Dang it. She'd make a terrible detective.

Before pulling out of her spot, she caught Mr. L. opening the garage door again and backing his car out. After the conversation they'd just had, she wasn't surprised he was defying his wife's order to stay put. He checked the road for traffic, backed into the street and punched the gas. And, by the way he hit that pedal and roared down the tight city block, he appeared to be in a hurry. A big one.

Most likely on his way to see Bart. Maybe to confront him face-to-face because that's how Mr. L. rolled. If he had an issue with someone, he went at it person to person. No distractions, no excuses, no slinking away.

With what Bart had put her through these last few days, it would be fun to watch Lutz nail him. Just rip into him.

Ooooh, that bastard. Selling fake paintings and bringing her in on it. She should report him to the police herself. Well, she sort of already had by telling Tim. But still, she was so strung out she wouldn't mind seeing Bart Owens in handcuffs. Locked in a cell. Feeling the way she had when she'd been arrested.

Yikes, what a week.

She shifted her car into gear, watched Mr. L. make the right at the end of the block. Where was he going?

Since she'd already decided traffic on the Kennedy would be a mess, she could kill some time, let the traffic die down.

And follow Lutz.

Just to see if he was about to confront Bart.

Had to be, right? He'd just been swindled and he was a man of action.

At the corner, Lucie looked right, watched for a second as Mr. L. made the next right, heading down the one-way street. She should be going left, making her way home for another night alone and working on financial reports for her growing business.

But that damned Bart Owens. She wanted to see him squirm.

Lucie made the right.

Lucie waited until Mr. L. entered the gallery then sneaked around the back to the office entrance where she usually picked up Oscar the Perv. Chances were he'd be in the office, but he wasn't a barker, so the worst that would happen is she'd get humped.

A silent hump.

As long as it didn't clue Bart in that she was in the office, the dog could get off on her all he wanted.

At the base of the stoop, she formed a plan. First, she'd peek in the door's window. If Bart was in the office and spotted her, she'd tell him she lost her watch somewhere and was backtracking the day's route.

Lame, but the best she could do on short notice. She

probably wouldn't even need a cover story since Mr. L. had already entered the gallery and Bart normally hopped up from his desk the second the door chimes sounded. Nothing stood between Bart and a customer.

Lucie climbed the steps, contemplated what she was about to do. She really should have checked with Tim on whether or not she could be arrested for this. It had to be trespassing since she was outside the function she'd been hired for. Sadly, snooping on the client probably wasn't included in her scope of services. At least she'd texted Tim to let him know she was coming over here.

That way, if she suddenly went missing, he'd know where to look.

And wasn't that a lovely thought?

She held her breath until her lungs ached and then released it. *Go to work.* She peeped in the door. No Bart. But Oscar lay sunny-side-up, snoozing on his Sniffany dog bed. Good boy.

The second she slid her key into the lock, Oscar bolted to his feet, faced the door and his tail whipped into action. *Please don't pick today to be a barker.*

She slipped inside, bent low to say hello to Oscar and heard voices from the gallery floor. Definitely Bart. Definitely Mr. L.

Lucie moved behind the closed door leading to the gallery and pressed her ear to it.

"You sold me a goddamned fake? *Me?*"

Mr. L.

Annoyed voice.

Lucie hated his annoyed voice. It remained steady in volume, low even, but the lack of shouting made it all the more fierce.

"Don't be ridiculous," Bart said. "I gave you the provenance."

A long pause and then, "I'm supposed to believe that crap?"

"Daniel," Bart said, "I know what you're thinking. I didn't give you fake paperwork."

"Lucie was just at my house. She feels guilty because she brokered a deal involving a fake painting. She's worried she's going to prison."

Darned tootin'. And if she was about to become someone's prison bitch, Bart was going with her.

"She's mistaken," Bart said. "Why would she think the painting is fake?"

"Give up already. She called the Gomez family. That damned dog walker she has—the art history major?—started asking questions. *My Darkest Night* is still in the hands of the family. They've never sold it. You dumbass. You should have at least faked a painting that wasn't still owned by the family. Flaming idiot."

Silence.

Yeah! *Get him Mr. L.*

"Which means," Mr. L. continued, "not only are you giving me my money back on that painting, we have to figure out a way to back Lucie off. We've barely gotten into this thing and you've botched it."

Hold up. Lucie hopped away from the door and stared at it. *We? Back Lucie off?*

"Daniel, don't panic. I'll handle Lucie. She knows nothing about art."

Hey! She knew enough to figure out Bart Owens was a thieving bastard.

From her pocket, her phone vibrated. Tim. Wanting to know what she was doing. She shot off a text.

Snooping at the gallery. Something might be up. Will call in a bit.

"Don't underestimate her, Bart. She's smart and she's grown up around criminals. She can sniff out a scam in no time. We should have anticipated this."

There was that "we" again. What did it mean? Was Lutz involved in selling himself a fake painting? That made no sense.

"I'll deal with her," Bart said.

"No. I'll deal with her. First, tell me where we're at on this thing. Setting aside what you owe me for that fake painting you sold me and the other deal you did, I want the rest of my money back. I'm out."

"Well fine, Daniel, but you'll have to wait. The money is tied up."

"Where?"

"You *know* where. I've got three guys on the hook. I've paid the artist with the money you gave me. He's one of the top forgers in the world. He'll have all three paintings done in two weeks. I'll sell the paintings and give you your money. I don't have that kind of cash lying around. If I did, I wouldn't have needed you!"

Just stop it. Mr. Lutz was in on this crazy scheme. Double-thieving rat bastards.

And they'd roped her into it. Lucie squeezed her fists tight, then bit back a stream of venom ready to fly. She'd been nice to them. Both of them. Tried to help them and make a little side money for herself. Oooh, she'd known the whole thing felt a little smarmy. *Knew it.* But with her father coming home, the lure of fast cash that would get her new headquarters completed led her to ignore her instincts.

Well, this is what she got.

And her cop boyfriend—was he even her boyfriend?—wouldn't be able to get her out of a fraud charge.

Dammit, these men. They'd betrayed her trust. That alone infuriated her. Rage, fast and sharp, shredded her, made her eyes throb. She closed them, took a long, slow breath. *Calm down.*

Calm.

Down.

If she confronted them, they'd know she'd been listening. Confronting them would give her some satisfaction, though. Just looking them straight in the face and letting them know that she knew what they didn't think she knew, but she did. Wait. What now?

She shook it off. Got her mind straight.

Tim.

She'd told him she'd be here. She could leave and call him. Relay everything to him and ask his advice. If nothing else, she could go to the police herself and confess. Ugh. How awful would that be? Joe Rizzo's kid, the apple that didn't fall far.

The gossips would have a grand time pulverizing saintly Lucie.

Once again, her father's reputation had put her in a place she never wanted to be.

"How the hell does this happen to me?" she muttered.

Well, however it happened, she wasn't about to put up with it. She hadn't known Bart and Mr. Lutz were scammers. Not a clue.

Who was she kidding? No one would believe that. Not of Joe Rizzo's kid.

The office door flew open.

Oh, no. Caught.

Lucie leaped backward, held up her fists. Fists? As if she knew how to fight.

Oscar barked at the sudden movement and Bart halted. He looked down at Oscar then, as if sensing someone, slowly lifted his gaze. Lucie narrowed her eyes—mean Lucie. *Very* mean Lucie.

His face stretched into open-mouthed shock. "What the *hell* are you doing?"

Her? The nerve. "Bart, I think the question is what the hell are *you* doing?"

16

———

TIM SAT AT HIS DESK READING AND REREADING LUCIE'S TEXT. What kind of message was that to send a cop? She was at a gallery owned by a known crook and thinks something is up. And expects him to do what? A phone call would have been nice. Maybe an explanation.

He tossed the phone on his desk. "She's got to be kidding me."

"Who?"

He glanced up at Rich Laslo, another detective in his unit. Rich, obviously on his way to the coffee pot if the mug in his hand were any indication, halted. He stood beside the desk in his wrinkled suit pants and shirtsleeves rolled to his elbows. Rich was an old-timer. One of those gritty twenty-year veterans with balding heads and barrel chests that were great for intimidating witnesses.

Given that, there was no way Tim could admit this one. *Hey, Rich, guess what? I'm hot for Joe Rizzo's daughter and she wound up in the middle of an art fraud case. She's innocent. Really.*

What was he supposed to do with this text? If he went

running over to that gallery and nothing happened, he'd tip off Bart Owens that they were on to him. Hell, this wasn't even an official case.

It would be soon, but he hadn't brought it to his superiors yet.

Stupid ass that he was, he'd known dating a mob guy's daughter—and not just any mob guy, but *the* mob guy—would be complicated.

But this topped any and all scenarios he'd imagined. And that was saying something for a Chicago cop.

"Women," he said to Rich.

"Please. I got two ex-wives. You're not telling me anything I don't know."

Tim read the text again, then set the phone down and tipped his head back to study the ceiling.

"Oh, boy," Rich said. "You got that look you get when a case strings you up."

Tim grunted.

Rich wheeled one of the rickety desk chairs into the aisle between the two rows of desks and sat. Right in the center of the aisle. Had to love cops.

He paddled both his hands. "Tell me. I can help."

"You got two ex-wives. Why would I ask *your* opinion?"

Rich laughed. "You don't think I learned a few things after two wives? Trust me, I got this. Go."

In a twisted way, it made sense. Plus, Rich was a cop. He'd understand the dilemma.

"I'm dating someone. It's fairly new."

"Good for you. Get a lawyer."

Tim shook his head. "It's not that serious, moron."

"Okay." Rich rolled his hands in front of him. "But you like her. More than just casual hook up stuff, right? Or we wouldn't be having this conversation."

True. "Yeah. Exactly. And she might be into something here."

"Something illegal? Get a lawyer. Now."

"Hey, she's a fraud victim. Sort of. We just figured that out. I haven't even had a chance to kick it up yet and I get this text from her that something's up with the guy running this scam."

"Okay. What's your problem?"

"I know where she is. I don't know whether to go there, see what's what or not. If I do that before I kick this up—and get warrants—the guy could bolt. And she's in a jackpot."

"Does this guy know you're a cop?"

"No."

Rich sat back, eyed him. "I'm thinking."

"Great. Got all the time in the world. Let me know when you're ready."

Rich slapped his hands on his legs. "I got it."

"Finally."

"If he doesn't know you're a cop, I'd go over there. Consider it an undercover gig. You check things out, make sure she's okay, and you come back, talk to the brass and get the paperwork going. Otherwise, you'll be sitting here with your thumb up your ass getting pissy. There's your plan."

Tim rolled his bottom lip out, considered it. Rich had a point. Down deep, Tim wasn't ready to go to his boss. A relationship with a mob boss's daughter might have career implications. Nothing wrong with having his ducks in a row before he went public.

Tim stood and grabbed his suit jacket off the back of the chair. "Never thought I'd say this, but you're right. I'll check it out."

"You want company?"

"Nah. I'm good. If I think something's hinky, I'll call you."

Because no cop should walk into an unknown situation without some backup. Regardless of the fact that his girlfriend was involved.

Girlfriend. Been a long time since he'd thought of a woman in that way.

Lucie. Girlfriend.

He liked it. A lot.

"You're trespassing!"

Rage in full circulation, literally tearing her apart from the inside out, Lucie bounced on the balls of her feet and swung her fists at Bart. "That's nothing compared to what you've done."

"What did you hear?"

"I heard it all, Bart. All. Of. *It.*"

She pushed by him, headed straight for Mr. Lutz, who was still in the main part of the gallery. "And you! I trusted you. How could you *do* this to me?"

"Lucie, now take it easy. I don't know what you heard, but I never intended to put you in the middle."

Lucie glanced back at Bart, who'd hustled up behind her. She needed to keep an eye on him. She didn't think Mr. L. would physically harm her, but who knew what Bart was capable of?

"Daniel," Bart said, "stop talking."

Mr. Lutz put his hand up, but kept his eyes on Lucie. "Bart, shut up. This is between Lucie and me. We've been friends a long time."

Totally playing her. That's what he was doing. Yes, they'd been friends a long time. She had, in fact, worked side by side with him, watching him close deals, negotiate terms, sometimes string people along.

Playing them.

Oh, he was the master.

And he knew it. His only problem was she knew it too.

The thing that really upset her was that he'd had the chance to come clean with her when she'd told him his painting was a forgery. When she couldn't stand the fact that he'd been swindled. Because she *cared* about him.

In this relationship, respect only went one way and it stabbed at her like a pick ax.

Heartbreaking betrayal. No other way to describe it. Something in her chest hitched and she cleared her throat, but...nothing. No air. She shook her head, scrunched her nose and forced another cough that released a gasping breath.

Good. Fine. She stood a little taller—as tall as someone so petite could—and tipped her chin up.

"We have been friends a long time. Which is why you should be ashamed of yourself."

"Okay. Hold on a second. Let's talk about this."

"This is stupid," Bart said. "You don't owe her anything. She's got nothing to defend herself with. Lucie, you're screwed. We've got you on the tracksuits."

Tracksuits. What? She spun on him. "What are you talking about?"

"A little insurance in case you decided to go to the cops. I bought those atrocious tracksuits from my cousin. He stole them. Brainiac didn't realize the damned things were out of season and got stuck with them. They've been sitting in his basement for months."

Oh, a fresh bout of rage burned right through her skin. "You," she said.

"Yes. *Me.* I planted them in your place. After you talked to Keegan about the Gomez. Keegan has a big mouth, Lucie. Never trust him."

Keegan. Another rat bastard.

"My dear," Bart continued, "he told me all about your conversation. I decided a little insurance was in order. Just in case I needed to prove the squeaky-clean Lucie had a taste for her father's lifestyle. That way, if you went to the cops, they'd have the tracksuits and think if you were involved in that, maybe fake paintings wasn't a stretch. You're in it just as deep."

Lucie's eyes burned. They'd set her up. After she'd cared for their dogs, loved them like they were her own, dealt with Oscar the Perv humping her leg every second.

"Bastards," she said.

Both of them. Not the dogs, the owners.

And then he laughed. A deep, annoying rumble that ravaged Lucie's mind. One thing she'd never been—at least until now—was a fool. All her adult life she'd known who she was and what people said about her. She'd risen above it.

Now, Bart Owens thought he could pigeonhole her, lead people to believe that she wasn't a legitimate business-woman, but simply Joe Rizzo's kid, leading the Joe Rizzo lifestyle.

Bart continued to laugh and the look on his face, that grin, that smug knowing, that *pity,* she couldn't stand it.

He half turned as if to walk away. Nuh-uh. *No one leaves.*

Lucie leaped—*whaaaaa!*—and landed on his back. Moving on pure and potent adrenaline, she wrapped her legs around him and hooked an arm over his shoulder, hanging on as he tipped forward and stumbled.

"Aaaaahhhh!" he screamed. "Get her off."

She slapped her hand across the back of his head. *Bam, bam, bam.* "You son of a bitch." *Bam*, she smacked him again. "You tried to destroy my reputation?" *Bam.* "Do you know how hard I've worked? I'm not some fraud, like you. I earn my living." *Bam!* "And now you think you're going to tear that away from me?"

"Aaaaahhhh! Daniel, help!"

Bart swung around, faced Lutz, and tried to buck Lucie off, but she hung on and locked her legs. She'd bloody him before she let go.

"And you," she said to Lutz, "you knew how I felt about stolen merchandise! You knew. I trusted you! And this is what I got?"

Bam. She smacked Bart again. Why not? Lutz would be next. For now, Bart deserved whatever he got.

"Whoa," came another voice.

All three of them glanced at the entrance where Tim stood, one hand over his holstered weapon.

Dear God.

"They set me up!"

Bam. She gave Bart another shot.

"Stop hitting me or I'll—"

"What?"

Another smack.

"Lucie," Tim said, his voice carrying a relaxed amusement she couldn't process, "as much as I'm enjoying this and think you have it under control, get off him before he gets hurt."

She bared her teeth. "I want him hurt. I want him to bleed!"

Mr. Lutz's head jerked back. "She's nuts. How did I not realize?"

Tim stepped into the room and shoved Lutz against the

staircase leading to the apartment upstairs. "You shut up. Stand there and be quiet or I'll unleash her on you."

He handcuffed Lutz to the bannister then turned back to Lucie, still on top of Bart but not swinging. "Off," he said, his voice so commanding she nearly wet herself.

Wow. Who knew the cute detective could be so fierce?

She hopped off of Bart and gave him one last smack for the fun of it. "Bastard."

"Okay," Tim said. "Everybody settle down." He grabbed hold of Bart and shoved him against the stairs next to Mr. Lutz. "I don't have another set of cuffs. If you move, I'll shoot you. Got it?"

Bart's lips peeled back. Apparently, he understood.

Obviously satisfied, Tim nodded. "Now, I'm going to call for backup and you nutcases are going to tell me exactly what happened here."

TIM ENTERED THE PRECINCT'S INTERVIEW ROOM AND FOUND Lucie sitting at the table with her lawyer.

Joe Rizzo's very expensive lawyer.

Tim nearly groaned. One thing he wasn't up for was a battle with a shark. But he supposed the guy was doing his job and since this involved Lucie, he'd be friendly.

Lucie sat with her hands in her lap. She still wore her dog walking clothes and her shoulder-length hair was flying all over. Her big blue eyes met his. Damn, this girl and her family would be a handful. If he had any sense, he'd run. Fast.

But apparently, that wasn't happening.

He swung the door closed behind him.

Seeing her beat the crap out of Bart Owens may have

sealed the deal. The woman had no fear. Maybe it had been a dangerous thing to do, but he loved her spunk. Her willingness to take care of a problem on her own.

Lucie Rizzo didn't depend on anyone or anything. She did it on her own.

"Detective," the lawyer said, "either charge her or we're leaving. She's been fully cooperative. My client is a victim here. How do you not see that?"

At the lawyer's condescending tone, Lucie's eyes flashed. "It's not his fault," she said. "Be nice."

Be nice. How flippin' cute was she?

The lawyer patted her arm. One of those I'm-sorry-you're-suffering-from-dementia pats, and Lucie drilled him with another look.

He'd better get in the middle of this before she jumped her lawyer too. Just as her mouth opened, Tim held up his hand. "You're free to go."

Her head drooped forward. "Free to... go?"

"Yep."

"'Bout time," the lawyer said. "No charges are being filed, I presume?"

"No charges." He focused on Lucie. "Lutz gave the whole thing up. Said you didn't know about the scheme. All you did was make the introduction between him and Owens. Even Lutz thought that painting was real. The guy scammed his own partner."

Lucie shook her head. "What an ass."

"Which one?"

She rolled her eyes, but laughed. "Both of them, I suppose." Then she turned to Mr. Slick Lawyer. "Would you give us a minute please?"

Slick didn't like the sound of that. This guy was good, but Tim had been around lawyers on both sides of the aisle enough to know their game faces. This bland stare was all about him not being happy.

"Ms. Rizzo," he said, "that's not a good idea."

"I know. I'll take my chances. Thank you. You can go."

Eee-doggies, I like this girl.

The lawyer packed up and headed out, but stopped at the doorway, asking one more time if she was sure. *Yeah, buddy, she's sure. Papa Rizzo won't hurt you.*

As soon as the door closed, Lucie let out a huge breath and dropped her head to the table. She'd had to sit here while they sorted out the Owens-Lutz mess, the entire time wondering if she'd be implicated. Throw in the three rounds she went with Bart Owens and she had to be fried.

While her head was still down, he twisted his lips, hiding a smile. He'd never forget the shock of walking in on tiny Lucie beating the crap out of that guy. Of course, his first reaction was to haul her off, but hey, she'd had the upper hand, so he let her get a few extra licks in. For what that guy had put her through, she deserved extended time.

But now, the day had obviously crashed down on her. Tim reached across and ran his hand over her hair. "You're okay, Lucie. All cleared."

She lifted her head, grabbed his hand, and squeezed. "Thank you."

"I didn't do anything. I would have if necessary, but Lutz manned up. He did the right thing."

"At least that's something. And hey, now I can call my dad off. No need for him to terrify people while trying to figure out where those stupid suits came from." She blew out a breath. "I can't believe it. They were going to use my connections to scam people. Bart doesn't know me that well. But Mr. L.? He knows how hard I've worked to be more than

Joe Rizzo's kid. *He knows*. How horrible is that? That he was willing to betray me that way."

The choke in her voice nearly killed him. Dug right down to the core of him and jabbed at every protective instinct he possessed.

That's when it hit him. When he knew he'd never walk away from this girl. That what he wanted was to be near her, keep her safe, and help her fight whatever battle she needed fought.

I'm so screwed.

"I'm sorry, Lucie. The guy got greedy."

"He makes millions as an investment banker. Millions!"

"Not lately. He's had a bad run. After you introduced him to Bart, they got together on this art fraud thing and Lutz said he'd be the initial seed money."

"I'm not sure I even understand what they were doing."

Tim sat back, rested his hands on his thighs. "Bart had a forger. The guy is good too. I guess he couldn't make it on his own work, so he started doing copies. Bart figured he could have the guy forge paintings and sell them as the real deal. He made up some story about how Renaissance wasn't selling and it would be a good investment for when the market turned around."

"That's how he got people to believe they were buying the real thing so cheap."

"Yep. The forger needed to be paid though. A lot. Bart didn't have that kind of liquid capital."

Lucie smacked her hand against her forehead. "That's where Lutz came in."

"Yep. He gave Bart the money to pay the forger." Tim shrugged. "When Bart sold the paintings, Lutz got half."

"They had to know they'd get caught."

"Not really. The art world can get pretty shady. And Bart

was smart enough to target people who were novices and wouldn't necessarily know the paintings were fakes. Along with the paintings, they received forged provenance." Tim brushed his hands together. "Scam complete."

"At least until my art history major employee spotted that Gomez."

"Yep. I'm seriously entertained over Owens selling Lutz a fake. That's some high-end street justice right there."

Lucie laughed. *Hey, I did that.* Made her laugh after her rotten day.

"I can't wait to tell Lauren this one. She'll probably write a paper on it. Good God. What about that Robert guy Bart was arguing with? Is that related?"

She set her hands on the table and he grabbed them. "Not to the fakes. Before he and Lutz came up with this scam, Owens was desperate for some quick cash and sold Robert's paintings to a gallery. He told Robert they were only on loan. How the hell he intended on getting out of that one, I don't know, but he's been ducking him."

"He *sold* them? What a creep."

"Yeah. We're gonna see what we can do there, but the guy might get screwed out of his paintings. Anyway, Lutz and Owens will probably both make bail and be out in a few hours, but they'll be punished. Owens mailed some of the paperwork involved in the Lutz transaction."

"U.S. mail. That's a federal offense."

And knowing what he did about the Joe Rizzo trials, Tim knew Lucie understood the penalties federal offenses could rack up. "Sure is. They'll do some time. Just depends on how good their lawyers are."

"Such jerks. I'm so angry at Mr. Lutz. He totally betrayed me. I trusted him. And that's not easy for someone like me. The worst of it is, I love Mr. Lutz's dog. Now I won't get to see him anymore. Everything was great and Lutz had to ruin it."

Yeah. He did. For breaking Lucie's heart alone, Tim wanted to pound on the guy. Make him think a little harder about his choices. She didn't deserve this. "You never know," he said. "Maybe the wife will divorce him and she'll want you to keep walking the dog."

"That would be great." The minute it came out of her mouth she gasped. "Wow, that sounded bad. I didn't mean..."

Tim cracked up. "I know what you meant. And, yeah, that would be great."

Someone knocked and a second later, Rich Laslo stuck his head in. "Her brother is here to take her home."

Tim nodded. "Thanks."

The door closed again and Lucie sat back, letting out a long breath. "If Joey is wearing that damned velour tracksuit again, I'll kill him."

17

———

"Close your eyes."

Two days later, Lucie and Ro stood in front of Coco Barknell while the workers removed the weathered Carlucci's sign. A cute winking poodle, Coco Barknell's giant-sized logo, would soon be splashed above the store's awning. The entire block would see that poodle, and Lucie took plenty of satisfaction in that.

Plenty.

Her entire life, people in this town had been divided into three camps when it came to Joe Rizzo, and by extension, his family. The worshipers, the tolerators, and the haters.

Oddly, the ones Lucie liked the most were the tolerators. At least they were honest. They didn't like Joe Rizzo's lifestyle, but enjoyed the lack of violence in Franklin. In many ways, Franklin fell under the protection of her father.

"Come on," Ro said. "Humor me. Close your eyes."

"Why? I've seen the place."

Ro flapped her arms. "Not finished you haven't. You saw paint and tile. Now it's done-done and I want you to close your damned eyes. Right now."

"Yikes. You don't have to get hostile."

"Apparently, I do."

Lucie closed her eyes. Might as well. Ro had pulled off a miracle and completed the project in plenty of time for them to move everything in and get the house back to normal for her father's return in five days. Lucie owed her, at the very least, this little indulgence.

"Okay. Just don't let me walk into a wall or anything. Tim is picking me up in half an hour and I can't have any drama or bruises. I'm trying to lay low after the art fraud."

"Honey, good luck with that."

They both laughed as Ro led Lucie through the door, complete with jangling doggie bells. "Little bump here," Ro said. "I talked to Joey about that. He'll have someone fix it so nobody trips."

Probably a good thing. A lawsuit they didn't need.

A burst of cool air puckered Lucie's bare legs. Yay. Working air conditioner. She should have brought a sweater though. Unaccustomed to dresses, something she vowed to change since she had a cute new guy who'd mentioned he liked them, she hadn't even thought about the sweater. Maybe Ro had one in her car.

Lucie stopped walking. "Can I look now?"

"No. Not yet. Stay here. One second."

Ro let go and stepped away, her high-heeled sandals clickety-clacking against the tile they'd picked out.

"Do you have a sweater in your car I can borrow for tonight? I forgot one."

Ro huffed. "Honestly, my work is never done."

Lucie grinned. In the next ten minutes, a sweater would miraculously appear.

"Open 'em!" Ro said.

Lucie did as she was told, blinking a few times to readjust to the light. Ro stood four feet in front of her, arms spread wide.

"Ta-da!"

Lucie drew a hard breath as she took it all in. The wooden blinds, the fresh paint, the silk screens separating the sewing area from reception. To Ro's left, gleaming in the sunlight, was a giant mahogany desk with two chocolate-brown upholstered chairs in front of it. Across from that sat a smaller desk, also mahogany. The guest chairs were different though. Still upholstered, but with a more modern fabric. Tan with red, green and brown intertwined circles. Pretty.

Along the wall sat a long table. Probably for meetings or looking at samples.

"Is that a *dining* table?"

In awe, Lucie rushed over to it.

"Sure is, babe. Amazing, right?"

Total understatement. The entire space screamed warmth and professionalism and class. Simply stunning. Lucie's heart froze. Just seemed to stop for a few seconds. Her BFF had most definitely pulled off a miracle.

Lucie held her hands out, swooping them around the room. "I'm... I don't know. Floored. I can't believe this is that rattrap we started with. It's spectacular."

"I know!"

Good old, Ro. Never one to mince words.

Lucie ran her hands over the gleaming top of the long table. Solid wood. Must have weighed a thousand pounds.

"Don't panic," Ro said. "I stayed in the budget you gave me."

How? The table alone had to cost ten thousand. Easy.

Which meant...oh, no. Lucie turned to her friend, her

best friend, but no, she couldn't do it. Couldn't ask where she'd gotten this expensive furniture so cheap.

"No," Ro said. "It's not off the truck, Dopey."

Lucie tipped her head back. *Phew.* "Thank you. I didn't want to ask."

"I know. And thank you for not insulting me."

"So how did you pull this off?"

"Thank the lady in Barrington who's downsizing her fifteen-thousand-square-foot house into a condo. Total fire sale. I got all of this from her. The desks, chairs, table, screens, everything. I even picked up some stuff for my house. Joey got a truck and we hauled it all back here. Tell me you love it. Please. I know it's a little more cozy than you probably expected, but with our clientele, I think it'll work."

"Are you crazy? It's fantastic. I'm so grateful. And I can't believe you got this done so fast."

"I can't take all the credit. Joey got the contractors in here so I could do my magic."

Her brother. The big lug. She'd hear about this for years, but that was okay. She'd thank him every time he reminded her what he'd done for her. "I'm a little surprised he was so agreeable."

"Eh. I made it worth his while."

Ro winked and the vision of Joey and Ro reenacting Position Seven popped into her mind. "Blech. I don't need those details. Thank you very much."

The doggie bells hanging on the door jangled and Lucie and Ro turned to see Tim walking through. A little ping happened in Lucie's ear and her chest blew open. Just a whoosh of happiness. Tim did that for her. Gave her a lightness she hadn't known in a long time. She wouldn't read too much into it because this thing was still in its early stages, but she'd enjoy him for now and not worry about the future.

He scanned the room. "Whoa, ladies, the place looks great."

"I know!" Ro said.

Lucie walked to him, popped a quick kiss on his lips. "Ro and Joey pulled off a miracle. We can get everything moved in now. And our sign will be here tomorrow."

Tim linked his hand with hers and gave it a squeeze. "I guess you're all set then."

Lucie turned back to the room, took it all in again, and visualized her mom sitting at a commercial-grade sewing machine and Ro sketching designs while Lucie handled the administrative tasks from the giant mahogany desk. *Coco Barknell.* Something told her this former rattrap would be the start of a very nice future.

She glanced down at Tim's much bigger hand wrapped around hers. He'd hung in there with the entire art fraud mess and never questioned whether she, Joe Rizzo's daughter, could be involved.

This was a good man.

She lifted their clasped hands and kissed the back of his. "Detective, I think you're right. I do believe I'm all set."

Book three in The Lucie Rizzo Mystery series:

Lucie stood on the sidewalk under a soothing stream of October sunshine while Fin, an eight-month-old Australian shepherd with more energy than a horny frat boy, sniffed at a giant maple tree on Chicago's West Side. After this stop, she'd call it a day. As soon as she got horny frat boy off the tree.

Not always an easy task.

Time to break out some Alpha Lucie. "Okay, Fin. Finish up. No more stalling."

Fin swung his head around, stared at her with his one blue and one green eye, and Alpha Lucie crumbled. Just completely melted. *I'm useless to the Alpha population.*

In her own defense, Fin's eyes—shades of tropical seas —could take down an entire army. She simply could not get mad at this dog.

Even when he hurled himself at her, blasting her in the chest with both front paws and knocking her on her butt. Or when he decided to stop, plop his furry bottom on the sidewalk and bark—*woof, woof, woof.*

Three rapid-fire barks meant, at least in Fin's mind, playing fetch. Which he could do for 90 percent of his waking hours.

But she'd been working on him. Giving him a treat every time he kept pace with her. He might be fifty pounds overweight by the time she finished with him, but he'd be a dog walker's dream. A graduate of Coco Barknell.

On the street, a car rolled by, slowing as it went. Probably someone looking for a parking space. They wouldn't find one on this block. Every parked car was squeezed bumper to bumper.

Fin's ear went up, and he barked at the car. Her hero. She bent low, gave him a nuzzle. "You make me crazy, but I love you."

A wet tongue slapped across her cheek. The bonus of working for dogs.

"Aw, you two are the cutest." A middle-aged woman hoofed down the sidewalk wearing a flowy skirt, an equally flowy blouse and a long cardigan against the late afternoon wind. She carried a briefcase in one hand.

Lucie scratched Fin's snout before standing tall. "He's a good boy and deserved some love."

The woman stopped just a few feet away. "Can I pet him?"

Something in Lucie's spine fused. After the dognapping of the Ninja Bitches last spring, she didn't take to strangers wanting to come near her clients. The woman must have sensed Lucie's sudden-onset Terminator and gestured to the auction house behind her.

"I'm Estelle. I manage Bendorf Auctions. I've seen you out here with this cutie."

Lucie let out a long, silent breath. "Fin."

"Sorry?"

"His name is Fin. You can pet him. Sorry. I'm protective."

Estelle glanced at Lucie's messenger bag with the screen print of a winking poodle wearing a diamond collar. The Coco Barknell logo created by the fabulous Ro, aka Lucie's best bud. And currently the squeeze of Joey, Lucie's ape of a brother. *Blech.*

"You're a dog walker?"

"Yes. I'm Lucie from Coco Barknell. We also have a line of dog accessories." Lucie slipped one of her business cards from the easy-access front pocket of her bag. There'd been a time when she'd been too shy to even tell people about her fledgling business. Now she was a pro and whipped out her card to anyone with even a passing interest. Her growing bank account helped inspire this newfound aggressiveness.

Estelle took the card. "Thank you. I have a little guy at home myself. A mutt, but the cutest darned thing. Maybe I'll buy him a collar or something."

"Sure. Check out our Web site. If there's something you see, let me know, and I'll drop it by next time I walk Fin."

"Oh, that'd be great. Thank you."

Finally, Estelle bent over and gave Fin a good rub.

"Stay, Fin," Lucie warned.

Please don't let him launch. With Fin, she never knew. One second he'd be calm and the next—airborne.

But, lookie here, he stayed put. He'd definitely get a treat for that.

"Good boy, Finnie!"

Lucie pulled out another treat. Peanut butter this time. Although the carob seemed to be his favorite.

He made a move to jump, but Lucie tightened her hold on the leash. "Stay."

"Well, now I've made a new friend." Estelle gave him one last pat. "I'll be sure to look out for you now, Fin."

"He loves people," Lucie said. *A little too much.*

"I see that. It was lovely meeting you, Lucie." She held up the card. "I'll check out your Web site."

Estelle wandered up the walkway to the entrance of the auction house, an old, brick building with a door the color of the purest blue sky. Such an interesting choice. Eclectic, yet elegant.

Fin finished his treat and stretched out on the sidewalk for one of his siestas. "Oh, no you don't, mister. Let's get this walk finished."

Lucie took two steps, but Fin—as usual—didn't move. "Come on, boy." She clicked her tongue—the treat sound— and he popped right up. Lucie sighed and tossed him another peanut butter nib.

In order to fix one bad habit, she'd created a treat monster. She'd deal with that later. After saving her precious schedule.

At the corner, they turned right and looped around the front of the auction house. Fin spotted something on the ground and charged, dragging Lucie with him.

As they approached she recognized the telltale eye—the blue in the middle—of a peacock feather. Actually, this one had two eyes. How cool was that? The sun glinted off the iridescent green and turquoise, and images of Fannie and Josie—the Ninja Bitches, a couple of shih tzus long on attitude and short on stature—wearing those colors flashed in Lucie's mind.

Gripping the leash so Fin couldn't snag the feather, Lucie bent low and scooped it up. She'd take it back to the office so Ro could create some sketches of peacock doggie coats.

"That, Fin," Lucie said, "would be a best seller. I just know it."

Want more? Don't miss the next Lucie Rizzo mystery.

A NOTE TO READERS

Dear reader,

Thank you for reading *Knocked Off*. I hope you enjoyed it. If you did, please help others find it by sharing it with friends on social media and writing a review.

Sharing the book with your friends and leaving a review helps other readers decide to take the plunge into the nutty world of Lucie Rizzo. So please consider taking a moment to tell your friends how much you enjoyed the story. Even a few words expressing what you enjoyed most about the story is a huge help. Thank you!

Happy reading!
Adrienne

ACKNOWLEDGMENTS

Thank you to my tremendous readers who take time out of their lives to read my books. I am so grateful.

John, Mara and Josh Leach, thank you for once again letting me use the beloved Otis in this book. I never get tired of looking at photos of him when writing his scenes. To Chris, Deb, Ralph and Josie Giordano for bringing the cuteness known as Boots into the family. And for those of you wondering, yes, his ears really do go up like that and we did once have a conversation about how he looked like the Flying Nun. Also, thanks to Deb for the great Botox line. Thanks also to Kevin and Cindy Palmer because even though Fannie and Josie were not in this book, I couldn't resist throwing their nickname in.

Scott Silverii and John Leach, thank you for always answering my emails and for sharing your law enforcement knowledge. Any mistakes I've made are mine, but I'm hoping I didn't blow it! To my plotting and critique partners and all-around great pals, Kelsey Browning and Tracey Devlyn, I could not make this journey without you. Amy Remus, you're a warrior! Thank you for helping me manage the business side of being an author so I can spend more time writing. To the fabulous Gina Bernal, you've been with me from the beginning, and I continue to learn from you with each book. Thank you!

Finally, to "my guys" who make me laugh every day and give me all the love a girl could ever want. I love you.

ABOUT THE AUTHOR

Adrienne Giordano is a *USA Today* bestselling author of over twenty romantic suspense and mystery novels. She is a Jersey girl at heart, but now lives in the Midwest with her workaholic husband, sports-obsessed son and Buddy the Wheaten Terrorist (Terrier). She is a cofounder of Romance University blog and Lady Jane's Salon-Naperville, a reading series dedicated to romantic fiction.

For more information on Adrienne, including her Internet haunts, contest updates, and details on her upcoming novels, please visit her at:

www.AdrienneGiordano.com
agiordano@adriennegiordano.com